THE LINDEN LEGACY

KENLEY DAVIDSON

D1563678

PAGE NINE PRESS

To all the fans who never gave up on this series or these characters.

This one is all for you.

ONE

THE STREETS SURROUNDING The Diamond Iris were nearly full. A line of high-end skimmers stretched halfway around the block, waiting to deliver their passengers, and all of the higher-altitude landing platforms were long since occupied.

The crimson carpet leading to the gold and etched-glass doors of the casino was likewise crowded, the air around it bristling with news drones, hoping to catch exclusive footage of anyone at all. Only the young, the attractive, and the obscenely wealthy had been invited, and one of them was sure to make a scene before the evening was over.

Callista Linden was determined to be that one.

She glanced over at her driver, who clutched the passenger seat armrest with bloodless fingers.

"Have a little faith, Barclay," she chided with a grin. "Have I killed you yet?"

"Three hundred twenty-two times and counting," her driver replied without pause, while staring resolutely through the front windscreen. "Allow me to remind you that my hair was *brown* when I came to work for you."

1

Callista chuckled and patted his perfectly trimmed white hair with genuine affection. "You know I don't trust anyone else with my babies."

"And how long will I be babysitting this evening?" Barclay responded stoically.

Tapping her diamond-tipped manicure thoughtfully on the control wheel, Callista considered the time. "I'll comm you," she said finally. "Or I'll have Xavier do it. Maneuvering might be a bit delicate tonight, so I don't want to rush things."

Barclay glanced at her wrist comm, which was cleverly disguised within a matching pair of silver filigree and diamond cuffs. "I suppose the favored daughter of Lindmark couldn't be caught dead doing something so pedestrian as ordering her own skimmer."

"Of course not." After all, she had an image to maintain. "Now hang on. I see a space about to open up, and I'm going to take it."

Barclay shut his eyes. "Just tell me when it's over."

Callista's grin widened as she yanked the control wheel to the right and dove.

Straight towards the milling mass of people, right through the cloud of news drones, her skimmer streaked like a silver arrow towards the spot at the end of the red carpet. Another skimmer had just departed, and the next one in line was getting ready to pull forward, but there was a gap...

The skimmer's drive screamed as she spun the wheel and threw the stabilizers offline. She'd had to customize the controls herself, or the safety mechanisms would have made this maneuver impossible.

But when she was at the helm? Nothing was impossible for Callista Linden.

The skimmer knifed sideways through the air—much too fast

and just fast enough. With a final wail of protest from the drive, she shut down the thrusters and slid into her chosen space— inches from the nose of the skimmer behind her.

The crowd erupted. The air exploded with flashes from the news drones. Casino security raced to surround her skimmer.

And Callista smiled. After months of planning, it was finally showtime.

The cockpit door slid back, and she emerged into the lights, booted foot foremost. Her pilot's shades concealed her dark eyes, but she let a smirk linger on her burgundy-red lips as the flashes from a thousand news drones reflected off her silver sheath dress.

Her hemline skated perilously close to too short, but never crossed that line. Four-inch heels (liberally encrusted with diamond chips) on her burgundy leather boots placed her solidly at eye level with most of the men she would encounter, while her bombshell makeup and carefully contoured neckline ensured that most of them would never bother meeting those eyes.

The moment she removed her shades and unleashed a smile for the cameras, Xavier emerged from the crowd to take her arm. Despite her four-inch heels, he was half a head taller and filled out his tux to perfection. Xavier was a pro at pretending to ignore the cameras, but with his flawless brown skin, shaved head, intense dark eyes, and cheekbones a model would kill for, he'd been confounding the society gossips for nearly two years. No one could ever seem to decide whether he was her body-guard or her lover, and both of them were happy to keep it that way.

"Is Alli already in place?" Callista murmured, throwing a cheeky salute at the casino's fuming security guards as she strode off down the red carpet.

"She's had eyes on your mark for twenty minutes," Xavier confirmed, his expression as stoic as Callista's was animated.

"Losses?"

"Moderate."

"Do I need to bait him, or do you think my entrance will be enough?"

"Your entrance," Xavier remarked dryly, "has probably already given your grandfather apoplexy. I imagine Maxim Korchek will be stewing sufficiently for your purposes."

If there was one thing she could be sure of, it was that Maxim would never willingly surrender the limelight.

"Excellent." Callista took a moment to pause, rearrange her dark curls, and pose for the vids. She looked every bit the quintessential society heiress, on her way to lose a fortune at the most exclusive casino in Haven Two—the largest neutral city on the planet, where everyone who was anyone went to see and be seen.

At least, that was the appearance she was aiming for. And by the time she and Xavier made it through the front doors of The Diamond Iris, her aural implant was streaming her a gratifying sample of the headlines already circulating on gossip feeds.

Callista Linden was well known to be flippant, mercurial, and unpredictable. An expensive liability. Dangerously close to being impossible to marry off, even for the sake of a merger. After all, Lindmark Corporation's status wasn't exactly untarnished, even before Callista's larger-than-life exploits. These days, there were frequent reminders of her drunken exit from a party a few months ago, after which she'd nearly crashed her skimmer through the roof of her penthouse apartment.

Nearly being the operative word. Callista Linden never crashed into anything unless she meant to.

She also never drank, but the world at large didn't need to

know that. All they needed to know was that she was rich, gorgeous, and out to have as much fun as possible before life got in her way.

"Tell Alli I'll need a vacant spot next to Maxim in about ten minutes," she informed Xavier as they made their way through the opulent foyer and onto the gaming floor. "I'm going to place a few race bets first."

He nodded and relayed the message, and somewhere, Callista knew her tiny blonde bodyguard would be working her magic on the son of some society family or other.

Alli was five foot nothing, with ample curves, golden waves, and innocent blue eyes. She was as deadly with weapons as she was with her dimples and mile-long lashes, and Callista had absolute confidence in her ability to clear a path pretty much anywhere.

After a detour to the private betting lounge, where she placed several random wagers on high-profile skimmer races, Callista meandered back out onto the floor and made a tour of the VIP tables, pausing to flirt with a few carefully chosen targets and sipping at a drink provided by Xavier. It was red and sparkling, just like the currently popular Scarlet Assassin, but Callista's was completely harmless.

Just another prop for the drama currently unfolding.

With a careless flip of her hair, she finally made her way to a baccarat table, where the criminally handsome Maxim Korchek was… winning. The stack of chips in front of him was far larger than Callista would have liked, but perhaps it could work to her advantage in the end.

"Callie." Maxim turned and aimed his patented smolder in her general direction.

Callista, in her turn, pretended to be affected by it.

"Max, darling." She offered up her diamond-chipped manicure to be kissed, and Max Darling obliged with a smooth wink.

"Couldn't help but notice your entrance," he murmured, half an eye on her as he slid his chips into place.

"That was the general idea," she purred, leaning closer and laying a hand on his shoulder. "But it's nice to be appreciated."

"Heard you nearly took out the wife of a Hastings cousin."

Was that who'd been in the skimmer behind her? She probably ought to be insulted by the consistent expectation that she would someday cause a crash. And perhaps she would be, if that hadn't been exactly what she wanted everyone to expect.

Turning half her attention to the baccarat table, Callista took note of Maxim's next few bets. He appeared to be playing it safe, Alli informed her through her implant. All bets on the banker. A few rounds proved her to be correct, which seemed on the cautious side for Maxim. Perhaps he needed some softening up. So Callista watched, made sparkling small talk, and sipped at her drink, which was kept consistently refilled by Xavier.

After about an hour, the moment seemed to be right. Maxim had lost five in a row, and Callista had consumed enough "cocktails" that anyone watching would assume her judgment to be sufficiently impaired. So she wobbled precariously on her four-inch heels, tripped over nothing, and spilled her drink directly down the front of Maxim's custom-tailored white tux.

He leaped from his seat, swearing viciously and scattering chips across the floor.

"Oh, Maxie darling, I'm so sorry," Callista cried, mopping ineffectually at his suit with a cocktail napkin. "Let me make it up to you."

"Make it up to me?" he snarled, all affability gone. "How about you stop flipping your hair and sit down so I can concentrate. If I win back the price of this tux, maybe I'll be willing to let it go."

Callie eyed the tux and almost didn't blame him for being angry. It was made with the newest generation of Korchek's patented nano thread, custom-engineered to maintain ideal body temperature while protecting the wearer from stun weapons and even some projectile attacks.

But Callista Linden wasn't supposed to know those things, so she only blinked innocently and tilted her head to the side. "But Maxie, I can't. You know I only ever bet on the skimmers. No dice. No cards."

He leaned in closer as a crowd formed around them. Xavier began to tug ineffectually on her arm, as if to remove her before she made a scene.

"Then maybe I'll take back the price a little more directly," Maxim said in a hard, dangerous voice. "Let's bet on a race."

"Ohhh, do you mean it?" She wobbled up and laid a hand on his arm. "I've always wanted to watch you race, Maxie."

Maxim blinked. Had he really offered to do that? He'd probably intended for both of them to choose professionals to represent their interests, as was common among the Conclave's upper echelons. But there were too many avid eyes on their little drama, and he was stuck now. Besides, Maxim Korchek prided himself on his flight skills. Why would he back out of a race with whoever might be chosen by the pampered daughter of Lind mark, who was all flash but had no idea how to survive in the real world?

Callista watched as indecision flitted across his face, and suppressed a shark-like smile. When he began twisting the signet ring on his right hand, she knew she'd won.

"I suppose I could consider that, as long as it's a friendly contest just between the two of us," Maxim responded, recalling his dignity in time to sneer condescendingly. "But as the offended party, I believe I should be permitted to set the terms of the wager."

Callista tapped her burgundy lips with one finger. "I don't know." She leaned closer. "You know my allowance was cut off after, well…" The near-crash into her own roof had infuriated her mother, as it had been intended to.

"Property then?" Maxim pretended to consider. "I wouldn't say no to wagering one of my smaller holdings against your penthouse."

Callista pouted for a moment. "But that's my home, Maxie. Where would I live?"

"I have no doubt you could find someone willing to take you in while you relocate." His smirk left no doubt about his meaning —or his belief in his own invincibility—but she chose to ignore both.

After a bit more pouting, she twirled a brown curl around her finger and said, "Fine. But what are *you* going to wager?"

Maxim shrugged, apparently unconcerned. "Take your pick," he said generously. "Dema-Steel Manufacturing, Gervasi Labs, Seren Biotech—"

"Seren!" Callista exclaimed, beaming. "I don't know what they do, but Seren was the name of my cat when I was little. Maybe it will be good luck!"

Maxim Korchek gave her a look that dripped with disdain for the woman who would choose her wager based on the name of a cat.

But he probably had no idea what Seren Biotech did either. He likely only knew that it was one of the smaller companies he'd been given control over as the second son of his family.

And small, to Maxim Korchek, equaled meaningless.

"As you wish," he said impatiently, summoning his bodyguard from the crowd with a peremptory wave. "Shall we say tomorrow morning? At the Canyon?"

Callista unleashed her most brilliant smile. "Of course! I'll find someone and be there."

"Bring your key code," Maxim said with a wolfish grin, "because you won't be needing it any longer."

And with that, he vanished into the crowd, while the onlookers began to disperse, content that the drama had played itself out.

"You know you won't be able to pull this off more than once," Xavier murmured from just behind Callista's elbow. "We may not be able to fully protect your identity."

"Once is all I need," she told him, turning to hand over her empty cocktail glass with a shrug. "This is the last piece before I go for the kill. Has mother commed yet?"

"Thirty-seven times at last count."

Callista let out a resigned sigh. "I suppose that means the fun is over. Call Barclay, would you? I'll chat with Mummy Dearest on the way home."

———

THEIR CONVERSATION WAS a near-exact replay of the last twelve, in which Satrina Linden bemoaned her child's complete incompetence, insensitivity, and inability to recall what was due the Linden name.

But the Linden name had been quite thoroughly tarnished long before Callista came along, so she wasn't really able to take such admonishments seriously. Nor did she care for her mother's approval. She'd spent her entire adult life ensuring that her mother and grandfather considered her a complete waste of air, so it was more than a little gratifying to know how thoroughly she'd succeeded.

As a child, she'd been both curious and observant, and by the age of eleven, had seen ample evidence of cruelty, corruption, and illegal practices that could be directly linked to her mother and grandfather. She'd learned early how to deflect their notice, but was forced to watch helplessly while they destroyed her brother, Phillip—crushing his conscience along with his heart.

Her oldest brother, Carolus, had responded to their mother's cruelty by caring for nothing except himself. Phillip had learned to care for nothing except the corporation.

And Callista? She'd found ways to remain independent. She'd learned to hide, to manipulate, and pretend. And she'd sworn back then that she would never allow them to control her. That she would someday redeem the name of Linden from the stain of her grandfather's legacy.

After the Daragh fiasco—and Phillip's subsequent disgrace and disappearance—Satrina had clearly hoped to turn Callista into something resembling a competent heir. And Callista, for her part, had every intention of taking control of Lindmark in the future.

But on her own terms. She would cut herself off completely before she agreed to become her grandfather's puppet, as Phillip had been since he was fourteen. That world had destroyed him and everyone around him, while Callista could do nothing but watch.

Now she refused to repeat her brother's mistakes, but there was one thing the two of them had held very much in common— a fierce love of the corporation their family had built. She was determined to protect the people who relied on it for their security and their livelihoods, but that would never be possible as long as her mother or grandfather held the reins.

Not when they saw nothing wrong with murdering their own family to protect themselves from the consequences of their own treasonous actions.

The hangar doors beneath her apartment opened automatically at their approach, and as Barclay slipped smoothly into a dock, he glanced in her direction with a worried frown.

"Will Diamondback be putting in an appearance tonight?" he asked, in his most neutral, professional-sounding voice.

Callista wrinkled her nose and shook her head. "Unfortunately, no. I need to make a few comm calls, and my legal team needs to be prepared for tomorrow." When Barclay said nothing in response, she dug her elbow into his ribs. "And yes, I know you're happy that my unsavory affiliation with the underground racing circuit is almost over."

She, on the other hand, was going to miss it. The less legal side of racing had given her the opportunity to test a vast array of new developments in skimmer technology. She'd also had the chance to rub shoulders with ordinary Lindmark citizens—something her mother and grandfather had never allowed—and understand more of what the people of Lindmark needed. And if it also allowed her to pit herself against the best and prove that she could win? That was just a bonus.

But starting tomorrow, everything was going to change. Starting tomorrow, her long-anticipated takeover of Lindmark would begin.

If she'd played her cards well, no one in the Conclave was going to see her coming until it was too late.

TWO

THE CANYON, as it was so inaptly named, was not an encouraging sight by daylight. An unsavory mix of testing grounds and dumping site, it lurked in the barren lands outside Haven Two and served as a home base for much of the shady activity that kept Haven's underground afloat.

Callista floated slowly over the outskirts, keeping a wary eye out for unexpected traffic. There were no laws out here that either prevented crashes or cared about the aftermath, and it was an easy place to be caught unaware. Pits, craters, and ravines pocked the landscape, interspersed with unnatural mountains of concrete and twisted steel—the abandoned remains of failed building projects, outmoded spaceships, and ancient bridges.

Much of it was uninhabited, but there were areas that had become a ramshackle warren of homes and businesses for those who preferred to operate outside the reach of corporate oversight.

Could the Conclave have chosen to crack down on these activities? Of course. But a thriving black market ensured that the corporations could keep their hands clean while retaining access to the less-than-legal goods and services this market provided.

And one of the more popular "services" was the underground racing circuit that operated in the midst of the ruins. Anyone could fly anything, and the only rule was that there were no rules. The race courses shifted according to the whim of the shadowy organizers behind the lucrative gambling operation, and they utilized the most hazardous parts of the Canyon with a ruthless zeal for danger.

Today's race, however, would be in the public eye. Maxim had enough contacts in the underground to set it up, but they would only allow the children of the corporate elite to race where accidents were less likely. If Maxim Korchek came to grief racing in the Canyon, Korchek's legendary rage would descend, and the entire area would be reduced to ashes.

Which was too bad, in Callista's opinion. Maxim was quite proud of his piloting skills, and she would love to see him tested in a night race at the heart of the Canyon—on a tangled course right through the labyrinth of hulking steel shells, where one wrong move could turn a skimmer into a crumpled ball of metal, or impale a racer through the heart.

But that was all part of what drew her here. Beyond the testing of new technology, she came back again and again for the high of riding that razor edge between victory and death. Of pitting herself against the impossible and coming out victorious.

Or maybe it was the knowledge that she was spitting in the eye of what everyone expected of her.

More than likely, it was all of those things, and as Callista eased into a gentle landing on the official starting platform, she tried to ignore the feeling of loss. This might be her last time.

Maxim was already there, standing beside his sleek black

racing skimmer with a cocky smirk on his sculpted lips. His helmet was tucked under his arm, and his blond hair was styled in its usual windswept waves.

Without leaving the cockpit, Callista sent a message to his comm.

Max, darling, my pilot has arrived. I'll be watching, so don't disappoint me.

Max Darling glanced at his wrist comm, then turned to stare at her skimmer. As if he could determine the identity of her pilot through the tinted windscreen and the bulk of her helmet.

He would find out soon enough, and she grinned as she transmitted her info to the tower.

When they realized both racers had arrived, a legion of news drones soared into the air around the starting platform. Across her aural implant, Callista heard the first waves of their transmissions and felt the familiar surge of fierce, adrenaline-fueled joy.

It was the last time, so she was going to make it everything she'd ever dreamed of.

"… a special event match race." The announcer's words crackled into her implant. "Maxim Korchek, three-time champion of the Korchek World Skimmer Circuit, against…" There was a pause, as if the announcer wasn't quite sure his information was correct. "He will be racing against Callista Linden, whose pilot by proxy will be…" He cleared his throat. "Friends, we're in for a hell of a show this morning. Please welcome back to the Canyon, the One, the Only, the Legendary… *Diamondback.*"

Her aural feed erupted. The news drones zoomed in, as if by getting closer, they could catch a glimpse of the elusive underground racer.

And Maxim Korchek's face twisted into an icy scowl of disbelieving rage. He stalked towards her skimmer, the expression on his face suggesting he intended to drag her out of it. But there was no way in, so he could do nothing but stand there, twisting his ring and glaring at the windscreen.

And then the starting lights illuminated, so there was no time for him to ruminate on his mistakes.

Maxim jerked as if coming to his senses, jammed his helmet over his perfect coiffure, and slid into his cockpit. A message flashed across Callista's wrist comm.

You're faking. There's no way you know Diamondback. And now I'm going to destroy you.

So she took a moment to respond.

Sorry, Maxie, but I really wanted Seren. Now stop twisting that ring, and let's find out if you race better than you kiss.

The light flashed green, and Callista's skimmer shot into the heavens like a sky-bound angel.

As much as she wanted to, this wasn't the time to press the limits of speed. This was her last race, so she knew she had to give the audience something to remember. It was all about showmanship, so she slowed enough to allow Maxim to ride the trail of her thrusters before dropping her altitude suddenly, right before the first checkpoint.

Maxim hit his accelerator and roared past her as they rounded the pinnacle of what had once been a skyscraper in Old New York. After that, the course took a steep dive into a v-shaped split in the earth, taking them rocketing along a narrow path with a sharp corner that served as the second checkpoint. No cheating here—they had to pass within ten yards of the beacon.

Drones overhead kept track of their progress, so Callista was careful to stay close to Maxim's tail as they soared out of the canyon and took a hard left towards the next series of checkpoints.

This part of the course required them to ping like giant pinballs across a debris field, zig-zagging through obstacles without hitting them, or each other.

Callista had run this course so many times, she could have found her way through the field with her eyes closed, so after the first checkpoint in the series, she increased her speed and flipped her skimmer upside down. A quick zag around the corpse of an ancient airliner and her left fin was tip to tip with Maxim's.

If he were another professional, she might have tried to run the whole course that close. But she didn't trust Maxim not to crash them both, so as they pinged the second checkpoint, she went into a horizontal spiral, circling Maxim's skimmer just fast enough to keep pace.

And the cameras loved it.

In her ear, Callista could hear the chatter and the cheers as she flipped through the channels. It made her grin, but if Maxim was listening too, his rage could make him dangerous, so she pulled out of the spiral and drew back.

He backed off at the same time, matching her pace.

Was he hoping to provoke her into making a mistake?

Their next checkpoint was a high-altitude beacon, meant to test their ability to control a glide. The maneuver was only difficult for amateurs, so Callista hit the climb at a moderate speed, Maxim stubbornly clinging to her side.

She didn't want to attempt a traditional glide with him that close, so when they hit the peak, Callista decided it was time to shake him off. She'd kept the race close as long as she could.

Instead of gliding back down at an angle, Callista opened up her thrusters, aimed the nose of her skimmer at the ground, and dove, straight down, thrusters screaming.

Her racing skimmer had no safety mechanisms, so there was nothing to alert her to the proximity of the ground. No alarms, no cushions, just the razor-edge of judgment telling her when to pull out. Just the rush of the wind past her cockpit, and the twitch of her fingers on the controls.

And because it was her last race, she let the dive linger until she knew Barclay would be screaming from the box where she was supposed to be standing.

Moments from impact, she reversed the thrusters and flipped the control wheel.

In any standard skimmer, she would have become a glittering silver pancake on the hard-packed ground.

But she'd spent years modifying this one, and it answered the controls like it was an extension of her mind, swooping close to the earth before rising again like a missile aiming for the heavens.

Then there was only one more checkpoint, at the end of a long, flat straightaway.

Time to show the watching crowd what her baby could do.

Callista rolled twice as she dropped back to Earth, opened the thrusters, and rocketed towards the finish line.

This was where she would live if she truly had a choice. As much as she cared about the fate of Lindmark, she longed for a world where the only things that mattered were speed and skill and the work of her own hands. But that wasn't where she'd been born, and no matter how much she wanted to escape, that wasn't an option—no matter how fast she flew.

Lindmark was in her blood and bone, and after today, it would become her world.

The finish line came in sight, with Maxim so far behind he

didn't even appear on her sensors. A fierce grin crossed her lips, and she considered doing a victory roll... but better to keep it professional. He was going to be angry enough as it was.

Less than a thousand yards from the end of the course, an impact punched through her skimmer's right fin.

What the... there was no debris on this part of the course, and drones weren't allowed to get too close. There was nothing to hit!

She'd been shot at.

Alarms blared as the skimmer's trajectory slewed wildly, and Callista fought for control, but she was going too fast.

The skimmer flipped end over end.

Hands locked on the control wheel, she gritted her teeth against the pain and fought the forces that threatened to press her into unconsciousness. A hard jolt indicated the skimmer had hit the ground. It bounced, tumbled, and hit again before Callista could glance out of the cockpit and see that her fins were gone.

She hit the button for the auxiliary thrusters and locked in the stabilizers. Only about half of them fired up, which threw the controls off balance. The blip of Maxim's skimmer appeared on her sensors, but Callista hadn't come this far to fail.

It took every bit of muscle to hold the controls steady, every ounce of her skill to aim for the finish and direct auxiliary power aft. But she'd built her baby herself, and it was designed to take a hit and keep going. The auxiliary thrusters flared to life, and the skimmer shot across the finish line, crashing into a makeshift barrier a full five seconds before Maxim's skimmer screamed across the line in her wake.

She'd won.

Even though someone had tried to ensure that she didn't walk away.

But she could think about that later. News drones clustered

overhead, filling the air with flashing lights and kicking up dust. Maxim had emerged from his skimmer and was headed her way with murder on his handsome face.

It was showtime.

The main systems were down, but her cockpit still opened manually, so Callista was able to slide back the door and exit with almost her usual grace and swagger. She was still a little dizzy from the crash, so she gave herself a moment once her boots hit the ground—a moment for the news drones to get a good look at her flight gear.

Her helmet was patterned with scintillating scales, and down the back of her custom flight jacket, a vertical row of diamond-shaped patches caught the light. She'd worn it ever since her debut on the underground circuit, and every racing fan knew it by sight.

Maxim stopped in his tracks when he saw her, and his mouth went slack. Until that moment, he hadn't quite believed he'd been racing a legend. For a brief moment, he almost seemed to relax. As if he could live with losing to someone like Diamondback.

So that's when Callista signaled her people and waited for the flashes of the news drones to stop before she reached up and took off her helmet. Shook out her dark brown curls, looked over at Maxim, and winked.

She was looking him in the eye, so she could see the exact moment when his brain basically exploded as he realized the truth. This was a body blow to his ego that he might never recover from and a public relations disaster for Korchek should it ever become widely known.

He couldn't even seem to process the potent combination of fury and disbelief. His knees wobbled visibly, so Callista decided to take pity on him. She crossed the remaining distance and held out her gloved hand for him to shake.

Maxim looked at it as if she might really be the desert rattler from which she took her name.

"Shake it, Maxie," she said softly. "Right now, it's just you and me. Those news drones have experienced an 'unplanned outage,' but if you prefer, I can make sure the whole world is watching."

"What. The. Hell," he murmured, his whole body quivering with the force of his rage.

"I think that's my line," she returned, her smile concealing the razor edge of her own fury. "Either shake hands and make good on your bet, or I will reveal not only the truth of this race, but the real reason why I crashed just before the finish."

"Good luck proving anything," he snarled through clenched teeth.

"Max, you might have the edge on me in a boardroom, but out here, I'm Diamondback. I don't have to prove it. The vids and the fin will show the hit, and you're the only one with anything to lose."

A guttural growl emerged from his throat, but he took her hand and gave it a single, vicious shake, attempting in the process to crush her with his grip.

She met his strength evenly.

When his eyes widened, she couldn't help it. She laughed in his face.

"Max, while you've been strutting around in your fancy suits, I've been working on skimmers since I was twelve. Me, not my people. Don't blame me if you overestimated yourself. Now, I believe we have business to attend to before we walk away."

When Maxim hesitated, Callista returned his poisonous glare

with an expression of serene confidence. "I want my winnings secure."

His lip curled. "Are you suggesting I would cheat?"

She raised an eyebrow and glanced back at the course, making her opinion perfectly clear. "I want confirmation that your legal team has made the transfer."

It was almost too much for his self-control, but Callista had planned her blackmail well. As long as she controlled the news footage, she held his reputation in her hands, and he had no choice. Maxim lifted his wrist comm and gave the order. Within seconds, Xavier's voice came across her implant.

"It's done. Seren is ours."

A weight fell from her shoulders. It had begun.

She turned back towards her ruined skimmer, preparing to walk away, when a hand landed on her shoulder. Twisting out from under it, she caught a glimpse of Maxim's fist as it descended towards her face.

Her body reacted almost without thought. Ducking left, she let his punch flash harmlessly past her face before twisting back to the right, turning her hips into a lightning-fast elbow strike to his right temple.

Skimmers weren't the only things she'd spent her life working on. She trained with Alli and Xavier four nights a week, so she knew where and how to hit.

Maxim's head snapped back with the impact, and he flopped like a dead fish.

Ugh. The Korchek scion never had learned to take losing well. It wasn't the finale she'd wanted, but it would probably play to her advantage in the end. Maxim would never risk this moment becoming fodder for public gossip.

Pulling her helmet back on and tapping her wrist comm, she

signaled her people to end the transmission blackout, but suddenly it didn't seem to matter anymore. The drones did not resume their flashing. Most of them were streaking away, and her aural implant had gone completely silent.

Curious now, she activated her voice comm and called Barclay.

"What's happened?"

The connection was solid, but he didn't answer.

"Barclay?"

She could hear him breathing, but he didn't seem to have any words.

"Are you okay?"

"I'm fine," he said finally, but his voice was flatter than the desert floor. "You need to see this. I can't..." Whatever it was, he couldn't find the words to tell her.

So in the middle of the dusty racecourse, Callista activated the viewscreen on her helmet and connected to the net.

Every channel was screaming the news—a transmission had just arrived via the Conclave beacons. It came from Concord Five, the busiest way-station in space. But Concord wasn't usually a significant source of gossip or novelty, so Callista activated the vid playback with burgeoning apprehension.

The face that appeared was the last one she would have expected. After all, the man staring at the camera was supposed to be dead.

But Phillip Linden, it appeared, was very much alive. Or at least, someone wanted the world to believe that he was.

"Greetings to Earth," he said, and Callista felt tears form in her eyes for no reason she could name.

She and Phillip hadn't exactly been close. But she had mourned the loss of the person he could have been and felt his pain at the injustice of the accusations against him. She knew all too well who had really been guilty of the atrocities on Daragh.

"Perhaps you remember me," he continued, "but perhaps you don't, so allow me to introduce myself. My name is Phillip Linden. Several years ago, I was tried and sentenced for serious crimes against the Conclave, crimes that blackened my name and doomed me to exile in the farthest reaches of space. I was stripped of my name and left to live or die according to the whims of fate."

Callista wondered if he was aware that everyone on Earth thought he was actually dead. Probably. If she knew Phillip at all, he would have found a source of information.

He paused for a moment, and she saw his blue eyes harden. "But the crimes for which I was exiled were not my own. I chose exile to prevent the collapse of Lindmark Corporation and the destruction that would inevitably have followed, but my period of silence has come to an end."

That definitely sounded like Phillip. The vid still might be a fabrication, but how many people knew her brother well enough to guess that he would fall on his sword for the sake of Lindmark's survival?

"I stand on the wreckage of Concord Five to tell you that war is coming. And not just a corporate war. This space station was brought to ruin by a destructive force beyond anything humanity has ever dreamed or conjured. And it is coming for Earth unless we can stop it."

Hold on…

Callista paused the vid, backed up, and played those words again. A destructive force? With the ability to destroy a space station?

Before starting the vid again, she commed everyone in her

inner circle. Had the source of the vid been confirmed? Was this an elaborate hoax, or was there a chance it was real? And if it was real, why had they not received news of it before now? If enough of the station was left for Phillip to send this message, surely others had survived.

She returned to the vid.

"I am returning to Earth," Phillip said, "to make every attempt to save it. But that attempt will not come without a price. I intend to see justice done for the crimes of which I was accused—crimes that can be laid at the door of Eustacius and Satrina Linden."

That would make two of them in search of justice. But Callista doubted they had the same goals in mind. If this was real, was there any way the two of them could possibly cooperate to achieve their ends?

"Believe me or don't. Ignore me or don't. That means nothing to me." Phillip's face was set, his expression taut and steely.

Callista knew that look. Her brother was win-or-die, and he had never learned to bend in pursuit of his end goals.

"I am coming," he said, "and I will be taking back what is mine. If you remember nothing else about me, remember that I will let nothing stand in the way of getting what I want. Justice *will* be served, and then we will face this threat together. Or, you can choose to oppose me and be annihilated."

He was challenging them all. Just as Callista had finally laid the groundwork for her own attempt to see justice done. If she wasn't careful, Phillip was going to ruin everything she'd spent the last few years achieving.

Would he class her with the ones who had wronged him and include her in his quest for revenge? And what did he mean about a threat?

But he still wasn't finished.

"Before I end this transmission, I have a special message for you, Grandfather." Phillip's even tone was a warning to anyone who knew him. "You should know that I remember every word you said at our last meeting. Know that I have finished bearing the weight of your crimes, your hubris, and your overwhelming incompetence." He leaned closer to the recorder. "Know that I am coming for you, and no matter what happens to the rest of Earth, I will ensure that you face the consequences for your actions. *All* of your actions."

He leaned back again and smiled.

"I imagine when you get this, you'll make a frantic attempt to lock me out of your systems and double the guards on the doors, but it won't matter. I'll always know how to beat you because it was never you that built Lindmark, Grandfather. It was me. I made Lindmark what it is today, and I am finished letting you destroy it. And because I made it, I will always be able to find a way in.

"No matter how far you run, no matter how well you hide, I will find you. And Lindmark will be mine."

The recording died.

Callista looked down at the crumpled form of Maxim, then let her gaze drift to the bent and broken frame of her beloved racing skimmer.

Both were as fully wrecked as her plans. And, if Phillip were to be believed, as the once-thriving space station, Concord Five.

It was time to see whether anything could be salvaged.

Striding away from the wreckage, Callista headed towards the tower and Barclay, already laying the foundation of strategies that might counter Phillip's damning revelations.

The more she thought about it, the less she believed his claim that the station had been destroyed, let alone that whatever had done it was coming for Earth. The Conclave beacons were clearly still working, so why would they not have received this news before now?

No, her brother clearly had a chip on his shoulder and every intention of ruining what she'd spent the last few years working towards, which meant she needed to gain control before he arrived. Given the distance, she should have between eight and nine weeks to accomplish her goals. She'd hoped for that many *months*.

But Callista Linden did not believe in the impossible.

Time to put on her big-girl heels and find a new path to victory.

THREE

BY THE TIME Callista returned to her penthouse, her team was in full damage-control mode.

As heads of her security team, Alli and Xavier were touching base with their contacts from the other four Conclave members.

Callista's business managers were waiting in her conference room. Priya and Jocasta had been with her since she was a teen, taking her first—secret—steps into the cutthroat world of corporate politics.

Jocasta was her mother's age, a severe-looking, white-haired grandmother of two, who still had more energy than Callista could dream of on her best day. She had the instincts of a piranha and the soul of a teddy bear, and Callista had entrusted much of the implementation of her plans to Jocasta's capable hands.

Priya was a stunning woman of not quite thirty, about the same age as Callista. She had flawless brown skin, huge dark eyes, and long dark hair that she typically wore in an elaborate braid. Her hiring instincts were second to none, and she'd been managing all personnel teams for Callista for nearly five years.

Both had what Callista essentially lacked—razor-sharp business minds to manage the corporate side of her ambitions.

It was Callista's unenviable job to deal with the Lindens and juggle the politics that came with being a part of a Conclave family.

"What do we know?" Callista asked as she strode into the conference room, her helmet still dangling from her fingers.

Priya's uncompromising expression softened slightly with compassion. Both women knew what Callista's racing career had meant to her, just as both knew that it was very likely over.

"The Seren handover is complete," Jocasta announced, crossing her legs and placing her folded hands on the conference table, posture as perfectly upright as always. "Our people are in the process of checking all on-site computers, downloading database content, and checking it against public records. We should have confirmation of the true extent of their research by tomorrow."

"Excellent." That was fast, but it was also necessary. If Callista hadn't had people in place, prepared to take possession the moment ownership changed hands, Korchek would likely have made every effort to destroy what made Seren so valuable—groundbreaking new discoveries in the field of biotechnology.

"As you requested, I checked into the validity of the bombshell comm vid from Concord," Priya announced when Callista turned her way. "More on that in a moment, but I've uncovered worrying discrepancies in communication patterns. There are usually comm logs arriving each day from all Lindmark ships coming or going from Earth. Only about half of our ships' comm logs have been updated for the past several weeks."

"And we're only just now hearing about this?" Callista raised an eyebrow as she dropped into the chair at the head of the table and propped one booted foot on the opposite knee. "Which ships have gone silent?"

Priya nodded. "That is, in fact, the correct question. Only the ships that were either coming or going from Concord Five are failing to update. But it gets even stranger."

She pulled up a reader and showed Callista the screen. "The ships are still functional, and all of them are on the move. They've been pinging off locator beacons, which show half of our fleet is returning to Earth at maximum speed."

This was not an accident. Callista shrugged off the fog that remained as a consequence of her crash and tried to make sense of the data.

"What do you think of the recording?" News outlets were still buzzing, hours after it had first been received, but there had been no official statement from any of the Conclave corporations. This, alone, would have been enough to arouse Callista's suspicions.

"More importantly, what do *you* think?" Jocasta leveled a piercing stare at Callista. "Is that really Phillip? Or an AI meant to throw us off the trail of something bigger?"

Callista drummed her fingers on the table as she thought back over the message in the recording. "My gut says it's really him." She shrugged apologetically. "I can't back it up with numbers or proof, but I've learned to trust my instincts. Phillip is alive. And he's no good at lying." Her lips twisted in memory. "The only way they kept him in line as long as they did was by feeding him so many half-truths and obfuscations, he genuinely believed in the value of what he was doing. Once he found out the truth about our family? He would have been gone whether they banished him or not."

And maybe he'd been right. Maybe there was no way to save

what corporate politics had created. But while Callista was fully as stubborn as her brother, she was more apt to view the world as a challenge to be conquered. The more impossible it looked, the more determined she was to find a way to win.

"If it really is Phillip," Priya noted, "our next move must take his warning into account. What did he mean by a destructive force that is coming for Earth?"

The door to the conference room burst open, admitting Xavier, with Alli at his heels.

Both of them appeared stunned.

"You need to hear this." Xavier set his reader in the center of the table and started audio playback.

Intermittent bursts of static were the first thing Callista heard.

"Where did you get this?" she murmured, as the bursts grew louder.

"It came in off the Conclave beacons," Xavier answered grimly. "All channels. Korchek tried to shut it down, but it was broadcast as a distress call, so they didn't get to everything in time. It's not even on the news yet, but one of my contacts in Korchek slipped it out before they locked down outgoing comms."

Korchek locked down comms? Callista swallowed the lump at the back of her throat that told her there was no simple reason for such a drastic action.

"... *Send assistance.*"

The recorded voice that suddenly echoed through the conference room was filled with panic.

Another burst of static. "...*On fire,*" the same voice screamed. "*We've lost all but one of our satellites.*"

Callista locked eyes with Xavier and wondered if she looked as horror-stricken as he did.

"They're everywhere! We can't stop them. I repeat, you must send assistance."

The transmission dissolved again into static… and then it died.

"Where did it come from?" Callista whispered into the silence.

"Vadim." Alli's tone was hollow with shock. "It's a Korchek mining planet—one of the farthest from Earth."

Callista's jaw clenched in response, and she lifted her wrist to tap viciously at her comm. "All of you, place our people on highest alert. Whatever this is, it becomes top priority until we figure out what exactly is happening and why we haven't heard about it through official channels."

"What are you…" Priya's question died at the fury in Callista's eyes.

There was only one place to get the answers she needed.

"I'm going for a little visit," she said.

———

SHE DIDN'T CHANGE out of her flight suit or stop to check her appearance. With only Barclay and Alli for backup, Callista headed straight for the hangar and took off, sending a cryptic message ahead of her. She informed her mother and grandfather that she would be arriving at the Tower and requested a meeting.

Then she ignored her mother's calls for the entire hour-long flight to Markheim—the operational center of Lindmark's holdings.

Lindmark occupied most of what had once been North America, and its chief city was built on the foundations of the old city of Chicago. Little was left of Old Chicago's ancient land-marks, but Lindmark Tower—the building that housed corporate headquarters—had been established on the site of that city's most iconic building, the Sears Tower.

Access to the upper levels of Lindmark Tower was keyed to Callista's genetics, so there wasn't much they could do to keep her out without restructuring security. And until now, Callista had given her mother and grandfather no reason to believe that this might be a mistake.

After all, she was flighty and irresponsible. Mercurial and uninterested in corporate concerns.

She was going to have to make this meeting count, because after today, there would be no mistaking her intentions or her ambitions. Only time would tell whether she could turn this situation to her own advantage in the end.

Security was tight around the Tower hangar, but no one tried to stop her, so Callista parked her skimmer in her usual spot. From there, she made her way towards the family-access-only tube. This was the most direct path to the topmost floors, from where Eustacius and Satrina Linden spun their webs and ruled their empire without conscience or compassion.

Along her path, Callista caught the sidelong glances of everyone from the cleaning staff to the commanding officer of Lindmark Security Forces. News of her bet with Maxim would have hit at the same time as Phillip's far more spectacular threats, but in Lindmark, at least, her stunt had likely still gained a fair amount of attention.

She'd been a wild card ever since she was old enough to know what it meant—ever since she began to understand the benefits of being underestimated. And everyone in this tower would know what it portended that she was here, now, under radically different circumstances than her typical visit to the family sanctum.

Their lives were about to change. And for those who lived close to the powerful few who ruled Earth, this could mean any number of things. It could mean the family they served was about to fall under the weight of scandal. It could mean restructuring—loss of power for some, immeasurable gains for others. It could represent either catastrophe or opportunity, and Callista could read both speculation and apprehension on every face that crossed her path.

No one survived Lindmark Tower without at least that much sense of self-preservation.

She stepped off the tube at its final stop, three floors below the tower's peak, and made for the office of her grandfather's secretary, Yolande—gatekeeper, and dragon in human form.

But the ageless, dark-skinned woman did not stop her. Instead, she pointed silently at the separate tube system that was the only access to the top three floors.

"You're expected," she said tonelessly, in response to Callista's wink.

Oh good. This should make things easier.

Barclay took a seat in Yolande's domain without needing to be asked, while Alli followed Callista into the tube. She was currently playing the part of a perfectly coiffed secretary, ready to do her mistress's bidding.

It wasn't likely she'd be allowed to witness the showdown that was about to take place, but her presence would irritate Eustacius — always a goal worth striving for.

Once the tube arrived at the topmost floor, Callista stepped out onto the gleaming marble of the hall and made her way to the executive office. Her grandfather's lair.

The door was open.

"Shut the door," Eustacius's cold voice intoned from his station by the window. "And leave your flunky outside. You should know better by now than to bring an outsider into family business."

"What business is that, Grandfather?"

Once, she'd believed him invincible. Eustacius Linden was well over eighty, but his face showed no more than fifty of those years. Anti-aging treatments had not yet advanced to the point of prolonging the human lifespan much beyond a century, but they were far more effective at obscuring the visible ravages of time.

And yet, now Callista could see how his hands shook where they hung by his sides. Could make out lines that he'd never before permitted to appear on his face.

When he turned to meet her level gaze, Callista almost took a step back.

In all her twenty-nine years, she had never seen that look in her grandfather's eyes before.

He was afraid. But he didn't want her to know it, so he struck like a viper before she could find her footing.

"I suppose you find your little stunt amusing," he barked.

Which stunt was he referring to? Her arrival at the Diamond Iris? Or had footage of her race somehow leaked out despite her team's drone blackout?

Callista jerked her head at Alli, who retreated silently to the hall outside. She would be keeping tabs on Callista's conversation through their aural implants—which neither Satrina nor Eustacius had. Most of the elite viewed them as an uncomfortable liability, so Callista kept hers a closely guarded secret.

"Which stunt is that, Grandfather?" she asked blandly, once the door closed on Alli's heels. "My gambling? My flying? Or the part where I won a wager against Maxim Korchek and gained control over a business you've been trying to buy for the past ten months?"

Satrina Linden stalked out of her corner on towering heels, ice blue eyes flashing with fury. "How dare you disrespect your grandfather?"

Once, Satrina had been habitually cool and detached, a professional wielder of ruthless instincts and emotionless efficiency.

But the loss of Daragh—and Phillip's "death"—had changed her.

Her fingers twitched continuously, clutching at her own sleeves as if they could somehow anchor her nerves. Desperation gave a hysterical edge to her voice, and her eyes darted from her daughter to her father in perpetual motion.

She, too, was afraid.

Afraid she'd failed to live up to Eustacius's expectations. Afraid that at any moment he would make the decision to cut her out—for her failed marriage, for her failure to raise up appropriate heirs, or for the losses that had reduced Lindmark Corporation to a shell of its former power and influence.

Because if there was one thing Eustacius Linden would never do, it was accept responsibility for any of his own actions.

"Now explain yourself," Satrina snapped. "Explain to me why, in the midst of a global crisis, I am forced to field questions about the instability of my heir. Explain why I am now embroiled in a legal conflict with Korchek, charging you with bodily assault and threatening to take action unless their property is returned."

Callista couldn't help a brief gurgle of laughter. She was a bit surprised Maxim had admitted to his father that she'd hit him.

He definitely would not have told the true story of the race, and would undoubtedly be furious that his family had stepped in.

But this wasn't really the time to be amused at Maxie's expense.

"I'm afraid," she said coolly, "that I have no desire whatsoever to explain anything."

Her mother's mouth dropped open a fraction.

"I am an adult, and my leisure activities are my own business. You have no say over whether I crash my skimmer or decide to join a troupe of itinerant acrobats."

This was not how Satrina had expected this conversation to go.

"However, I would like a few explanations of my own." Callista walked forward to face her grandfather over the top of his gleaming onyx desk.

"Perhaps you can explain the comm message from my not-so-deceased brother, whom you declared *dead* over a year ago. Perhaps you can also explain why half the Lindmark fleet is currently making its way towards Earth under communication blackout. Or why the entire Conclave has been conspiring to conceal the truth of Concord Five's destruction! An entire space station has been destroyed, and you're trying to *hide* it?"

"You have no right…" Satrina's attempt to berate her daughter was cut off by a silently raised hand from Eustacius.

"So you know," he said, his hard, calculating gaze boring into Callista's face.

"I know a lot of things, Grandfather." Callista held her ground, and her stare never wavered.

"You've been playing us for fools." He did not appear angry about it, and Callista fought back a shudder at the look of calculation he was now directing her way.

"No." She shook her head. "If you believe you've been made to appear a fool, look to your own house. I play my own game, and I always have."

She didn't give him a chance to say whatever insulting thing he would come up with next. Such as offering her a job. Because she knew her grandfather well enough to believe he just might do it.

So she struck again, from another angle. "Tell me about Vadim," she said.

Eustacius seemed to consider her for a few more moments. Then, to her surprise, he abandoned his station by the window, returned to his desk, and sat down.

This was no longer a confrontation. It was a conference. He wanted something from her.

"Concord Five suffered a collision with an alien creature of unknown origin," he said abruptly. "The integrity of the station's gravity and environmental systems was destroyed, and it has been abandoned until the appropriate repair crews can be sent to deal with it."

For a handful of moments, Callista found herself utterly speechless.

A collision? With an *alien creature*?

"What kind of creature?"

"All we know is that it is the size of a spaceship and appears to be individually capable of interstellar travel."

Callista did not permit her feelings to appear on her face, but she was stunned by the idea. Stunned, and then utterly appalled as she connected the dots.

"So that's the reason for the information blackout—all five corporations decided they wanted to be first to arrive back on the scene with science teams." Either that, or they were arguing over who would pay for repairs.

Eustacius didn't bother to deny it. "The creature, whatever it is, represents almost limitless potential in terms of advancing our understanding of space flight. We cannot afford to waste this opportunity."

His attitude was unsurprising. But it did not explain the content of Phillip's message.

"Then why did Phillip seem more concerned with the possibility of war and destruction affecting Earth?"

Eustacius's frown indicated his disdain for the direction of this conversation. "I could not possibly care less about the mumbling of a useless screw-up. He's probably hysterical and desperate to regain his power by any means possible. Attempting to frighten the gullible into retreating from this opportunity so he can seize it for himself."

"So you admit he's not dead?" Callista returned bluntly.

Her grandfather shrugged, but she could see the discomfort in his shoulders. "Perhaps I was overly optimistic."

And that was her family. Love had never once figured in their relationships. But that was not why she was here. There was no fixing the Lindens' dysfunctional family dynamics. No going back to a time before she realized she'd been born into a nest of vipers.

"If he's so hysterical," she said, slowly and clearly, "then what is happening on Vadim?"

It might be a Korchek mining planet in the sector of explored space farthest from Earth, but there weren't so many explored planets that her grandfather wouldn't know the name.

"That's Korchek's problem," Eustacius sneered. "Probably a fake, to draw our attention away from the situation on

Concord. Or an industrial accident. Or pirates. Nothing to do with us."

"'They're everywhere,'" Callista quoted. "'We can't stop them.' Does that really sound like pirates to you?"

"And what would a professional gambler and partier know about pirates?" her grandfather asked, a curl in his lip that belied the focused gleam in his eye.

"At least as much as a decaying corporate figurehead who never leaves his ivory tower."

Instead of growing angry at her jibe, Eustacius Linden smiled.

It was a terrifying sight.

"You've grown up, Callista."

The way he said it made her want to fly straight home and shower.

"In spite of your mother's hysterical carping, I believe you may have potential."

Potential for what? To be turned into a monster, just as they'd attempted to do with Phillip? No, thank you.

"Perhaps," Satrina burst in, rushing towards her father's desk. "But we cannot afford to be distracted in the midst of this crisis. And she has hardly contributed to the success of Lindmark—only created more messes for us to deal with."

"By acquiring Seren, as I asked you to do months ago?" Eustacius didn't even glance at his daughter. "That's not a mess—it's an opportunity. Perhaps her methods are unorthodox, but I never argue with success."

He looked up at Callista. "If your managers will set up a meeting with mine, I will ensure that the transfer of ownership is swift and uneventful. You'll be compensated, of course."

Then he leaned back. "And if everything is in order, I feel that we ought to consider some changes to the command structure.

Perhaps you can be of greater use than I previously considered. Your mother is, I believe, becoming increasingly weary of the weight of her responsibilities and would welcome your willingness to share her burdens over the coming months."

Callista fought the urge to… to… What was there to be done? She couldn't physically assault an old man, and destroying his office would serve no purpose. And in any case, she doubted there was any way to make him see how despicable his offer really was. How arrogant and self-absorbed he'd become, sitting here at the top of his kingdom, like a spider in a vast web spun from money and power.

He'd offered to take her property off her hands, and then suggested she replace her mother, like putting on a new pair of shoes.

"It seems there's been a misunderstanding," Callista replied, turning and making her way to the window. It was all she could do to stand motionless, staring down at the city while she gained control of her fury.

Finally, she turned and regarded the old man with both pity and contempt. "Seren is mine. I will not be signing it over to you, now or ever. And my life is my own. I will never take my mother's place, because I will never make the mistake of putting myself in a position where you have the slightest power over me."

She stalked back to his desk and loomed over it—over him—while he remained in his chair, watching her like he might watch an unknown animal suspected of rabies.

"I am not here to help you, Grandfather. I am not here to be a part of what you call a family. I am here to save Lindmark from the disaster it has become under your leadership."

Eustacius began to laugh. "You dare?" He sounded amused. "You have not the smallest idea what it takes to run an enterprise of this magnitude. Even less the spine and guts to do what must be done to keep it alive. Your brother didn't either, and that's why he's now trapped on the ruins of an abandoned station, raving about aliens and making impotent threats. Don't make the same mistakes he did, or you'll find this old man is nowhere near as helpless as you seem to think."

She shook her head. "Tell me, then, if you're not helpless. What are you doing about Concord? About the loss of jobs and lives? About the loss of a refueling stop our ships are counting on as they take supplies to our colonies? What are you doing about the concerns of our settlers as they hear the reports from Vadim? Will you protect them? Ensure they have access to the goods and services they need to survive? Is that why you've rerouted all our ships and refused to communicate with our people?"

"Our?" Her grandfather raised one dark eyebrow. "Don't be presumptuous, granddaughter. I built this corporation, and I will do with it as I please. Neither you nor anyone else has a say in how I allocate resources, and if you persist in this challenge to my authority, I will withdraw my previous degree of indulgence."

"Oh really?" Callista mocked. "Exactly what indulgence do you claim to have granted me?"

He did not move, and his expression did not change. "I can destroy everything you think you have, everything you love, and everything that gives your life meaning. You were made by me and my money, and there is nothing I cannot take away from you."

Callista heard a whimper from her mother but did not permit herself to be distracted. The real threat was behind the desk.

"Perhaps," she said. "But perhaps I'm not the only one being presumptuous. You think you own me?" She shook her head. "You haven't been paying attention."

She turned on her heel and made for the door.

"If you walk away now," her grandfather said, "you lose everything. I will take it all, and I will destroy you."

Callista looked back over her shoulder, and winked.

"Go ahead," she said softly. "Try it. I dare you."

And then she walked out.

FOUR

KILLIAN AVALAR, former pirate and smuggler, exiled prince, and unwilling defender of humanity, stood on the landing strip and asked himself what in all the hells he thought he was doing.

A cool wind ruffled his hair, and he put up one hand out of habit to rearrange it. But it was no longer styled in the rakish spikes he preferred. It was blond instead of brown. Short. Businesslike. Fuss-free and unremarkable.

Because Killian Avalar was wearing another man's face.

It shouldn't bother him after all this time. After all, his kind had been borrowing DNA and adopting different shapes for the span of many lifetimes.

But he'd spent so many years now as Killian Avalar. Pirate and rogue. Charming, dashing, and unmistakably dangerous. That body felt right in a way this one did not.

But that body could no longer take him where he needed to go—into the heart of the corrupt political machine that ruled Earth. That body was nothing, and no one would listen to him. And at this moment, what he needed more than anything else was to be heard. The lives of everyone on this pitiful planet—including his—now depended on it.

Which was why he'd plotted this desperate gamble. Why he was even now standing on an abandoned airstrip outside of Haven Two, waiting for a meeting with someone he already despised.

Killian had spent the two-week journey from Concord Five diving deep into the world of corporate politics. He'd paid special attention to any information he could find on the Linden family —founders of Lindmark Corporation, one of the five members of the Corporate Conclave. Lindmark owned twelve percent of Earth's landmass and, depending on who you asked, were responsible for anywhere from ten to twenty percent of its economy.

Over a billion people relied on Lindmark to protect them from threats both physical and economic, and that was not counting the colonies even now growing and thriving on far-flung planets beyond Earth's tiny star system.

But all those people were relying on corrupt, conscienceless monsters. The Linden family had committed crimes so numerous they had to be categorized to be understood, and Killian still felt nauseated when he recalled his first perusal of the data chip he'd stolen on Concord Five.

He winced at the memory of what he'd done there, then shoved it to the back of his mind as he saw a skimmer pulling up from the direction of Haven Two.

This would be his first test—the first challenge to his hard-won skills. If he couldn't convince this human that her brother had returned from the dead, he stood no chance of surviving the gauntlet of Earth's full scrutiny.

Fortunately, he expected this to be an easy victory. According to every source he'd been able to uncover, Callista Linden was notorious for precisely two things—beauty and privilege. She was spoiled, mercurial, and vapid, and made little of her money and time beyond messes for others to clean up. But if his sources were correct, she should also be easy to fool. If he could make inroads with her, he stood a better chance of being accepted by the rest of Earth as who he claimed to be.

Phillip Linden. Villain and disgraced son of Lindmark. Bogeyman of the Daragh scandal, and as of a report from just over a year ago, officially dead.

But he'd returned bearing evidence of his innocence—enough damning information to shake Lindmark to its core and hopefully win his way to the head of one of Earth's most powerful corporations.

Only from there could he implement his true plan. Only from there could he hope to save Earth from the disaster that was coming.

But first, he had to convince a spoiled rich girl that he was her long-lost brother, returned from exile and in need of her support, as he was innocent of all crimes.

If Callista Linden was as clueless as everyone claimed, he should be established in her good graces before his ship's drives even had a chance to cool down.

The moment the gleaming silver skimmer came to a stop, the door slid back, and the driver stepped out. A tall, middle-aged man with silver hair, he wore an understated suit and immediately stepped around to the other side of the skimmer to assist his passenger.

Callista emerged from the cockpit with languid grace, donned shaded lenses, and adjusted what looked like a bulky, purple shawl. When she stepped out from behind the skimmer, Killian could see she wore a short, glimmering black dress and high-heeled purple boots—not exactly a practical outfit for meeting an unnamed ship at an abandoned airstrip.

But practical didn't seem to be in Callista Linden's vocabulary.

When she saw Killian standing at the foot of the *Fancy's* ramp, she tilted her head in her driver's direction before heading towards the ship, her stride slow and faltering as she crossed the uneven ground of the unused airstrip.

Killian took advantage of the moment to confirm that yes, it was Callista Linden, and she appeared exactly as advertised.

When she was within ten paces, she whipped off the shaded lenses, and Killian almost didn't manage to contain his surprised reaction.

Her eyes...

They were dark where her brother's were blue—deep and luminous—but they were unmistakably the same eyes. They weighed, calculated, judged, and dismissed, all in the space of a moment.

"It really is you," she said, and he could not determine whether she was happy, sad, or simply indifferent.

She was, however, undeniably gorgeous, and he was far from immune. Her curling dark hair was just the right amount of windblown as it fell over her shoulder in a calculated cascade. Her face appeared to have been planned by a master—smoky dark eyes, straight nose, perfectly shaped lips, and flawless cheekbones—and her dress hugged her form as though custom tailored.

But all of those could be faked, he reminded himself. Humans might not have developed the use of nanotech to change their shape, but they had certainly mastered the application of artifice in their appearance.

"You expected otherwise?" he responded, in Phillip's clipped, often sarcastic tone.

"I just can't believe you're alive." Callista's tone turned soft and melting, and her eyes began to glimmer with a hint of tears. "Phil, darling, you have no idea how awful it's been."

And without so much as a moment's warning, she raced forward and threw her arms around him.

Without making any conscious decision to do so, Killian closed his arms around her in return, recalling a moment too late that Phillip would never choose such a demonstrative action.

But he'd just returned from the dead, so perhaps he was permitted a moment of weakness.

Half a second, no longer, then he released her and stepped back, keeping his expression cool and impassive as he surveyed his "sister's" face.

"Why are you here?" he asked abruptly.

"When I heard you were coming..."

"No." He had to determine her intentions. "Why did you come to meet me all the way out here?"

"Phil..." Her voice trailed off, and she searched his face. "Are you angry with me? I thought you would be happy to see me."

There had been no indication from any of his sources that Phillip and Callista had shared anything more than their DNA. But Phillip was a master of hiding his feelings, and the Linden family had done their best to remove his capacity for sentiment. If he and his sister had been close, it made sense that they would have kept their relationship out of the public eye.

"Happy?" he enquired derisively. "What part of the past two years was supposed to contribute to my happiness? Being unjustly accused of murder and genocide? Being disowned? Exiled from Earth? Or being declared dead so the family could wash their hands of me?"

Callista's lips began to quiver. "I know, Phil, and it was just awful. And now there are all these scary stories about aliens and... Is Concord really gone?"

So she *had* seen that vid—all the more reason to move swiftly. Killian hadn't counted on Phillip being able to restore the comm system on Concord Five quite so swiftly, or on him delivering such a ridiculous ultimatum. The man was stuck on a dead hulk, surrounded by pirates and malcontents. It would take months for him to fight his way off, and months more to reach Earth using a standard fusion drive.

But in some ways, Phillip's hubris had aided Killian's cause. He'd broadcasted the existence of the Bhandecki threat, when the Corporate Conclave had seemed determined to lock down all information in the name of profit.

"The station has been all but destroyed," he confirmed. "And before you ask any more useless questions, yes, it was done by a spacefaring alien race."

Callista's eyes went round with shock. "And you think it's coming here. To Earth."

"I don't think," he said coldly. "I know." He knew all too well. Knew how swiftly the Bhandecki would respond now that they knew of humanity's existence.

Killian's own race, the Wyrdane, had encountered the Bhandecki long ago and learned a great deal about them over the millennia. But the most important thing they'd learned? The Bhandecki cared only for conquest, and explored continuously in search of other species that might be a threat to them.

Now that humanity was on their radar, it was only a matter of time before they reduced every human planet they could find to a dead, smoking hulk.

"What are we going to do?" Callista said plaintively, pulling him out of the deep gravity well that was his thoughts on that particular topic.

"We?" He raised one eyebrow as he met her eyes—level with his due to the towering heels of her boots.

"Well, of course I want to help," she insisted. "Phil, darling, you know Grandfather isn't going to be very happy that you're back. And everyone thinks you did all those awful things on Daragh, so they probably won't believe you about the aliens."

His lip began to curl, and Callista took a step back. "As I said on the vid, this time I have proof," he reminded her softly. "I plan to take down everyone who stands in my way until Lindmark is mine. And once it is mine, we will find a way to protect Earth."

Callista's mouth rounded in apparent awe. "You're so much braver than I am," she said with a sigh, just before her brow began to wrinkle. "But Phil, what I don't understand is... How did you get here so fast? We only saw the vid two weeks ago."

Fortunately, he'd prepared for this question. Human technology was so hopelessly backward, he'd been covering up the differences for years. "Did you think I was hiding in a hole for the past two years?" he asked harshly. "I've been places you've never dreamed of, and discovered there is more than one spacefaring race out there. This ship"—he jerked his head in the direction of the *Fancy*—"is only the beginning. I have knowledge of what is needed to defeat the threat that is coming, but to implement it, I must have the trust of the people of Earth. And soon."

His sister nodded enthusiastically and grabbed his arm. "In that case, maybe you'd better come home with me."

At his skeptical look, she stomped one booted foot and tugged him towards her skimmer. "Oh, don't be like that, Phil. I have a nice place here, in Haven Two. You can stay with me, and I'll keep you safe while you come up with a plan." Her lips curved downward into a pout. "Please say yes. It's been so boring lately, and I can't wait to hear about your adventures."

Something here wasn't quite right. Killian would have bet his ship on it, but he also didn't have any reason to refuse. He did need a base in neutral territory, and he needed the connections Callista had with the other Conclave families. Social connections, true, not business ones, but it was a start. And even if Callista Linden betrayed him, he wasn't exactly an amateur at dealing with betrayal.

"Fine," he said shortly. "But this isn't a social visit, so don't expect me to make nice with your friends."

Callista was suddenly all sunny smiles and flipped her hair back over her shoulder. "Phil, everyone knows you don't know *how* to be nice," she said, with a trilling laugh that bounced off the ship and echoed across the otherwise empty landing strip.

Suddenly she glanced back at the *Fancy*. "But what about your crew? I don't have room for that many people right now. Maybe we could put them up at a hotel?"

Her eyes blinked up at him innocently, but for some reason, Killian's instincts were still insisting there was more to her questions than hospitality.

"They'll be fine." If she was fishing to find out how many people were with him, she was doomed to disappointment. He almost couldn't bear the reality that answer represented.

Four. Four people remained out of the fifteen that had joined him in exile from their homeworld.

Some had been forcibly punished along with him. Some had

chosen to join him out of loyalty. But he had been responsible for them all, and he'd failed them.

But he couldn't exactly tell Callista that his crew was made up of shapeshifting alien space pirates who weren't as accustomed to dealing with humanity as he was.

"My crew is not composed of perfect, law-abiding citizens," he said instead. "They prefer to stay on the ship for now."

His "sister" seemed to take that statement at face value, and her sunny smile reasserted itself. "Then shall we go?" she asked.

"After you."

Killian followed her in the direction of the skimmer, with a carefully concealed smirk lurking at the corner of his lips. His first mission was a success. Callista Linden had welcomed him with open arms and seemed more than willing to support his cause. It would be a simple matter to use her connections to establish his identity, and from there, he would be well-placed to use the damning information currently in his possession.

One week, at the most, and Lindmark would be his.

———

CALLISTA RELAXED against the back seat of her skimmer, legs crossed and face arranged in an expression of angelic innocence while she considered multiple potential methods of murder.

It wasn't so much that murder was difficult. More that extracting information first could prove a bit tricky.

The man sitting next to her was blessedly unaware of her thoughts. He stared out the window—brooded, more accurately —and seemed content to ignore her completely.

He looked just as she remembered, if a bit older. Short, sandy blond hair, and a lean, handsome face, with piercing blue eyes and a fit build.

But the man sitting next to her was most emphatically *not* Phillip Linden.

She knew it the same way she'd first known her mother was a sociopath and her grandfather was a liar—her instincts about people were rarely wrong.

And her instincts had been confirmed when he hadn't once pinned her with his patented, ice-cold stare for calling him "Phil."

There was a whole host of evidence, really, starting with the fact that everything about the way he carried himself screamed, "Not Phillip Linden." Perhaps the average citizen of Lindmark wouldn't notice, but to Callista, he might as well have been wearing a flashing drone advert on his head.

And yet...

The man who sent the message from Concord Five *was* Phillip. Her brother was alive and headed for Earth.

So who was this? How could he mimic her brother with such near-accuracy, and how had he known to contact her?

Were the two of them working together?

No, she decided almost immediately. Phillip would have given his doppelgänger far better information. Whoever this was, he was not Phillip's ally, which meant Callista could trust him even *less* than she would have trusted Phillip.

It was a complication she didn't need. The past two weeks had already felt much like a skimmer race—flying too fast, perpetually on the edge of disaster as she and her team moved swiftly to counter her grandfather's attacks and sow the seeds of unrest within Lindmark's lower echelons.

She'd expected to have eight or nine weeks to cement her hold on the corporation before her brother arrived. Enough to establish herself in a position of power from which to judge his claims and determine the best path forward.

But two weeks? It was impossible, which meant she could not immediately dismiss the newcomer's claims of encountering alien technology. Nor could she rule out the probability that Phillip's message from Concord had simply thrown an unwelcome hitch in the stranger's plans. He might have been on his way to Earth for months and was only now forced to concoct a story to cover up the fact that he had not, in fact, been anywhere near Concord Five.

She threw him a glance from under her lashes and felt the familiar, welcome buzz of adrenaline racing through her veins. The sudden intrusion of a mystery—and a new opponent—into her well-laid plans ought to have made her angry, but instead, she felt a surge of anticipation. It was like a course change in the middle of a race, a test of her ability to adapt and respond to new challenges.

But how much of a challenge would he prove to be?

This man claimed to have the same proof that Phillip had mentioned in his vid. He also claimed to have the same goals. But if he was not truly her brother, he might not have any idea what an uphill battle he faced. Convincing Earth to forgive him, let alone trust him, would not be a simple matter.

Callista knew all too well who was truly responsible for Daragh, but she'd never bothered trying to convince anyone of the truth. After all, Phillip was dead.

Now she could only be thankful for that hesitancy and wonder how to use it for her own benefit.

Even better, she'd managed to keep the enemy on her own territory. He would be staying in her apartment, with her people in control of every scrap of communication that went in or out.

If she had to sleep with one eye open, it was a small price to pay for the security of knowing he could not twitch so much as a finger without her knowing about it.

Tapping lazily on her wrist comm, Callista notified Alli and Xavier of her impending arrival and the presence of a guest. There was no time to explain fully, but she managed to convey the basic situation. He was to be treated as her brother, while being watched as if he were the son of a rival corporation. Which he might very well be for all she knew. Beauty could be bought through advances in aesthetic medicine, so perhaps a new identity could be procured just as easily.

Alli's voice came across her aural implant a moment later.

"Message received, boss. We'll ready the Galaxy Suite and prepare a surveillance detail. Board meeting in the War Room at midnight."

Board meeting meant a gathering of Callista's most trusted staff. They would spend hours together, considering the new threat and proposing counter-attacks, and suddenly Callista wished she could tell every one of her people how grateful she was for their tireless energy in support of her cause.

In truth, they were all as motivated as she. All of them had family who had suffered due to the conscienceless leadership of her mother and grandfather, and none of them cared to see Lindmark remain in the hands of a man like Eustacius.

Or, if she were honest, a man like her brother. At least, the man they believed him to be. Phillip had been far less the monster than he pretended, but after so long adrift in an uncaring galaxy, who knew what he might have become?

But that was a worry for later. Now, she had only enough room to worry about the man sitting next to her—a man who somehow possessed all of Phillip's old passcodes to Lindmark's infrastructure. Xavier had intercepted multiple attempts to access their databases before the imposter's ship had even landed on Earth.

But why? What did he truly want? And how far was he willing to go to get it?

The success or failure of all her plans might depend on the answers to those questions, so for now, this was her top priority. And if she decided she didn't like the answers?

Well, then, there were plenty of creative ways to make this imposter regret his decisions.

FIVE

KILLIAN HAD SPENT JUST enough time skulking around Earth to recognize privilege when he saw it.

The penthouse apartment that housed Callista Linden and her staff was somewhere past opulent, verging on obscene. On the top floor of a glass and transparisteel apartment tower, with a rooftop garden and a private hanger, it did not give the impression that Phillip's sister had suffered any loss of luxury when her family fell into disfavor two years past.

The moment they landed, the woman shot him a smile, exited the skimmer, and led the way into a unit that probably cost more than his entire ship. Done in gleaming white marble, onyx, and titanium, it featured floor-to-ceiling windows, scarlet accents, a fountain and a statue in the atrium, living trees growing right through the ceiling, and crystal lamps flickering with what appeared to be real flame.

An honest-to-goodness river flowed down the side of the entry hall and into some other part of the expansive living space, and when Killian looked closely, he saw bright red koi fish swimming in the cheerfully rippling water.

But all of this would be quite familiar to Phillip Linden, so he made no remark as he followed the clicking of Callista's heels through the atrium. They crossed a room filled with mirrors, deep pile rugs, and uncomfortable-looking chairs, and passed into a less ostentatious space that was half kitchen, half sitting area. The couches were black leather, the pillows fluffy and white, and there were glossy leather-bound readers on the table, making the space look actually lived-in.

He was still getting his bearings when something collided with his leg.

A cat. Tall enough to butt its head against his knee, the animal had glossy black fur with shadowy rosettes scattered across its coat. Its eyes gleamed gold, and it regarded him with an intelligence greater than what he was aware Earth animals were capable of.

And Killian had no idea whether he was supposed to have met the creature before.

"Katsi, darling, don't scare poor Phil," Callista cooed, crouching down on the floor and tugging her pet away. "He doesn't care for animals, poor thing." She scratched under the cat's chin while it closed its eyes and arched its back in bliss. A smile of genuine affection tugged at her lips as she knelt on the floor, oblivious of the creases she was putting in her boots.

So perhaps the heiress was not all flash and no substance. Or perhaps she simply reserved her genuine humanity for her cat?

Two people entered the room and stood to the side as if awaiting her notice. One was tall, with dark brown skin, a shaved head, and the build of a man who kept himself fit for reasons besides appearance.

The other was a small, curvy blonde woman, with blue eyes,

dimples, and an expression that suggested she wouldn't mind flirting with him given half a chance.

"Alli!" Callista stood and greeted the woman with a sunny smile. "Please show Phil to his room, and then we'll all meet back here for dinner. Does that sound all right?" She addressed that last to Killian. "I've already canceled all my engagements for tonight, so we can spend our evening chatting just like we used to."

Killian was pretty sure he hadn't imagined the way the tall man's eyebrow jerked when she said, "just like we used to," but had no idea what it could mean.

And he needed the intelligence Callista could give him, whether she meant to or not, so he didn't protest when the blonde woman led him to a bedroom the size of the *Fancy's* bridge. She showed him where to stow his belongings, demonstrated how to send a message to any of the staff should he need anything, and definitely winked at him at least twice before departing and leaving him to a few moments of blessed silence.

He used them to stare into the mirrored wall of a bathroom big enough to serve as crew quarters for eight people and ask himself why he was bothering.

Why was he here, attempting to convince a stranger that he was her brother? Why risk his life trying to infiltrate Earth's government, on a quest to protect the planet from a threat none of its people believed in?

Once, he'd believed in his mission because he'd had nothing else to believe in. He and his crew were part of a warning system meant to protect the galaxy against the predations and violence of the Bhandecki, but they were part of it because they'd been exiled from their home.

And much like Phillip Linden, they'd been exiled for no fault of their own. They'd been sent here because Killian's brother, Fourth Prince of the Northern Wyrdane Protectorate, had decided he required more territory, and Killian was very much in the way.

His exile had kicked off a silent war of conquest and left the lands he'd once loved in the hands of his brother. And the only way for Killian to return home and take back his birthright? To meet the Bhandecki threat and defeat it. To provide the humans with a defense against the alien invasion and ensure their survival.

Then, and only then, could Killian and his crew claim redemption and present themselves for reinstatement to their former positions.

But it was a condition that no one had believed would ever be met. The Bhandecki had been roaming other sectors of the galaxy for generations, and Killian's brother had exiled him with confidence that he would live out the rest of his life buzzing helplessly around the human hellhole that was Earth and her recently claimed planets.

Killian splashed water on his face from a crystal tap and reminded himself that his chance had finally come.

His chance to remove his traitorous brother from power. His chance to return the last members of his loyal crew to their families.

But first, all he had to do was save a species that didn't believe it needed to be saved—one that wasn't likely to react to his revelations with gratitude. Humans were irrational, violent, and xenophobic. If he came straight out and told them the truth—about himself or about the Bhandecki—they'd be just as likely to lock him up in a laboratory as listen to his warnings.

His only way in?

Callista Linden. He might have the proof, but she held the keys, so he needed to stay in her good graces until she led him straight to the source.

Eyeing his reflection, Killian noted that he would need to acquire new clothing soon. His spacer jumpsuit would be ill-suited to enduring the kinds of publicity he would be attempting to generate. But at least Callista should be well-qualified to help him with that part.

Whether she was qualified for any of the other obligations that came with her family name was another question. She was, he could acknowledge, undeniably beautiful, and provoked a puzzling thrill of attraction whenever she looked his way. Particularly when that quizzical gleam of intelligence entered her eyes, or the corner of her mouth curved with some secret amusement.

But those obviously had nothing to do with her willingness to take responsibility for her position. If nothing else, however, Killian could probably use her appearance and reputation to distract from his own intentions. If she continued to draw as much media attention as her past history suggested was usual, he could potentially conceal his own movements until it was too late for anyone to counter them.

But first, he had to convince Callista to play her part.

To back his claims and show him the path to victory. Then he could leave her—and her indulgent lifestyle—behind.

WHILE "PHILLIP" remained in his rooms, ostensibly freshening up or doing whatever else men did before dinner, Callista briefed her staff on her suspicions. Alli would be responsible for keeping the closest eye on him moving forward, as men tended to be distracted from their purpose whenever she made herself part of their orbit.

Xavier insisted on remaining closer to Callista while the imposter was in the house. Though she privately considered his caution unnecessary, she could not argue with his logic. Whatever the fake Phillip wanted from her, it was likely to include removing her from whatever position of power he thought she might have. If he intended to take over Lindmark, he would eventually come face-to-face with her own burgeoning ambitions, and she could not be sure he wouldn't resort to violence to assure his victory.

It had been decided that their first evening together would be devoted to learning his plans. And to irritating him as greatly as possible in the hope of throwing him off his stride.

Once Callista had him trapped at her formal dining table, surrounded by elaborate dishes and plied with wine, the campaign commenced in earnest.

"So, Phil darling, do tell me more about these aliens. I simply can't believe"—here she shuddered delicately—"that they intend to harm us here on Earth."

Her guest raised an eyebrow in a manner that was, in fact, quite a solid imitation of her brother's most sardonic expression. "I don't see what's so confusing about sapient, extraterrestrial life forms wanting to destroy humanity. After all, humanity has done a rather neat job in the opposite direction."

Callista took a sip of wine to hide her amusement. "But what can be done about it? You said you intend to take over the company and then protect Earth, but how?" She let her eyes grow wide and pleading. "And is there anything I can do to help?"

The fake Phillip nodded. "There is, in fact. My plan is simple. I intend to release the records proving my innocence to the press, using the identity of an anonymous Lindmark employee. The files will show that Mother and Grandfather are the true agents behind not only the atrocities on Daragh but multiple other crimes stretching back decades. Once they are discredited, public outrage will require their removal, and the other corporations will go in for the kill. But if I can prove myself capable of taking up the reins, administering justice, and providing stability in the midst of a power vacuum, the others will have no choice but to relent unless they want to be accused of fomenting war."

It was indeed simple—too simple—and Phillip would know better. He would understand that the takeover process would require a small army of experts in everything from security to finance to labor laws. They would need muscle. Public relations professionals. A ruthless approach to loyalty testing. All of which Callista already had in place.

Which meant that whatever this man's game might be, he wasn't here for Lindmark. Not really.

For him, this was about the alien threat.

Mind running swiftly down this new path, Callista set down her wine glass and toyed with her fork. "That sounds like a lot of work," she said, with a bit of a pout. "But what about the aliens? What are they? And when do you think they'll be coming?"

She asked about them like they were slightly unwelcome dinner guests and watched as the man across from her took a firm grip on both his fork and his temper. It was hard not to feel smug. Very little in her life was more fun than irritating people who took themselves too seriously.

"The alien threat is from a species known as the Bhandecki, and they are capable of arriving here within mere hours."

Callista allowed her eyes to widen once again, but this time her surprise was genuine. How could he already have a name for them? Where had this man come by his information? He claimed to have been places she never dreamed of, but just how far had he gone?

"They are a sapient, space-faring race, and they travel the galaxy by way of living spaceships known as fireworms. These creatures form rifts in space that they use to cross vast distances —similar to the idea of wormholes."

Her mind spun as she processed this information and wondered whether he was feeding her lies in hopes of distracting her.

"The Bhandecki first appeared in this galaxy millennia ago, destroying star systems as they came, but eventually, a race of beings known as Wyrdane learned the secret to countering their attacks."

"Wait," Callista interrupted breathlessly, "you mean there are *more* sapient races? More life out there that has already reached the stars?"

She must have sounded more fascinated than her surface persona warranted, because "Phillip" gave her a sharp look before continuing his story.

"More than you can imagine. But the important facts are these: the Bhandecki are numerous and powerful, but they are also technologically primitive. Much of the damage they do is caused by the fireworms themselves—which have the capacity to disintegrate metal hulls in minutes."

Callista allowed her lower lip to tremble and her wine to slosh in its glass. "But you said you know how to stop them. They won't actually destroy us, right?"

"That," her guest replied flatly, "is entirely up to the people of

Earth. If I can convince them to trust me in time, we might have a chance. But if they choose to fight amongst themselves? We would be better off returning to my ship, charting an unknown course, and hoping for the best."

She wished she could dismiss all this as an attempt to distract or frighten her, but Callista was quite sure of at least one thing—whoever this man was, he believed wholeheartedly in his words.

And that frightened the hell out of her.

So much so that she forgot herself and asked an intelligent question.

"Space is rather big, all things considered," she mused aloud. "How will they find us? And why?"

His answer was prompt. "The Bhandecki are vulnerable to a narrow band of frequencies on the electromagnetic spectrum. Though they seem capable of shielding themselves, they still continue to seek out anything and anyone capable of producing those frequencies. Whatever they find, they destroy."

Callista glanced across the room to where Alli and Xavier waited and saw her own horror mirrored on their faces. If this was true? Unthinkable.

But she'd heard the transmission from Vadim. She knew Concord Five had truly been rendered uninhabitable by some creature outside of human experience.

There was most assuredly *something* out there, but whether this man was lying about it, only time would tell.

And time, he seemed to believe, was the one thing they didn't have.

"What can we do?" It was not hard to allow her voice to waver and her lower lip to quiver along with it. "If they've destroyed so many other planets, how can we defend ourselves?"

"Biotechnology," he said, with a certainty that was as

comforting as it was worrying. "Because the fireworms are adapted to life in deepest space, they have little to no resistance against certain types of aerial microbes that can thrive in planetary atmospheres, such as Earth's."

Callista blinked as though she didn't understand. This conversation was rapidly accelerating to the point where she would be forced to abandon it. The last thing her public persona would be interested in was a conversation on microbes in the atmosphere.

"With access to the right labs," her guest was saying, "we can create engineered microbes and seed the atmosphere in a way that will pose a danger to the fireworms without significantly harming Earth's ecology. An atmospheric shield, of sorts. But all we can do with this method is hold them off. Once the enemy learns of it, they simply won't cross the barrier."

The right labs... Callista's heart began to pound as she thought of her most recent acquisition.

Seren. She'd been intrigued by their advances in biotechnology and the implications they held for every field of human advancement. If anyone could do this, they could.

"It will take every resource at our command," the fake Phillip continued, leaning forward to place his elbows on the table. "And likely will require the cooperation of every corporation on Earth to make this a reality. And even if we succeed, it is only the beginning. Every remaining human planet will be vulnerable until this technology can be deployed, and the microbes will have to be engineered for survival in each individual atmosphere."

A challenge... Callista felt a familiar surge of adrenaline as she confronted the enormity of the task, and the lure of the impossible took hold.

She was still lost in contemplation when Alli stepped forward, casting off the illusion of silent subservience to voice Callista's own next question.

"But what then?" she insisted. "You said we can hold them off, but how do we kill them?"

"Phillip" leaned back in his chair and let his hands drop to his sides. "No one has managed that yet," he said softly, "but I believe it can be done. Fireworms cannot be damaged by energy weapons or lasers, but perhaps there may be some benefit to using projectile weapons. The fireworms have no armor against such things, as they've apparently never needed it. At the least, it is worth trying rather than simply enduring a siege that could conceivably go on for years."

Worth trying. Years.

All those words meant was that he didn't know. And until Callista could determine his true identity, she didn't dare assume that anything he said could be trusted.

She hoped he was lying about all of it.

But neither could she afford to dismiss him entirely. As of this moment, those in this room were the only ones on Earth who might know the truth. If she disregarded the warning and later learned it had been true?

She could be responsible for the extinction of the entire human race.

No, she would have to prepare for either eventuality—to embrace this man as an ally and humanity's only hope, or to destroy him as a liar and a fraud. Both roads must remain open until the last possible second.

It was time to play out the strategies she knew so well, but with higher stakes than she'd ever before imagined. All without letting anyone know she was even in the game.

It was exhilarating and terrifying at the same time, and as Alli and Xavier stepped in to continue the conversation, Callista lost herself in the planning of next steps.

There was still her takeover plan to consider, the actual fate of her brother to determine, and at least thirty new outfits to buy. Unless she was very much mistaken, her social calendar was about to become extremely complicated.

SIX

AFTER ONLY A HANDFUL OF DAYS, Killian was forced to acknowledge a certain degree of grudging respect for his hostess. Vapid, spoiled, and irritating she might be, but she had mastered the art of manipulating the vast machine of social connections within the Corporate Conclave.

Callista Linden wasn't exactly respected everywhere, but she knew everyone, particularly the younger generation of Conclave heirs. And with a history of wildly unpredictable behavior, wherever she went, the eyes of the press were glued to her every move.

So when his release of the information on the data chip stolen from Phillip Linden coincided with Killian's first public appearance at her side, the resulting news vids were seen and judged by everyone who was anyone around the globe.

As the responses began to roll in, Killian distantly recalled the real Phillip's assurance that it would be impossible for the people of Earth to believe in his innocence, and wondered briefly whether he hadn't misjudged the man.

The early hours were brutal. That night would probably

linger as one of his most painful memories, despite the fact that he was not actually Phillip Linden. First, the Lindmark public relations team struck, with a reminder of his trial in absentia and a list of the crimes of which he'd been convicted. They played footage of his public excoriation. Aired interviews of a tearful Satrina Linden, weeping over the depths to which her beloved son and former heir had now sunk.

There was a swell of renewed public outrage, followed by a general conviction that this new "evidence" was a poorly constructed fake, particularly given the suspicious nature of Phillip's claims about an alien threat.

But buried deep within these responses were the beginnings of doubt, as evidenced by a report first broadcast in Haven Two. An independent investigative journalist had begun to wonder why Lindmark Corporation had assured the world that Phillip was dead, when he was in fact very much alive.

This report was, of course, seized on by the other four Conclave members, who stood to gain a great deal should Lindmark fall. But as their questions began to mount, Callista was already preparing a response—Phillip's second public appearance, in a much more visible setting than the first.

She'd secured invitations to the most anticipated party of the year, a glittering anniversary celebration in honor of Haven Two's tallest building—the Victory Spire. The crystalline tower was a two hundred fifty floor monument to humanity's never-ending appetites, and it was the very last place Killian wanted to go.

But he went anyway, teeth gritted, wondering whether he wasn't wasting his time following the lead of an overdressed socialite who cared more for her cat than for the corporation her family had built.

They arrived at the party under the blinding lights of news drones and to the deafening shouts of crowds who seemed determined to catch a glimpse of him, whether they considered him monster or man.

Callista stepped out of the skimmer into the chaos and waved, a mysterious smile on her painted lips. She seemed unaffected by the noise and the publicity, and as she drew him out to follow her into the glittering storm, Killian began to wonder yet again whether there wasn't a bit more to her than she allowed anyone to see.

"You don't have to be happy," she murmured in his ear, "but do try not to look chastised, Phil, dear. You're swimming with sharks now, so let them see your teeth."

Strangely sage advice.

Then she took his arm and brushed some non-existent speck off his sleeve. "And for heaven's sake, don't freeze up. They're all going to want to talk to you, so don't forget—you're innocent." Her dark eyes held his with unshakeable sincerity. "You were framed. And it's only a matter of time before you're running things at Lindmark."

She really seemed to believe it, and somehow, the thought gave him comfort. At least someone believed in him, even if it was only Callista, who had little interest in anything outside of clothes, makeup, and parties. Only Callista, who still might be hiding something beneath that gorgeous, mysterious facade.

They made their way inside, and it took blessedly little effort to don the icy, distant mask that Phillip seemed to maintain as a matter of habit. There was nothing here that he wanted, and even less that interested him.

"Callie."

Callista's head turned, and she nodded to acknowledge a tall, gorgeous woman with dark brown skin, dark eyes, and close-cut blonde hair.

"Adanna." Callista leaned in, and the two women gave one another a brief peck on each cheek.

"You're back," the woman said to Killian, her tone slightly curious, verging on admiring. Did Phillip know her?

He doubted it. From what he'd been able to uncover about Phillip's past, the man had operated mostly from within Lindmark's walls. He was an almost obsessive loner and confined himself to business dealings rather than the social side of corporate politics.

"I'd say I'm happy to see that you're not dead, but…" Adanna's teeth flashed in a sudden grin. "That would be a lie."

Callista pouted for a moment before letting out a light, airy laugh. "Adie, what a terrible thing to say. If you're not careful, poor Phil might believe you're being serious."

The other woman shrugged. "Maybe I am, maybe I'm not. But Olaje stands with the victims of your family's crimes. I've not yet seen enough evidence that your brother had no part in the Daraghn genocide."

"It was Grandfather," Callista said, with a sudden fierceness that surprised Killian. "Not Phillip. Why else would they punish him even after they claimed he was dead?"

Adanna smirked. "That's certainly what my father would like to believe. He'd love nothing better than to see Eustacius locked away for the rest of eternity. Well, he'd love it better if he got his claws into Lindmark's territory, but with an innocent Phillip Linden returned from the dead, that's not very likely, is it?"

Her dark eyes bored into Killian's, and it took effort not to let her see his anger. He didn't have time for this. And yet, he had to *take* the time, so he forced himself to continue playing the part. "I'm not here to play games, Adanna Olaje." He revealed no pain, no anxiety—no emotion at all. "I'm here to see justice done, to retake what is mine, and to save Earth from a threat that none of you are prepared to face. If you choose to stand in my way, I will go over you, through you, or past you, but I will not stop. Not for you or for anyone else."

Adanna chuckled. "Hasn't changed, has he?" she said to Callista. "Just don't let him bite anyone, and he might have a chance."

Bite anyone?

But she wandered off before he could respond.

Was that how Phillip was viewed by the rest of the Conclave? As his grandfather's rabid attack dog?

"Don't worry." Callista patted his arm. "She's going to like you in the end. We just have to convince them all of what I've always known."

"And what's that?" Killian asked, curious in spite of himself. He couldn't help but wonder what she truly thought of him.

No, not him, Phillip.

Callista smiled, her eyes just a little too wide and a little too innocent. "That you might be a stuck-up pain in the ass, but you're not a murderer."

His mouth opened to answer, but she was already moving on, forcing him to follow with the uncomfortable conviction that she'd scored a point in a game he hadn't known they were playing.

———

BEFORE THEY'D BEEN at the party even a full hour, Killian found himself irritated, exhausted, and utterly unconvinced that the effort he was making would be worth it.

Why was he fighting to save these people? Why couldn't he return to his ship, head for the farthest planet he could reach, and leave humanity to its fate?

Right. Because his people had already sacrificed too much. Because he owed it to everyone he'd lost to finish this mission and get the last of them home.

But he hated it. Hated the necessity of pretending. Hated the feeling of doom rushing towards them while he could do nothing but stand and wait and watch as others determined the outcome of his attempts to save them.

It was madness, and his rage only continued to grow the longer the evening dragged on.

He tempered it somewhat by focusing on Callista and watching her drift through the crowd. And as he watched, he began to notice what it seemed no one else in that glittering assembly had yet been able to see.

She might present herself as shallow and pretentious, but there was a certain kind of canny intelligence required to exist in the glittering high-stakes world she inhabited. Somehow, without seeming to employ either artifice or effort, she flitted from one social circle to the next, never entrenched enough in any one entourage to be rejected in any of the others. They saw her as not quite embarrassing enough to shun, not quite clever enough to fear, not quite powerful enough to respect.

And as he followed in her wake, everyone in that space eventually seemed to relax in his presence. Somehow, her sponsorship transformed him from the bogey-man they feared into just another part of their world. They weren't sure of him, and they might eye him and his ambitions askance, but they made space for him.

There was one exception to the general tolerance for Callista's eccentricities—Maxim Korchek. The second son of Lindmark's biggest rival seemed to glare at her all evening, and to regard her more as one would a poisonous predator than a harmless socialite.

An ex-lover, perhaps? Or had Maxim simply taken her measure more accurately than anyone else?

The idea nagged at him, so Killian made sure to give the man an opening to speak with him while Callista was too far away to overhear. When Maxim appeared at his elbow with a drink and a sneer, looking as though he'd already had one too many, Killian reflected that if this was the future of Earth, saving them from the Bhandecki might not do any good.

"Look, Linden," the blond man drawled, "I know we've had our differences, but just this once, I think I can find enough compassion in my heart to warn you."

Killian said nothing, just raised an eyebrow and began to turn away while silently begging the spawn of Korchek to tell him more.

The spawn complied, catching Killian's sleeve to prevent him from leaving. "You all think she's harmless," he said in a low voice, "but she's not."

"Should I infer that you're speaking of my sister?" Killian kept his voice icy.

"Don't pretend the two of you are close," Maxim sneered. "You barely more than tolerate each other. Which is why you can't see it."

Killian waited. Maxim leaned closer.

"She's just waiting for her moment to strike," he said in an overloud whisper. "She'll lure you in with her innocence, play the clumsy fool, and then before you know it, you've been bitten, and there's no way out."

"I really don't want to hear about my sister's sordid affairs," Killian responded, with very real dislike.

Maxim burst out laughing—the loud, over-confident laugh of a drunk man. "I wouldn't sleep with her to save my life," he said, and suddenly Killian felt the urge to quiet him down. Keep the man from saying whatever it was he was about to spill in front of the worst gossips on Earth. Killian might not know for sure whether Callista could be trusted, but he didn't care to see her humiliated.

"And if I'd known who she really is," Maxim went on, a bitter sneer crossing his lips, "I would have made sure they didn't miss."

Somehow, despite the crowd, Killian's gaze lifted and locked with Callista's. She was watching, and even without her saying a word, he knew she'd heard. And while her painted smile never wavered, something in her eyes went tight and worried.

He probably should have turned his back on her and encouraged Korchek to spill everything he knew. But he needed Callista to make his plan work, and he needed her to believe he was on her side.

Though he also needed her alive, and if he was not much mistaken, Maxim Korchek had just admitted to making an attempt on her life.

But why? And should he be worried that Korchek might try such a thing again?

If only he could still use mind-speech and ask his people to investigate. But in this human body, he was weak, without many of the advantages he had once taken for granted. He would have to wait and comm the ship later when he had a secure channel.

And maybe he would just ask Callista. He'd assumed her life was all fashion, frivolity, and parties, but if someone had attempted to kill her, apparently even the most harmless of the Conclave heirs could not escape the consequences of their families' power.

————

IT WAS the longest night Callista could remember. Besides playing her own games, she was forced to keep half an eye on the stranger wearing Phillip's face to ensure he didn't get himself into anything too deep for him.

But whoever he was, he seemed more than capable of faking his way through a party, in part by donning the icy mask her brother had adopted at an early age.

The most worrying moment had come when Maxim Korchek approached him, but fortunately, Max had been drunk enough to be easily distracted. Once Xavier tipped off the Korchek security detail about their charge's condition, the guards had whisked him away before he could commit any further indiscretions.

If only she could be sure he hadn't said anything too damning. But they'd been too far away, and she'd been too distracted by Jocasta's voice in her ear.

Her grandfather was up to something. They didn't know what yet, but Jocasta had caught wind of significant restructuring inside Lindmark's upper echelons. Security had been tightened around Lindmark Tower, and a large percentage of the Lindmark Security Forces had been recalled and re-stationed in Markheim.

Eustacius was afraid, and when people were afraid, they became unpredictable. But they also made stupid mistakes, which was what Callista was counting on. She'd just assumed that she'd be able to give those mistakes her full attention, but with her focus now split between Lindmark and the imposter in her home, she was forced to lean even more heavily on her team and pray they didn't miss anything.

Once the party concluded, and they returned to her apartment, Callista intended to plead exhaustion, "retire" for the night, and hold several important meetings with her staff. But no sooner did the door close behind them than "Phillip" blocked her way and fixed her with a cool, serious stare.

"I think we should talk," he said.

Callista sighed and attempted a pout. "Phil, I'm tired. What is it that it can't wait until later?"

"Maxim Korchek."

A surge of adrenaline shot through her, but she tamped it down with ruthless control and rolled her eyes.

"Really, Phil, I can't believe you're listening to anything that poisonous little toad might say."

"So I don't need to do anything about his failed attempt to kill you?"

For just the tiniest moment, her control slipped.

Her eyes darted to meet her guest's, and she wondered what it would have been like to have a brother—or anyone at all—who actually cared about that sort of thing. How would her life have been different if her family had been willing to stand up for one another when they were threatened?

She wasn't sure her imagination was equal to the task. Her family might be willing to protect their public reputation, but if she died, they would no doubt gather in private to complain that she was dead because she was weak. Because she was a failure. A disgrace to the Linden name.

And this stranger was not really asking because he cared. He was doing his best to pretend to be her brother, so perhaps he simply believed it was the sort of thing a real brother would do—defend his sister's person and her honor.

As if a Linden could afford to have honor.

But right now, she had to deal with the situation at hand. What had Maxim revealed while he was too drunk to care about the consequences?

"He said he…" She let herself stagger a little on her heels. "When did he try to kill me? I mean, I thought we were friends. How could he…" Grasping her clutch in white-knuckled hands, she leaned against the wall and slid down it to the floor.

While "Phillip" was still staring at her as though unsure how to handle her reaction, Katsi padded around the corner on silent paws.

Revived from a long-extinct strain of wild felines, the phantom cats had been briefly popular as pets among the corporate elite, but most had found them difficult to keep due to their size and intelligence.

Callista had adored Katsi from the start, and the two of them had bonded early. The cat was an astonishingly good judge of emotions and character, and a fierce protector when she thought her person was threatened.

And if Callista were honest, it was Katsi's initial acceptance of her guest that had fueled her willingness to trust him as far as she had.

Even now, the cat first approached Callista and licked her face briefly before moving on to rub her cheek against "Phillip's" knee. And even more surprising, he crouched down to scratch beneath her chin before fastening his gaze on Callista's face.

"I suspect," he said thoughtfully, "that you already know about this attempted murder. And that Maxim had his reasons. What is it that you're not telling me, Callista?"

She sniffled as her mind raced, wondering how far he would go. Was it time to confront him with what she knew? Time to find out who he truly was and why he was here?

Her mouth opened, their eyes met, and the world shattered.

If they hadn't been crouched in the entryway, they would have been shredded by the shards of her windows as they exploded inward.

The high-pitched whine of energy cannons assaulted her ears, and she watched as an energy beam scored a deep groove across the wall of the atrium. Steam hissed as the beam connected with the water feature, and the statue of a skimmer that she'd commissioned when she first moved out on her own flew apart in an explosion of formless chunks.

While she'd acknowledged the possibility of an attack, she'd thought it unlikely that anyone would risk the repercussions of such an action in a neutral city. If the perpetrator were caught, they would face the outrage of the entire Corporate Conclave. It was just one more mark of her family's desperation, and yet, for those first few moments, it was still a shock.

But somehow, she was even more surprised when the man wearing Phillip's face leaned in and braced his arms against the wall on either side of her body.

As screams echoed from other areas of her apartment, he remained steady, shielding her from flying debris. Placing himself between her and the violent destruction of her home. It was yet another piece of proof that he was not who he claimed to be—her brother's youthful desire to shield those around him had been long since destroyed.

The onslaught paused for a brief moment. Katsi crouched and

hissed, and Callista heard a series of thuds from overhead. The attackers were on the roof.

Placing her hands on the stranger's chest, Callista pushed him back and rose to her feet.

There could be no more hiding. No more pretending. Her home and her people were under attack, and she was about to let them know exactly who they were messing with.

SEVEN

WHILE CALLISTA CROUCHED, frozen, against the wall of her apartment, Killian commed the *Fancy* with an emergency alert. He had no idea who was attacking or why, but he wanted his crew to be on standby in case he needed to be flown out.

He couldn't afford to die here just because a spoiled socialite had offended someone one too many times.

Could this be Maxim's answer to whatever history he'd nearly confided?

Or was this not about Callista at all? Could it be that someone had decided to silence Phillip Linden before he could reveal any more damning facts about his family's misdeeds?

But before he could reach any conclusions about the attack or his own culpability, Callista pushed him back and rose to her feet.

The energy fire had paused for a moment, and he could hear a distant thud overhead that suggested troops may have been deployed to finish what the aerial attack had begun. It was time for a retreat. They could return to the hangar, abandon the penthouse, and regroup somewhere safer.

"This way…" He reached for her arm, but it wasn't there anymore.

She was two steps away, reaching into her clutch as she strode not in the direction of safety, but towards the center of the destruction. Her hand emerged from the clutch holding… a compact palm stunner.

"Leave if you want," she said, and threw him a glance over her shoulder. "This is my fight."

He met her eyes, and in that instant, he knew that Maxim Korchek had told nothing but the truth.

Her entire body language had changed—as if he were looking at a completely different person. Ruthless intelligence stared back at him from the glittering depths of her brown eyes, while her posture and aggressive stride proclaimed she could not only deal with the threat, she welcomed it.

Callista Linden was anything but harmless. But whatever Killian had started by allying himself with her, he was curious enough to see it through to the end.

"What are you going to do?" he asked, as if dumbfounded. "Flutter your lashes until they succumb to your fatal charms? That only works on second sons and incompetent fools."

"I don't have time for you right now," was her harsh, clipped reply. "Either run for the hangar and get out, or stay close if you want to live."

Behind them, Alli and Xavier burst in through the door that led to the hangar. They'd obviously been delayed on their way back from the party, no doubt by design.

"Are you hurt?" There was no flirting in Alli's tone this time, just cool competence.

"No, just pissed off." Callista's reply was equally cool. "Did you see anything?"

"They took a few potshots at us, but they missed," the blonde woman reported, drawing a laser pistol from somewhere on her person. "Our pursuers' IDs were blacked out, but their security is crap, so Marcus hacked their comms."

Callista's eyebrows lifted, and Alli responded with a brief nod.

"Bold," Callista remarked, and it sounded almost like respect. "Or desperate." Here she threw Killian another glance. "But we'll need to fall back before they hurt anyone on the lower floors. Alli, you're in charge of getting Jocasta's team out. Xavier, activate the traps and fail-safes. I have a message to send before I leave."

Her tall guard was feeling visibly mutinous, but she stopped him with a single raised hand. "You know I've got this, X."

He threw a glance at Killian.

Callista grinned suddenly. "He can be my backup. Now go. Take Katsi. We regroup at the safe house."

She tossed her curls back over her shoulder and took off at a run. Into the apartment. Towards the attackers.

So Killian swallowed a heartfelt curse and followed her.

As the first living area flashed by, he took in the shattered windows, the shredded art and furniture, and the winds that swirled around through the debris.

A winged shape loomed in the darkness outside, hovering a hundred and forty floors above the ground. Not a skimmer—it was a fully space-capable craft with energy weapons that fired up as Killian followed Callista across that open ground.

She never paused. Never faltered, even when the whine of the energy weapons kicked up, and they fired at her heels.

But she was moving too fast. They passed into another hallway before the gunners were able to track them, and then she was racing up a set of stairs.

"Are you armed?" she snapped over her shoulder.

Was he armed…

He was always armed. But was he ready for Callista to find out what he truly was?

"Yes."

"Then you should know that if you shoot me in the back, you will die before you set foot off this tower. My people are well-trained, and, unlike Maxim's, they don't miss."

She paused, and seemed to be listening for sounds from up ahead.

"Why would I shoot my sister in the back?"

Callista lifted her stunner and favored him with a bitter smile. "Maybe for the same reasons my mother and grandfather are trying to do the same? Because you want to keep Lindmark for yourself? Or perhaps because no Linden has ever known the meaning of family, trust, or honor?"

He had no answer for that. She clearly believed this attack was meant for her—that the Lindens were trying to take her down.

"Or maybe," she continued, her dark eyes boring into his, "because you were never a Linden in the first place."

Before he could react, she charged up the stairs and out of sight.

He heard shots. A strangled grunt. Shoving aside his shock, he burst into action, but by the time he peered around the corner into the hall at the top of the stairs, all he saw was two bodies in dark combat gear, lying motionless on the floor.

He stepped past them cautiously, but they were clearly unconscious. As he passed the second, he bent down to investigate the soldier's gear and uniform.

Unmarked. Pockets empty. The helmet had a top-notch

screen visor with low-light vision and targeting options, and the weapon was a high-powered laser rifle, more suited for hunting large game than a targeted op in a highly-populated area.

They hadn't come just to frighten—they'd come to kill.

Rising from his crouch, Killian jogged to the end of the hall, taking the laser rifle with him. No sense in betraying himself any sooner than necessary.

In the room at the end, he found two more bodies and Callista. She'd already ditched the halter dress she'd worn to the party, and now stood in the shadows wearing dark pants, a spacer jacket, and buckled leather boots. Her hair was back, and she was speaking urgently into her wrist comm.

"...no," she was saying. "Leave the prototype for me. I need to be able to draw them off so they can't follow you. Get Jocasta out." A pause. "No. You know I can handle this. Just do your job, and let me do mine. We'll regroup and discuss what this means for our timeline later." Another pause. "If he tries, I will eviscerate him and leave him for Grandfather's stooges to find." She tapped the comm to end the transmission and glanced his way.

"Nice weapon. Can you shoot it?"

Killian gave in to his worst impulses and bared his teeth at her in a feral grin. It was not an expression Phillip Linden had ever worn in his life. This was his own—a predatory smirk that would probably tell her more than he intended about his true identity. "Shall we find out?"

Her answering grin was as vicious as his. "Most hits gets to ask the first question?"

"Deal."

She picked up a backpack off the bed. "There's a secret hangar on the roof. We just have to get past the troops before they blow the rest of this place to splinters."

"Plan?"

"Follow me," she said. "And don't whine if you die."

Killian heard himself laugh. "Oh no," he said softly. "I'm much too interested to die today."

"That," Callista replied, "makes two of us."

———

SHE'D UNDERESTIMATED her grandfather's desperation, Callista realized bitterly as she crouched behind a ventilation unit and typed in the code for her rooftop hideaway.

She'd expected him to throw a fit. To throw his weight around and try to destroy her life.

But not like this. Not a public attack in a neutral city, where thousands of others could be hurt, and the fallout would be disastrous if anyone discovered who was behind it.

Rather than go down alone, he would take all of Lindmark with him.

But she would have to worry about that later. Right now, she had to survive, and to do that, she would have to fly out of here in a prototype skimmer she hadn't used in months.

At least the man at her back was a decent shot, she reflected, even if she didn't trust him as far as she could spit. Since they left her bedroom, he'd been as silent as he was deadly, and she thought their contest was pretty well even.

But his smile…

Where he had been bitter and closed off, he suddenly seemed to be enjoying every minute of this. He was dangerous, unpredictable, and not to be trusted, and for some reason, that intrigued her far more than the icy distance of his "Phillip" facade.

She couldn't wait to pin him to the wall and crack his secrets open...

The pad beneath her fingers flashed green.

"Watch my back," she murmured, keenly aware that this was the moment of greatest danger. Her unknown guest now had access to her skimmer and could easily decide he was better off without her. "At the end of the wall up ahead, we turn right, go around the corner, and enter what looks like a ventilation tube. It's a fake. There's a gate in there that's now open. At the end of the tube is my hangar. Once we're there, you take passenger, and we're out of here."

"You can fly?"

His doubt almost made her chuckle. "I guess we're about to find out."

She took a deep breath and darted out into the open.

Laser fire lit the night, flashing at her heels as she ran. She didn't have time to shoot back. Only to run faster, digging in for every bit of speed she could manage. Behind her, she heard a brief curse, then more shots, as her companion returned fire. Hopefully, he wasn't hit.

Eight more strides. Seven...

Red-hot agony stabbed through her shoulder, and she stumbled.

They'd hit her. She got up and staggered forward, gritting her teeth and narrowing her eyes against the pain.

A hand caught her arm on the other side and pulled her the last few strides until they hit the end of the wall.

She tried to shrug him off, but he didn't let go, only fired one-handed over her shoulder before tugging her into the tunnel.

"I can walk," she gasped out, steadying herself against the wall of the tunnel.

The man raised an eyebrow, but let go and followed as she made her way unsteadily past the gate. A few moments later, they emerged from the tube into the narrow space where her skimmer waited, shrouded by a dusty cover meant to conceal the truth beneath.

Using her good arm, Callista yanked the cover off and hit the button to slide back the cockpit doors.

They responded, and she breathed a sigh of relief.

"I closed the gate, but I don't know how to lock it," her guest said in a clipped, neutral tone as he approached from behind.

"It'll be fine. Get in."

He raised a cynical eyebrow, laser rifle propped over one shoulder. "You aren't flying in your condition."

In her condition?

"I am flying out of here in about three seconds," she said between gritted teeth. "You have the option of coming, or you can choose to stay. But nobody is touching my baby except for me."

After a moment's pause, he shrugged and made his way around to the passenger side. "If you crash, just be sure to make it a good one. Wouldn't want to be embarrassed by the news vids after I'm dead."

Callista scrambled one-handed into the cockpit, strapped in, and punched the remote that opened the hanger doors. Then she fired up the thrusters and threw him a vicious look. "As you wish."

The repulsors whined as she drifted up... up... past the edge of the hangar roof... far enough.

She saw when the remaining attackers spotted them, but it was too late.

This was the experimental prototype she'd used before

building her racing skimmer. It had no safeties. No warning sirens. None of the modern technology meant to prevent crashes. She flew by instinct and experience, and in this craft she'd built with her own hands, there was nothing to hold her down.

Callista slammed the thrusters into reverse and shot backward so fast, it drew a grunt from her passenger.

Five seconds later, she reversed direction again and dove, straight towards the ground, through four levels of traffic, ignoring the screaming of automated beacons in her ear.

Ten feet above the ground, she leveled off and increased her speed.

It was four in the morning, and even Haven Two had to sleep. The streets were mostly empty, except for automated cleaners, taxis waiting for a fare, and a few straggling pedestrians.

The streets went by in a blur, or maybe that was her eyes. The pain was making it difficult to concentrate.

"Where are we going?" Her passenger sounded a little too deliberately nonchalant.

"Relax, I'm not going to kill you today." She glanced over at him. "We're headed to a safe house. We'll regroup and get a look at the news vids of the attack before we decide how to respond."

"You're certain it was Lindmark?"

Callista smiled in spite of herself as she dodged a median and darted through a public park. "They're the only ones who know about my ambitions, and I should remind you that's two questions in a row. You seem very certain of your victory."

"I am," her passenger said smoothly. "The score was tied, up until the roof, but you lost all your points when you forgot to dodge."

"No sympathy for my pain?"

"Sympathy isn't one of my many talents."

Callista almost laughed. That had certainly been true of Phillip, but was it true of this man? After tonight, she wasn't entirely sure. Not after the way he'd tried to protect her, in spite of his disdain for the woman she'd been pretending to be.

Flashing lights behind her indicated that her traffic violations had caught the attention of one of Haven Two's law enforcement drones. Hardly surprising, but not precisely worrying. Her prototype had never been intended for public use, so it had no identifying marks.

But still... She increased her speed as they approached the edge of the city, fully intending to lose the drone before making her way back to the quiet, out-of-the-way neighborhood where her staff would be waiting.

They were almost past the last of the city lights when she brought the skimmer to an abrupt, fish-tailing stop.

Something was wrong.

Callista tapped her wrist comm. "Xavier, can you hear me?"

Nothing.

She cycled through the channels on her aural implant and again got nothing. Not even static.

"We're being jammed," she said grimly. "Full blackout, which means they're using a localized suppressor."

"How close do those have to be?"

"Quarter of a mile or less," she confirmed, "which means they know where we are. Probably set up a net outside the city. The safe house may be compromised."

Slamming both hands on the control wheel in frustration only bought her a spike of pain. She had no way to contact her people. No way to know whether they'd been caught in this trap, or it was meant for her alone.

How could she have made the mistake of underestimating her

family *again*? She knew they were desperate and unprincipled, but they had to have hired mercenaries for this. Lindmark didn't have access to the type of craft they'd used to demolish her apartment—at least not according to legal records. And the fact that her adversaries had tracked her through the city meant they possessed both a great deal of manpower and some significantly illegal tech.

But even more worrying? They'd been willing to violate the sanctity of a neutral city, which meant that all the gloves were off. Her family now considered it more important to take her down than to preserve the legacy of Lindmark.

"We can rendezvous with my ship," her passenger suggested, almost casually.

Callista shook her head. "My grandfather has probably had eyes on your ship since the moment you transmitted your identity. If you're lucky, he hasn't sent someone after it yet."

"He won't find it." The man sounded irritatingly sure.

"Which is another way of saying no one will find my body if I agree to your proposal," Callista snapped. "I don't trust you that far."

"I could have shot you in the back a thousand times," he countered reasonably. "But I need you. And right now, you need me. The devil you know isn't always the safest option."

The flashing lights of a security drone appeared once more from behind her. And out in the dark, past the fitfully illuminated streets, a deadly chase awaited them, which meant her options were rapidly dwindling.

"What are you proposing?"

"A truce between us." Her brother's face twisted with what looked like self-mockery. "I thought myself done with human allies for good, but it appears the past is determined to haunt me."

Callista let his words echo through her mind for a moment before they finally registered past the insistent voice of her pain.

Her conclusion was preposterous, but it was the only thing that made sense. The only thing that could make a complete picture out of the puzzle pieces thrown her way over the past few days.

"You're not human."

Her passenger grinned, not noticeably perturbed by her statement. "If it's any consolation, your brother was considerably slower on the uptake than you."

Callista breathed slowly and steadily—in through her nose, out through her mouth. She wasn't panicking exactly. Just processing a great deal of information in a short time.

"Why are you here?"

"Other than my identity, everything I told you was the truth." He didn't look happy about it, though. "I'm here to save Earth, whether I want to or not. And to do that, I need your help, which means I need your family not to kill you." He paused. "It would be nice if they didn't kill me either, but if they do, it isn't like I'll care much one way or the other."

It wasn't the way Callista would have preferred to make this discovery. Nor was it the best place for a confrontation. Her passenger had the advantage here, and he knew it. She was wounded. Isolated. Out of options.

"What kind of truce?"

He cocked his head in the darkness, and she could feel the pressure of his steady regard. "My crew and I will provide you with a safe haven until you're able to reconnect with your people. In return, you will use every asset at your disposal to aid us in saving Earth."

"Where's the downside for me?" Callista asked. "I'm not sure how to trust a bargain where I'm winning in both directions."

"You will come to hate me before the end," he predicted bluntly. "And you may lose everything in the process. Because I'm not here for your corporation. I don't care about Earth politics. What matters to me is that the Bhandecki are defeated, and I will do whatever is necessary to achieve that goal."

She might not like it, but she could respect it. And she was nearly at a dead end.

Oh, she could dump him by the side of the road and make a run for it. But with her injury and the pursuit she knew was waiting, she was unlikely to make it on her own, and she was unwilling to endanger her team by asking them for help. Wherever they were, she could only hope they were safe.

"One condition," she said, as she rotated the repulsors and revved the thrusters.

"Name it."

"As soon as we're safe, you're answering all my questions. And if I find out you're lying, I get to kill you."

He shrugged. "You get to try."

"Deal."

She opened the accelerator, and with a sudden roar of thrusters, they shot into the night.

Here went nothing.

EIGHT

KILLIAN AVALAR, free-trader and merchant of questionable ethics, had been roaming this part of the galaxy for years before he found himself locked in the cockpit of a skimmer with Callista Linden.

He considered himself an excellent pilot. He'd flown dozens of different types of ships, and he'd had many years to perfect the art.

His crew pilot, Rill, was even better. She had a decade's worth of experience on him, and he would have staked her against anyone he knew when it came to piloting small craft.

Callista Linden was something else entirely. Less a pilot than another piece of the machine she flew. Or perhaps she simply made the machine a part of herself.

She didn't fly as though she'd learned it—she flew as though she *knew* it. No one, he was sure, had ever taught her the insane maneuvers that she used to escape the trio of security ships that awaited them on the outskirts of Haven Two.

Because no one else would ever have attempted them. On several occasions, he was positive she defied the nature of gravity itself, spit in death's eye, and laughed as she skated along the razor edge of destruction.

After the path he'd traveled to get to that point in his life, very little in the universe could frighten or surprise him, but Callista Linden managed both when she flew her skimmer screaming into the night, twisting and sliding through the intended barricade like a steel minnow through a trap.

It was hard to believe, watching her at the controls, that she had ever been the vapidly smiling socialite he'd met when he landed. This—this was where she was meant to be.

And it was where she would kill them both if they didn't reach the *Fancy* before she succumbed to her injuries. As they finally slowed in the shadow of an abandoned fueling station, the light of the city and the sounds of pursuit far behind them, he glanced over to see her sweating and gritting her teeth as she gripped the controls.

"I assume you moved your ship?" Her voice was tight and carefully controlled.

"I don't recommend assumptions," he returned calmly, "but yes. It's no longer at the landing strip, but it is tucked away somewhere near here. If you'll give me access, I'll input the location to your computer."

She had enough energy left to shoot him a look of withering scorn. "Tell me the coordinates. As I said, nobody touches this skimmer but me."

He almost laughed but did as she said, and ten minutes later, they were touching down just outside the *Fancy's* weapons bay. The bay doors opened before the skimmer's thrusters were fully shut down, and the gangway slowly extended.

Callista's head fell back against her seat, and Killian watched as her hands began to shake. "Just how much am I going to regret agreeing to this?" she asked softly, her eyes on the open bay door. "What am I about to see that I can never take back?"

"If I thought you were in the habit of dwelling on your regrets," he returned, "I would never have brought you here."

She surprised him again by laughing quietly. "You might not be my brother," she said, her words beginning to slur together, "but you seem to have taken my measure more accurately than he ever did."

It sounded rather like a compliment.

"I believe," she continued, "that I am about to lose consciousness. Ordinarily not something I would do in front of a stranger. I suppose now is your moment to prove yourself. Will you pass or fail this time, I wonder?"

Killian had begun to wonder, too. There were so many ways he could take advantage of this situation, now that she had no choice but to trust him. So many opportunities for him to seize the upper hand in their partnership and never let it go.

It was undoubtedly what he *should* do—the shortest path to achieving his goal. After all, hadn't he said that he would never again trust a human at his back?

"You'll find out when you wake up?" he suggested, letting the corner of his mouth quirk into a smile. "After all, what fun would life be if you already knew how it ends?"

And even as her eyes began to close, he heard her laugh again. "Well played," she whispered. "I may kill you when I wake up, but well-played indeed."

Then her body went limp, her hands dropped from the controls, and Killian Avalar was forced to confront his own worst impulses.

What should he do now? How would he proceed now that his most valuable ally was entirely within his power?

No matter how he considered the problem, he could not shake the conviction that the key to all his plans—and possibly the rest of his life—was the woman now unconscious beside him in the cockpit. How he proceeded from here could mean the difference between victory and defeat, and for the first time in many, many years, he wasn't feeling overly confident in his own decisions.

————

HE WAS STILL ATTEMPTING to extricate Callista from her harness when Rill appeared in the weapons bay door, silhouetted against the light from inside the ship.

"Another one?" she grumbled, but only rolled her eyes a little when Killian tasked her with moving the skimmer into the cargo hold and preparing the ship for flight.

Telling himself he wasn't really that concerned, Killian lifted Callista out of the cockpit and cradled her carefully against his chest as he carried her into the *Fancy* and up two levels to biotech. She was going to be fine, even if her face was far too pale. Even if it bothered him somehow to see her so limp and vulnerable.

"You're starting to make this a habit," Harvey grumbled, once Killian reached the bay that doubled as biotech and a human medical ward. "I don't like it."

"What habit?"

"Bringing home humans and expecting me to save them from their own bad decisions."

Harvey was the only one of his crew to understand much about human medicine, but a less likely figure of a doctor would be difficult to imagine. Hopefully, Callista wouldn't find him too intimidating whenever she finally returned to consciousness—though the chances of her finding *anyone* intimidating hardly seemed worth mentioning.

Killian felt strangely reluctant to leave her, but even more reluctant for Harvey to find out how Callista affected him. So he left her a message before returning to the bridge, where he sat in his command chair, chin in hand, considering the next stages of his plan.

He had not counted on Callista's cooperation. Nor had he counted on her being a razor-sharp competitor in her own right. Despite her distrust, despite the setback posed by Lindmark's attack, he somehow felt more hopeful than he had since the moment he saw the fireworm, thrashing as it died in the wreckage of Concord Five.

Now with Callista tucked in the sleep tank—and with Harvey's assurance that her injuries were painful but non-lethal—Killian was free to assemble his crew on the bridge and begin discussing their next move.

They listened as he outlined the current situation, and it was Dinah who was first to voice the concern he knew all of them were feeling.

His engineer, mechanic, and second-in-command, Dinah was tough, competent, and perpetually annoyed, and Killian trusted her instincts beyond even his own on most occasions.

"You say this human has discovered your secret. How long before she tries to use us as a ticket to ensure her victory in one of humanity's messed up political games?"

"I don't know." And he didn't. Callista Linden was still largely a mystery to him. A beautiful, fascinating, and incredibly dangerous mystery. "But I see it as unlikely, and the benefits of a partnership still outweigh the risks."

"You admitted she's been lying to her own kind for years. Why would you trust her at our backs?" That was Harvey. No dancing around the issue, just straight for the throat.

It was a question Killian wasn't sure he wanted to answer, not because he didn't know, but because he didn't like the conclusions he'd reached. And yet, they'd all been together too long for him to start lying to them now.

"Because," he said softly, "she's too much like me."

Everyone else on the bridge turned to stare at him.

But it was Patrick who spoke first. The nanotech specialist had been nearly silent since Concord, but after what he'd been through at the hands of the pirates who'd killed eleven of Killian's crew, no one was willing to press him.

When they'd first rescued him, he'd been little more than bones and bruises, held together by pain and rage. Now, thanks to new nanotech and regular meals, his warm brown skin was free of injury, and his shoulder-length dark hair was bound back in a neat tail.

But his eyes remained dark and full of pain—the same pain that shadowed his voice no matter how hard he tried to hide it.

"We all respect you as our captain," he said slowly, "and we would not have made it this far without you. But I will not try to hide what we all know. Your bitterness at your brother and your rage at our losses has made you dangerous, and willing to consider actions you never would have considered before."

It was no less than the truth.

Killian's shoulds, coulds, and woulds had gotten rather tangled over the years, and his relationship with Phillip Linden had only complicated them further. He'd done things over the past few months that he couldn't take back. Things he'd thought at the time he *must* do in order to accomplish his mission, and yet still somehow filled him with nagging unease.

He could have waited for Phillip. He could have simply taken Persephone with him on the *Fancy* instead of leaving her at the mercy of Concord's descent into lawlessness. He'd had his reasons at the time, but in the end, either of those actions would have slowed him down when every second counted. Either of them would have forced him to deal with his rage at the humans who had brutally murdered his people.

His dead crewmates had done no wrong and were only trying to save the human species from annihilation when they were killed. Their deaths were senseless tragedies, and the only way to make them count was to complete his mission at any cost.

Or so he'd thought, and in the heat of his fury, he'd thrown feelings and relationships aside, realizing only too late that he was capable of experiencing regret.

Regret was a new emotion—a profoundly human one—and he didn't much care for it. Anger, bitterness, and resentment he was all too familiar with after his brother's betrayal, but it was regret that had puzzled, confused, and enraged him ever since he learned of his people's deaths at their hidden base. Ever since Concord. And now, it seemed likely to trouble him again, as his crew began to question whether they could trust him.

"If this human woman is like you," Patrick continued, "and if your guesses about her ambitions are correct, how can we trust that she will keep her word? You suspect she has dedicated her life to disguising her true purpose until she can seize power from her family. If she sees a path to power that does not require our involvement, why would we not assume she will take it?"

A fair question. And one Killian would have been asking for himself had he not recalled her words back at her penthouse.

Had he not heard her pain when she said that no Linden had ever known the meaning of family, trust, or honor.

He had forgotten what those meant, and had trampled on them when given the opportunity. But Callista would not, he was certain. Not unless he betrayed her first.

Just as his family had done to him.

Without warning or remorse, his younger brother had destroyed his world—overrun his household, corrupted those closest to him, and turned the tide of public opinion against him with lies and fabricated evidence.

Killian had gone from prince to pirate in the space of a single day.

For years now, he'd existed only in the shadows—banished from his world and his people, with no choice but to live in exile among humans who could not be permitted to learn the truth of his origins. For years, he'd been waiting for his chance to fulfill his mission and return home to reclaim his stolen birthright.

And over the course of those years, he'd almost lost hope that his chance would ever come. He'd come to think of himself as the clever, sarcastic human rogue, Killian Avalar. Changeable and unknowable—a tantalizing mystery with no fixed ties and loyalties that changed as easily as money changed hands.

But then the Bhandecki appeared in human space, and every wound he'd buried, every bit of rage and bitterness he'd harbored, had returned to the surface.

He'd taken out that rage and bitterness on the two humans he'd least wished to hurt—the two who knew him best—because he thought himself willing to sacrifice anything to get revenge on his brother and return to the life he'd once known.

He was wrong, but he hadn't known it until it was too late.

He'd crossed that line, and there was no going back. But regret did not change what he needed to do now.

"Callista has not yet lost hope," he told his crew. "She hasn't spent years in exile, or watched her people be slaughtered before her eyes." Or so he believed. He prayed that tonight had not been for her what his brother's betrayal had been for him. "When I said she is like me…"

He'd meant in all the intangible ways he'd only just begun to see. Her love for living on the edge. Her willingness to embrace the unpredictable. Her ability to lead and inspire loyalty… he'd possessed all of those once.

"…I meant that we want the same things," he finished, not sure how to convey what he'd intended by his original statement. And this was true to a point. They both wanted Earth to survive. "I've made it clear that she needs us as much as we need her, and she's pragmatic enough to make the right decision."

"Then what's our next move?" Rill, his pilot, was the least likely of his crew to question his decisions. She was better with computers than people and cared only that the ship was in perfect working condition at all times.

"There's a dumping ground outside the city, called the Canyon. It's where the humans put everything they don't want— from old buildings to broken tech to people. We'll find a spot there to hide the ship and wait until Callista wakes up."

"I thought we weren't planning to wait for the humans before we act." Harvey was the least patient of them all, especially when it came to humanity.

"We've set the original plan in motion. The truth is public now, and the Lindens are scrambling to save themselves. But Callista is the key to gaining control without smashing what we may need to use, and I don't intend to let that kind of resource go to waste."

"Resource." Dinah eyed him steadily. "You're sure that's all she is?"

A flash of anger—or maybe it was guilt—stiffened his limbs, but he forced himself to sprawl in his chair like the old, care-for-nothing Captain Avalar.

"If anything changes, I'll be sure to let you know," he said.

———

CALLISTA AWAKENED WITH A JOLT, expecting her pulse to still be pounding with adrenaline. She remembered the chase. The pain. The frustration. And the man beside her in the cockpit… the man who was not her brother.

Who wasn't even human.

She jerked into a sitting position, only to discover that she wasn't wearing much besides a loose shift. The bed beneath her was a strange, slightly springy material that had molded itself to her body, and the room…

"Are you finally ready to stop lazing around?"

An unfamiliar man strolled into view, and Callista was forced to calculate whether she thought she could handle him should the occasion demand it.

Tall and barrel-chested, with a wild gray beard and a perpetual scowl, he wore a tight, sleeveless black shirt, gray cargoes, and heavy black boots. Muscles strained the material of his shirt, and he probably outweighed her by well over a hundred pounds.

What was he doing in this room with her? Had he been the

one to change her clothes? And what had happened to the laser burn through her shoulder?

"Depends," she said slowly, running careful fingers through her hair and assessing the state of her body as she did so.

No pain. Her mind seemed clear, and she didn't feel tired.

"On what?" the man responded flatly. "I'm sick of having to listen to you breathing, so tell me the quickest way to get you out of biotech, and I'll see what I can do."

Callista chuckled in spite of herself. "Find my clothes and answer all my questions, and I'm out of your life for good, Handsome."

His eyebrows shot up. "That easy? Hell, what do you want to know?"

Where to even start?

"How long have I been here?" Her people were probably going crazy with worry, assuming they'd survived Lindmark's attack.

"Eight eternal hours," the man responded without hesitation.

Callista took a moment to consider her tactics. Should she return to her helpless, socialite persona? Or was it far too late, considering that the last thing she remembered was fleeing through the night at the helm of her skimmer, with the man who was not Phillip beside her?

Whoever this man was, he probably knew all too well that she wasn't helpless. It might be more to her advantage for him to think twice before trying anything.

So she looked the man directly in the eye. "Do I have to beg or kill anyone before I can make a comm call?"

He grunted. "Guess that depends on who you're calling, but since I'm curious now, I think I'll say yes and see what happens."

Ordinarily, she would have gone with the second option. There were numerous ways to disable a man of even his size if she could catch him off guard. But at this point, she wasn't completely sure her body would respond to her commands.

So she opted for batting her eyelashes and throwing the man a deliberately fake smile. "Please."

He raised an eyebrow, but reached into a compartment next to him and tossed her... her wrist comm. "I think I would have preferred your attempt to kill me."

"I'll remember that for next time," she replied, and activated her comm, just as a section of the room's wall simply disappeared.

She almost dropped the comm. There hadn't appeared to be a door there, but there was one now, and Phillip Linden came strolling through the opening as if it were an ordinary, everyday occurrence.

No, not Phillip Linden. Not even human.

He admitted he wasn't human, which meant everyone and everything around her probably wasn't of human origin either. She was on an alien ship. Surrounded by alien tech.

And the aliens themselves, who were doing a remarkable job of feigning humanity. Not a single tentacle in sight. "Should I ask what kind of evil alien experiments you performed on me while I was asleep?" she asked, only partially joking.

The look on her brother's face was just a tiny bit wicked and a tiny bit mocking. "You could. Or you could just find a mirror."

"Maybe later," she said, swinging her legs off the bed and testing them gingerly to see if they would hold her weight. They did, so she took a step, and her knee buckled.

The bearded medic was closer, but it was "Phillip" who caught her before she could fall.

"Can you do something about that face?" she asked, a little breathlessly, her arm thrown hastily around his shoulders.

"Every time you do something he wouldn't do, it's a little disorienting."

"Maybe I prefer to keep you disoriented," he said, turning to look at her with a peculiarly intent expression.

Callista held his gaze and refused to show how strange it made her feel. He was the exact image of the brother she wasn't sure she'd ever really known. But she *had* known how to expect him to act, so the counterfeit version was constantly throwing her off.

This situation, for example. Phillip never touched other people if he could help it. Never displayed emotions except over matters of business. If someone fell, he would look at the floor and call for a flunky to clean up the mess.

"I'm not too confused to remember that you promised to answer all my questions," she said levelly. "And that I get to kill you if you lie."

He set her carefully back on her feet, stepped back, and nodded. "That was our deal. As soon as you're dressed, come to the bridge. You can meet my crew, and we'll tell you what we can." He turned around and left the same way he'd arrived—through the door that was not a door, which turned back into a wall the moment he was gone.

Callista turned to the medic. "Do you have a mirror?"

He made a choking sound and gave her his handheld.

She held it up, tilted it until the reflective surface of the screen showed her face, and nearly dropped the unit on the floor.

Her hair was limp. Her skin was pale, and her eyes were haggard and bruised-looking.

And someone had drawn an elaborately curled mustache across her upper lip.

She glanced at the medic, one eyebrow raised, but he shook

his head, and somewhere on the inside, she gave a nod of amused respect.

The man wearing Phillip's face had been sending her a message—he'd had her at his mercy and done nothing but this harmless prank. Was it a plea for her trust? Or an attempt to lull her into complacency?

Either way, she was looking forward to teaching him that neither of those would be simple to achieve.

NINE

CALLISTA APPEARED on the bridge about an hour later, and Killian did his best to behave as though he hadn't been completely distracted by waiting for her recovery.

Not that she noticed. She strolled onto the bridge in Harvey's wake and barely glanced at him. She didn't gawk at his crew, nor did she seem noticeably perturbed by anything she'd seen on the way from biotech. It should be evident by that point that she was not on a human ship, but her serenity remained unruffled.

The mustache, Killian noted, was gone.

Had he passed or failed? And why did he care so much?

"Welcome to the *Fancy*," he said, rising from the chair in front of the command console and bowing elaborately.

"Interesting name," she responded, striding across the deck and glancing around with no more than clinical interest.

"Christened after a pirate ship of old Earth," he informed her. "She captured some of the richest prizes ever recorded and was never captured or sunk."

Callista's glance told him she understood the message. "So

you're an interstellar pirate? I can't say that inspires me with an overwhelming desire to trust you."

He chose to ignore that for the moment. "My crew," he said, and pointed to each of his people in turn. "Dinah, my second in command, Rill, my pilot, and Harvey, who deals in biotech and does the cooking. Patrick is our nanotechnology expert and will be handling the details of our plan to repel the Bhandecki from Earth."

After the introductions were complete, Killian indicated a chair beside his, and after only a moment's hesitation, Callista took it. She crossed her legs gracefully, showing no indication of the nerves he suspected she was feeling.

When the chair suddenly reformed itself around her—curving up and around her shoulders and flowing to meet the back of her knees—she only subjected it to a curious gaze before returning her attention to him.

She might appear wealthy and polished, but she'd trained in a harsh school—one where only the most powerful had nothing to fear. Much like her brother, she seemed to have learned early never to show when she was shocked or afraid.

"I'm impressed," he noted. "That one always seems to catch humans by surprise."

Her dark eyes narrowed. "And just how many humans have enjoyed your charming hospitality?"

"Two," he said, startling even himself with his prompt answer. How much did he want her to know? How much had she already guessed? "At least, two that were invited."

"And was one of them my brother?"

She kept on surprising him. Sometimes she was as elusive as fireworm spawn, and sometimes she shot straight for the heart. It was a tactic he could approve of, even when it made him uncomfortable.

"It's quite refreshing to find someone who knows the right questions to ask," he told her, unable to resist an appreciative smirk.

And suddenly, the wealthy socialite was looking back at him with a raised eyebrow that suggested she was less than amused.

"Perhaps you could stop doing that with Phillip's face," she suggested coolly. "It's not making me feel more inclined to trust you."

Killian leaned back in his chair, marveling at her transformation. She wore different faces as easily as he did, and after a few moments, his curiosity finally got the better of him. "What was it that first gave me away? Humans don't typically notice fine details if you give them what they're expecting to see on the surface."

Her lips curved into a secretive smile. "I knew a few moments after we first met," she told him. "When you didn't threaten to eviscerate me for calling you 'Phil.'"

Ah. He probably should have known better. But he'd underestimated her then, a mistake he hoped not to repeat. "Would he truly have threatened you? Or merely frozen you out with one of his legendary ice-cold glares?"

She chuckled. "In most respects," she assured him, "you've captured Phillip's public persona quite well. So I'm forced to conclude that either you know him well, or you've spent a lot of time watching footage of his public appearances."

"Both," Killian admitted. "For the past two years, I was as close to him as he allows anyone to get." Phillip had been the nearest thing he'd had to a friend since the beginning of his exile. *Had* been. Until Killian betrayed him and left him behind to sink or swim on the wreckage of Concord Five.

"And does Phillip know who you really are?" Callista's dark eyes bored into his, almost begging him to tell an easy lie. "Does he know about your plan to save Earth?"

It only benefitted his cause to answer those questions honestly. And yet, his answer would lead to other questions, and part of him couldn't bear the idea of her knowing everything. It was all too probable that she would never be able to trust him fully after what he'd done.

Killian looked down at his hands. Then back up at her.

"He knows," he said. "I begged him to help me save it, but he refused. After these past few days, I understand more clearly why he believed my plan would never work. But I had to try, and so I left him on Concord. If he ever gets off..."

Callista waited, silently, for him to hang himself.

Oh well. Far be it from him to disappoint a lady.

"If he manages to find his way to Earth, he will probably try to kill me."

"Why?"

"Because I shot the woman he loves, stole information from her, and then left her to live or die in the wreckage of Concord Five."

Callista's mouth dropped open a little.

"The woman he..."

Killian cocked his head and considered what her words revealed—that she was more shocked by her brother's love affair than the news of Killian's betrayal. Telling, he supposed, about all of them.

"Yes," Killian said with a crooked smile, "I was as surprised as you. Her name is Seph, and she brings out a side of Phillip I never thought I'd see. Deep down, he's a better man than he wants anyone to know, and somehow, she makes him want to live that way."

The recording Phillip had sent from Concord made the former Lindmark heir's intentions very clear, at least to Killian. Phillip intended to save Earth, but he wasn't doing it for humanity—he was doing it for Seph.

Callista remained still for a moment, as if considering his revelations.

"You've answered my questions," she noted, "but your answers haven't given me much inclination to trust you. I've seen no proof that you're telling the truth about yourself or your purpose here. All I know for sure is that you attempted to impersonate my brother in order to take over Lindmark Corporation, and that you claim to have done so to counter an alien threat." She glanced around at his crew members, all of whom looked back in grim silence.

"Tell me why I should believe your story. Convince me that you are who you say you are, and I will do everything in my power to help you."

Killian cocked his head at her and considered his options. There were so many truths he could tell her. Show her.

But in the end, there was only one thing he could do that would thoroughly convince her of his identity. And for some reason, he wanted her to see him as he truly was. Longed to leave off this pretense and feel like himself.

So he stood and glanced at Patrick. "I think I have enough nanotech remaining to make the change," he said, "but be prepared in case I overextend."

Patrick looked back with a bitter edge to his expression. "You know we're down to emergency supplies," he pointed out. "If we can't get help from the homeworld, we'll have a few years at most, and then none of us will be able to change. Let alone make vital repairs to the ship."

"This is important."

He didn't give Patrick a chance to protest. Just stepped away from his chair and began the change.

First, he would assume his true form—the natural form of all Wyrdane when they were between shifts.

It was as simple as pouring water from a vessel, and when he was finished, he knew what Callista would see.

A tall, humanoid shape, with four limbs and a head—human-like, in many ways. But his Wyrdane body was translucent and changeable, its biological material flowing continually in loops and swirls that glowed with energy as connections sparked within it.

Once he returned to that shape, it was the nanotech swirling within his bioplasm that enabled what he did next. A few of those tiny seeds of biotechnology held the memory of a DNA sample taken from a chance meeting with a real pirate captain, and it took only an instant to activate a fresh change.

The fluid material of his body began to swirl faster, change color, and acquire texture. Thankfully, the clothing he'd worn as Phillip remained in place, so as he once again took on human skin, there was no risk of showing Callista more than she'd ever wanted to see. And within only a handful of moments, the transformation was complete.

He stood on the bridge as… himself.

But no. This form was not his true one. When had he begun thinking of his human skin as his real self?

Somehow, he hid his surprise at the turn of his own thoughts and turned to Callista with his lips quirked.

"It's a pleasure to have you aboard the *Fancy*, Miss Linden," he said, offering his hand. "I'm Captain Killian Avalar."

———

KILLIAN. At least she finally had a name. Something to call him in the privacy of her head—something besides "not Phillip."

And it fit him. Fit with the sudden rakish grin, the short brown hair, and the sparkling brown eyes. Knowing his name seemed to suddenly emphasize the cleanly-cut angles of his face, which Callista found rather disturbingly attractive.

Even in her heeled boots, she discovered she was slightly shorter than the *Fancy's* captain. He was less muscular than her brother, and wiry, but despite the loose fit of the clothes he'd worn as Phillip, she could see lean strength in his build.

His brown eyes were fixed on her intently, and she received the impression of both competence and a relaxed confidence in his own abilities. He was at home in this form, as he had never been at home in Phillip's. And despite that in-between form she'd glimpsed during his jaw-dropping transformation, Callista suspected that she had only now met his true self. Whoever that turned out to be.

On the outside, at least, he was unmistakably appealing— handsome, dangerous, unpredictable, and likely to give her family fits. But she'd known more than a few men who fit that description, and thus far, they'd all ended up disappointing her. Should she take the risk of hoping Killian wasn't about to do the same?

After a long pause, she stood and accepted his hand, and in a rather predictable move, he kissed the back of it instead of shaking.

"Very well, Captain Avalar," she acknowledged casually. "You're not human. Perhaps you should tell me what sorts of things you've already learned from humans. Besides flirting, obviously," she added, with a slightly sardonic edge.

"A great deal," Killian responded. "But my personal favorites are lying, stealing, and murder." His smile remained, but its edges were sharp and meant to cut.

"Then I can see why you must have got on well with Phillip," she returned, her own smile a brittle, dangerous thing.

"Then you *do* believe the charges?" The tilt of his head was almost predatory.

"It doesn't matter what I believe." She deliberately returned to her seat, crossed her legs, and rested an elbow on the side of the chair. "It matters what he believes."

Killian watched her for another moment before his smile changed to something almost grudgingly real. "You hide your true self in much the same way that he does," he told her. "Even if I hadn't known you for his sister, the layers you use to conceal your emotions would have given you away."

"Survival is a cruel teacher."

Their gazes clashed, hard-edged and looking for an opening, which neither gave.

"If you have questions," Killian said at last, "now is your chance. I don't particularly enjoy explaining myself to humans, but I'm willing to do it one final time for the sake of your curiosity."

"My curiosity?" She tilted her chin but gave no ground. "Or my trust? Those are very different things, Captain Avalar."

"If you trusted me," he replied, "your curiosity would look rather different. Perhaps I hope to gauge your sincerity by your questions."

He fenced well, for a man not born to the harsh realities of the corporate boardroom.

"Very well." She allowed herself a glance around the bridge. "I am willing enough to believe that none of you are human. I also believe that you know my brother. No one who merely mimicked his public face would have attempted to perpetrate such an audacious claim as a romantic involvement on his part.

"What I require now is an explanation of how you've come to be here. You've known about humanity long enough to impersonate us, but apparently, you never cared enough to make contact. So why would you be concerned enough about the survival of Earth to go to such lengths on its behalf?"

"What's in it for us?" Killian translated mockingly.

"You told me you were here to save Earth whether you wanted to or not. No one says that unless the real answer is 'not.'"

He did not answer immediately.

"You also admitted you don't care about Earth politics, only about the enemy's defeat—that you would do whatever was necessary to achieve it." She stared him down. "If by that you mean you have no care for human lives, our alliance can only go so far."

His sharp-edged smile returned. "Should I attempt to convince you of my altruism, I wonder?"

Callista regarded him steadily. "I'm not convinced you have any."

"I don't." He admitted it without hesitation. "Once, I might have said differently. But I have been betrayed by humans far too many times to care whether the majority of them live or die. All they need to do for my purposes is survive as a species."

It was unexpectedly painful to hear him say it. To have him

confirm her suspicions that she didn't dare trust him too far. "And what are those purposes?"

He leaned back in his chair. "What I told you of the Bhandecki is true. The threat is real. My people have been aware of them for millennia and have created outposts across the galaxy to watch for their eventual return."

"You're one of those outposts," she concluded. "Why?"

He probably didn't realize how much pain was visible on his face. "I was betrayed by my brother. My birthright was stolen, and we were exiled here until we fulfill our mission of protecting this part of the galaxy from the Bhandecki threat."

She thought about that. Recalled what he'd told her previously and made the connection.

"They never believed it would happen," she guessed. "You were meant to be stranded here and never return."

A brief look of surprise crossed his face. "Yes. I came with a crew of fifteen—the most loyal of my people, who were exiled with me for the crime of that loyalty. Thanks to *humans*"—he all but snarled the word—"all that remains is what you see here."

Callista had to fight not to let him see her shock and dismay.

Or the strange feeling of disappointment that suddenly assailed her.

It was surprisingly easy to accept his identity. Humanity had encountered dozens of alien races since space exploration began, so it had always seemed sensible to her that eventually, they would find one with more advanced technology than humanity had yet achieved.

Shapeshifting alien space pirates were, strangely, the least of her worries.

What frightened her more was that they were the only ones

capable of countering the threats facing humanity. And that their captain had no particular desire to preserve human life.

When Killian first told her of the threat, she hadn't realized how much comfort she'd taken from having an ally. Someone who knew the enemy and was willing to confront it.

Now?

She was on her own. She might have these aliens' assistance in taking on the Bhandecki, but it was up to her to protect the people of Earth.

Up to her to determine whether her staff had survived the attack on her apartment. Up to her to ensure they'd reached a safe haven.

And in her free time, she would have to prevent her mother and grandfather from burning down the world before she could manage to save it.

But Callista Linden did not believe in the impossible.

Or did she?

She raised her eyes to Killian's. "I'm sorry for your losses," she said softly. "But *I* have never hurt you. Nor have the billions of people now working, sleeping, laughing, crying, or simply existing on the face of this planet. If you must blame someone for your dead, blame the one who sent you here. Don't you dare hate us just because we're convenient."

Their eyes caught and held, and it was Killian who looked away first.

TEN

SHE WAS RIGHT, and Killian knew it. But his rage was all he had left. He'd done things in the depths of that rage that he couldn't take back, and even if he could, remorse wouldn't stop the Bhandecki.

But it could stab him with surprising force as he saw Callista's response to the weight of his revelations. Saw when disappointment shadowed her eyes as she accepted the burden of what he'd revealed.

But still, she did not bend. If anything, she sat taller, and the fire that drove her burned hotter than ever.

He'd been a prince, once, and so knew what it meant to lead. Knew what was required of a leader.

And if anyone could lead Earth through the coming days, it would be a woman like Callista Linden. Assuming she would accept the task. And assuming she managed to survive her family's attempts to kill her.

He would simply have to make sure she survived.

"Captain." Rill's voice broke the tension between himself and

Callista. "There's an emergency transmission coming in through the Conclave beacons."

He blinked, spun his chair, and tapped on his console to activate the forward viewscreen. "From where?"

"From Galloway. It's a Hastings planet. A bit farther than Concord, but closer than Vadim."

He'd stopped there a time or two on his free-trading adventures. Like Vadim, Galloway was a mining planet, and most of the settlements there were underground.

"Let's see it."

The forward viewscreen shifted to silvery static before snapping into focus on a scene straight out of the hell depicted in numerous Earth mythologies.

Galloway was burning. The rocky, mountainous surface of the planet glowed with hot molten rock, and in the glow, he could see...

"What in the name of all hells is that?" Callista had shifted to the edge of her seat, eyes glued to the screen.

"That," Killian replied, "appears to be part of a dead fireworm."

He could feel almost sorry for her at that moment, because until you saw them—until you came to appreciate their true size and menace—it was possible to pretend they were only a distant potential threat.

The vid came into focus, then wavered, then focused again. Someone in the background was speaking, but the transmission was garbled, so Killian took a moment to marvel that someone had gotten that close to a fireworm and survived.

It appeared to have crashed on the surface of the planet after doing tremendous damage. Or perhaps the devastation they could see had been caused by the explosion of the fireworm itself. Whether the Bhandecki had lost control or had used the creature like a living bomb, it was impossible to tell.

From the size of the remaining pieces of the worm relative to the humans scrambling around nearby, it had been an adult. Easily the length of an interstellar cargo craft when whole, the creature would have been cylindrical in shape, with each end tapering to a rounded point. Running parallel down the length of its body, four rippling frills—almost like sails—were its only appendages, but only a small piece of one could still be seen on the vid.

The audio crackled, and they could finally make out a voice in the background.

"This is Commander Carlton... Hastings Security Forces. If this makes it out, we've come under attack by... took out Vadim. There are thousands of these things. *Thousands.*"

Despite the poor quality of the transmission, they could hear his voice shaking.

"We don't know why this one crashed... why they're attacking. They're shrugging off everything we can throw at them. Lasers and energy weapons don't even leave a scratch... the damned *rocks* are melting." The commander sounded as though he were near tears. "We're trying to get our people out, but... may be no point. Hundreds of them are darting in to hit us... rest just sit there past the atmosphere, like they're waiting for us to come to them."

No one moved as his desperation filled the otherwise silent bridge, and his words grew even harder to make out.

"We're trying... weren't prepared. We have no way to fight them. If this message gets out... everyone else get ready. Don't waste your time... energy weapons. And if you have to... stay in your planet's atmosphere. I don't think they like it."

A burst of static filled the bridge, then the vid shook violently.

"Another hit!"

Killian heard screaming, saw as flames erupted on the viewscreen.

"We're about done for," said the voice, "but I hope someone else figures out how to beat these sons-of-... Carlton out."

The video feed died, and the bridge fell utterly silent. Callista was still staring at the screen as if struggling to process what she'd just seen.

No doubt it was shocking. He'd seen historical accounts of fireworms and their destruction many times, and it was still jarring to confront the reality of their size and capabilities.

"Those poor people."

The quiet sound of Callista's voice brought his head around to stare at her.

"They never had a chance." She looked at him, and he could see the shimmer of tears in her beautiful dark eyes. "They died wondering if all of humanity was about to die with them."

Killian cocked his head and contemplated this new information about Callista Linden.

Her first thought had not been for the lost planet, or what this might mean for her personally. She hadn't responded by digging for information. She'd first considered the *people*. A spoiled society heiress was grieving for the senseless deaths of people that weren't even hers.

Was this the truth of what drove her? Did all of her ambitions truly revolve not around money or power, but around protecting the people that Lindmark was so willing to use and then throw away when it became expedient?

And if true, what did it mean for his understanding of her as a

Linden? As Phillip's sister? How could it help him predict her actions?

Killian understood what made Phillip the way he was. The man had been born with a soft heart, and his family had shattered it because it suited their purposes. They'd taught him that caring was pain, and Phillip had learned to protect himself by feeling nothing for anyone, to the point that he'd nearly forgotten he had a heart.

Callista, though...

She jumped to her feet. "We have to get a transmission out to all the other colonized planets." Her arms folded, and her eyes narrowed. "Can you hack us in, or do I need to contact my people?"

She was about to give him whiplash. "What does this have to do with a plan to save Earth?"

Her stare was like looking down the barrel of a laser rifle. "This isn't just about Earth, Captain Avalar. This is about saving everyone we possibly can. We need to send everything you know about fireworms and Bhandecki to every planet still connected to the beacon network. We have to give them a fighting chance."

"We don't actually know how to beat the Bhandecki yet," he countered. "Why terrify people if they're only going to die in the end?"

"Because some of us haven't given up yet," she said, her voice dripping with quiet condemnation. "Now, can you do it or not?"

"I can do a lot of things." But he couldn't sit by while she misunderstood the situation. Misunderstood *him*. She needed to know the truth, as painful as it was.

"I can probably hack your beacons. And I can probably prepare a briefing for what your people should expect." He rose from his chair and looked Callista in the eye. "But I won't ever pretend in order to make you feel better. I know too well what we're up against. And these planets of yours, out there alone on the edge of space, already struggling to survive—they don't have the technology or the kind of infrastructure needed to make my plan work. If the Bhandecki find them, they *will die.*"

She didn't even blink. "Tell me, Captain Avalar—what makes you angrier? The situation we're in, or the fact that you feel helpless to change it?"

Even in the midst of his anger, he froze.

Then, as her words seemed to echo across the silent bridge, almost against his will, his fingers curled slowly into fists. He wanted to lash out, to tell her why she was wrong, when the real problem was…

She was *right.*

Once, he'd hidden the truth of his helplessness behind the flash and swagger of a free-trading captain. He went his own way and owed no one his allegiance. Now, he was hiding behind his bitterness and rage, but Callista had seen past all the barriers he put up and told him a truth he hadn't wanted to acknowledge.

He'd been able to control nothing since that long-ago day when his brother had somehow told lies upon lies and never been questioned. When the younger prince had stolen everything Killian once believed gave his own life meaning. When he either exiled Killian's people or stole their loyalty for himself.

There had been nothing Killian could do.

Since then, he'd built his own tiny empire, trading with anyone and everyone but building alliances with no one, because anything you depended on could be torn away in a moment.

And yet, he'd still felt helpless. After years of trying, he'd found no way to accomplish his goals—no way to ready humanity for a Bhandecki invasion, and no way to ensure that his people would be able to return home. Then, just when the opportunity finally presented itself, the lives of his people had been violently ripped away. Since then, he'd felt that same sickening pain and anger at being powerless to change what had happened, or even what was still happening.

But the only alternative was to stop caring and to do nothing.

He'd been tempted—so many times—to take his ship and go far, far away, leaving humanity to their fate. But if he did so, the other members of his crew would be stuck with him. Forever unable to go home. Permanently exiled from the world and the people they loved.

As he'd once told Phillip Linden, Killian was a cold, inhuman bastard, but not that cold. That final step of fully giving in to his helplessness wasn't one he was willing to take.

And yet, what could he tell Callista that wouldn't lead her to despise him? He needed her, and whether she knew it or not, she needed him.

So it would have to be the truth.

"The helplessness," he said baldly, and heard a tiny gasp of surprise from one of his crew. "Maybe you've lived in privilege for so long you've never known what that feels like. But I do, and I will not court that feeling again."

"So you'll choose to do nothing?" Her tone was studiously neutral.

"I choose to put my time and energy in the only place it truly has a chance of success."

She would never be able to accept his choice, this woman who cried over the lives and deaths of people she would never know. But he couldn't let himself care about that. Couldn't let himself feel her disappointment. He had to focus on his goal. Nothing else mattered.

"You're wrong, you know," Callista said, almost gently. "I know exactly how it feels to be helpless. When Phillip was exiled, and when I realized what my mother and grandfather had done and continued to do... I was powerless. And you're right—it's the kind of pain I wouldn't wish on anyone. So I've decided to do what I can to prevent others from feeling it."

He wanted to snarl and snap like a wounded animal in a corner.

"That's why we're going to take the time to hack those beacons," she went on relentlessly. "That's why we have to send messages to every planet we can reach. Because even if they're going to die, they shouldn't have to feel helpless. They deserve a chance to fight for their own lives."

Was she right? If Killian were in those people's places, would he want the gift of hope, even if it were false?

He wasn't sure he knew the answer.

He only knew that he was still responsible for the people under his care. For Harvey, Rill, Dinah, and Patrick. That he would do whatever it took to keep their hopes alive.

And for that, he needed Callista, so he had to do whatever was necessary to convince her to cooperate.

"Then I propose we make our partnership official," he said, regaining enough equanimity to present an unruffled exterior. "Find your people. Set them to work on locating the resources required to create and deploy an atmospheric shield. If you will commit to that much, I will commit myself to providing the data they need and deploying a message to whatever planets can still be reached."

She didn't hesitate. "Done."

He extended his hand again, in a very human gesture meant to seal the deal.

She took it and held it steadily. "I believe we can do this. But if you betray me, Captain Avalar…"

"I know," he answered, a self-mocking twist lurking at the corner of his lips. "Your face will be the very last thing I see before I die."

———

HE *DID* KNOW. And he didn't sound as though he were making fun of her.

Was it weird that she found that deeply gratifying? His confidence in her ability to gain her revenge probably shouldn't have made her happy… but it did. After a lifetime of being underestimated, Killian's recognition of the threat she posed felt like a gift.

He didn't say she would have him "taken care of" as if the only way for her to accomplish anything was through her "people." He saw her as a threat in her own right, and that confirmed her decision to trust him like nothing else could have done.

More than likely, she was making a mistake. Or maybe she was just gambling on that tiny chance that Killian could do what he claimed.

"I'll need my skimmer," Callista said, "and a drone to do some reconnaissance. Something with comm capabilities, in case we can move it close enough to the city to get a message in without being traced."

"And just what are you planning to do with your skimmer?" Killian raised an eyebrow in that thoroughly irritating way he seemed to have perfected.

"I need to either join my people or rescue them." She pointed at her wrist comm. "I haven't been able to communicate with them since we left my apartment last night. They may have reached the safe house and be waiting for me to contact them, but the longer they go without any message from me, the more likely it is they'll do something desperate and compromise their own safety."

"So you'll compromise your own safety in order to find them?"

She turned to leave without bothering to respond. Either he understood, or he didn't, and she didn't have time to change his views.

"Then I'm coming with you."

Callista whirled back around to stare at him, suddenly remembering that moment in her apartment when he'd shielded her with his own body. Did he care more than he pretended? Or was this some other plot he was hatching?

"I don't need your help, Captain Avalar, and I certainly don't need your protection. That wasn't part of our deal. This is *my* city, and these are *my* people. I'm fully capable of functioning on my own."

"But I think we can both agree on the importance of protecting one's investments," Killian answered smoothly. "You're my only way in, and I would hate to lose you to a stray energy blast or an overzealous mercenary."

She was a bit surprised and disappointed in herself when her heart sank a little at his words, and she wasn't even totally sure why. Such a vulnerable part of her shouldn't be remotely involved here. She'd believed he respected her abilities, yes. That he saw her as an equal—fully capable of taking care of herself. But that had nothing to do with her heart.

Perhaps she simply wasn't used to having anyone stand in her way. In that respect, he wasn't wrong about her—she was extremely privileged. And she'd become accustomed to protecting herself while masquerading as Diamondback.

And yet, from a purely pragmatic standpoint, she could also appreciate Killian's concerns. If the two of them were the only ones capable of preventing Earth's destruction, it made sense for them to be extra cautious.

"Maybe you should send someone else," she countered. "So that we can't both be taken out at the same time."

"None of my crew members are as comfortable interacting with humans," Killian responded glibly. "Nor do they all have experience with piloting, weapons, and interfacing with human technology."

She didn't like it, but it didn't sound like she had a choice.

"Fine. But you can't go as Phillip. You'll go as yourself, and when we find my people, we explain the situation fully."

"And can you promise me they won't react badly to the revelation of my identity?"

Callista laughed. "Oh, they'll react badly. But if for some reason you can't cajole your way back into their good graces, I'll let them know they aren't allowed to murder you outright."

A tiny smile grew on Killian's lips. "Oh, but I'd really rather you not. It's been a distressingly long time since anyone tried to kill me."

If only she didn't think he was serious.

"Give me an hour," he said. "That should give me enough time to prepare what we need. Then we'll go looking for your people, while Rill and Dinah work on getting the message out on the beacon network."

An hour. While her grandfather plotted and the Bhandecki drew closer to Earth... an hour felt like an eternity.

But she'd been waiting and planning for so many years now.

She could manage one more hour.

———

AT PRECISELY THE ONE-HOUR MARK, Callista sat in her skimmer, finger poised to start up the thrusters and leave Killian behind.

But at precisely the one hour and one minute mark, he appeared in the cargo bay and leaped into the cockpit beside her with languid grace, as if he'd had no doubt she would wait.

For an instant, she wondered whether he'd done it on purpose, but was distracted almost immediately by the change in his appearance.

Apparently, he'd decided to embrace the "pirate captain" look, and if Callista were honest, she didn't blame him.

Her new ally now sported a leather spacer jacket over a perfectly fitted jumpsuit and wore a narrow comm-band around the back of his head. The outfit seemed deliberately designed to complement his elaborately spiked hair and the gleaming blue hoop in his right ear.

It was a good look on him—more attractive than she cared to admit—but Callista knew protective camouflage when she saw it.

"If 'trustworthy ally' is what you're going for, you aren't helping your cause," she remarked as she fired up the thrusters.

"Trustworthy is Phillip's job, not mine."

An odd remark.

She twisted to look at him as the bay doors opened. "Do you think he'll make it here in time?"

Killian's jaw hardened. "I haven't the smallest idea, and at the moment, it's the least of my concerns."

"Yes," Callista murmured with a small smile. "I'm worried too."

He ignored her so completely, she knew she'd hit the mark.

"So what *is* your plan?" he inquired, seeming more than ready to change the subject.

Callista decided to allow it. "Do your people have the drone ready?"

"In the air, just outside Haven Two."

"Excellent." She nodded in acknowledgment. "Its first job is to give us a look at what's happening around my apartment. I'll also need updates on any news that's circulating about the attack and any current gossip involving Lindmark."

"Done."

Killian tapped his comm band. "Rill, I'll need you to patch through the visuals from that drone, and then get a secure link to Haven's news feeds. We need anything you can find on Lindmark."

He threw a glance at Callista. "She'll need access to your skimmer's computers."

Callista snorted. "Do you really expect me to believe you didn't have her hack into my baby the moment it landed in your cargo bay?"

"If you believed I would do something like that, why did you trust me enough to accept this alliance?"

She eased the skimmer forward, clearing the doors and emerging into the sunlight of early afternoon.

"Because," she said absently as she searched the area, both visually and with her onboard scanner, "I have security systems that would let me know if you'd done anything beyond creating a basic access portal. And, it's what I would have done in your place."

Killian let out a short laugh. "I feel like I've wasted far too much effort trying to convince you to work with me. Why all the warnings about betrayal if you don't intend to do anything about it?"

"A healthy sense of caution is a valuable trait in an ally," she reminded him as she moved off through the Canyon in the direction of Haven Two. "And it is not the same as betrayal. You've poked at my defenses, yes, but never gone beyond testing them. Would it make you feel better if I told you I *will* shoot you if I genuinely feel threatened?"

"Maybe not *better*," he said, eyes glittering oddly, "but it would definitely make me feel more interested."

"In what? Our alliance? Or in me?" She threw him a deliberately icy glance, despite the small voice that insisted she wouldn't mind if he *were* interested. "I already know enough men who are only interested in women as objects to be conquered. If you're looking for a challenge, I'm not it."

Killian, however, did not rise to the bait. "I'm not interested in playing some kind of game with you, Callista. Saving humanity is enough of a challenge for both of us."

"But?"

His answer caught her completely by surprise. "But I am human enough in this form to find you intriguing."

Intriguing… The word sparked a buzz of adrenaline—one she typically only felt before a race. "What does that mean?"

"It means"—he seemed surprised by his own admission—"that for whatever reason, you make me curious enough to want to ask questions. That I find myself unaccountably interested in what you're going to do next. And"—his lips quirked oddly—"that I was strangely reluctant to send you off on this little errand with someone else at your back."

She didn't dare tell him that she understood, because that would reveal far more of her own feelings than she was ready for him to know.

So she deflected as best she could. "Perhaps you simply understand how important it is that we both survive. After all, you already said you wanted to 'protect your investment.'"

He shrugged. "It wasn't entirely untrue," he said. "You can be both the key to our strategy and…"

Their eyes locked.

"And what?" Callista murmured.

"And surprising," he said finally, after a long enough pause that she suspected it hadn't been what he first intended to say.

It was ridiculous to feel disappointed again, but she did.

"For example," he continued, "ruthlessness and idealism make an odd pair, and yet you seem to possess both in equal measures."

Perhaps he was only fascinated because he'd gotten the wrong idea about her. If that were the case, it would be a simple enough task to set him straight.

"Captain Avalar, I have lines I won't cross, but if you're expecting some kind of saint, you'll be disappointed. You can only afford so much idealism when you're fighting a Linden."

He didn't seem deterred. "Why would that disappoint me? Surely you realize that a pirate has no idealism at all."

Despite her confusion, Callista almost laughed. Killian Avalar might be a shapeshifting alien with dubious motives, but he was strangely honest when it counted. And he seemed to accept her, despite her own deliberate attempts to mislead him.

No, not just accept… respect. He respected the Callista Linden she'd always tried so hard to conceal.

For most of her life, she'd hidden almost everything real about herself. Not everything about her public persona was a lie

—she loved dressing up and stepping out into the crazy social whirl of Haven Two—but much of the Callista everyone knew was designed to camouflage the truth.

The truth of Diamondback, who never dared show her face.

The truth of her corporate ambitions, known only to her most trusted staff.

And the truth that she would rather get her hands dirty than stand back and let others do the work for her.

Killian had seen it all. He'd seen her flirt, seen her fight, seen her fly, and seemed to respect her skills and the threat she posed without being in any way intimidated.

It was disturbingly appealing, even in a man she wasn't sure she should trust. Or maybe that was part of the attraction?

Callista reflected wryly that if she had a type, it was probably the sort of man she wouldn't have dared take home to meet her parents, even if she had normal parents who cared.

He would be dangerous. Slightly mysterious. A rogue with a conscience, who loved speed as much as she did. Someone who wasn't afraid of risk, because Callista's entire life was a risk.

Thankfully, she'd yet to meet a man who fell into all those categories, so she'd never stopped to ask herself what she might do if he suddenly appeared.

At least, she'd never asked herself that until now.

But it was a mistake, because she wasn't entirely certain Killian Avalar had a conscience. Only time would tell, so she would have to contain these inconvenient feelings until he betrayed himself—one way or another.

ELEVEN

KILLIAN HAD no idea what was happening, but Callista had completely thrown off his game.

He was used to playing the smooth-talking, all-knowing, mysteriously sardonic pirate. He wasn't used to having someone push his buttons, challenge his morals, and laugh at his flirtations.

In short, Callista Linden drove him crazy, and yet he kept signing himself up for more.

Clearly, the pressure of the looming apocalypse had twisted his mind to the point that he no longer cared what was good for him.

The screen on the console flashed with an incoming transmission from Rill, distracting him from his frustration.

"… patching through the news feeds. Looks like security is tight, so you may want to turn around, Captain."

Callista slowed and turned her attention to the screen, which was suddenly filled with multiple vids and voices, all playing at once. But somehow, it didn't seem to bother her.

"Looks like Conclave peacekeepers are patrolling the

perimeter of the city," she mused, somehow splitting her attention effortlessly between piloting and processing the incoming information. "Sarat and Olaje have lodged formal complaints, even though there has been no official announcement of who was behind the attack."

She glanced at Killian. "Haven Two is a neutral city. All Conclave members have equal rights to territory, and residents are considered free agents unless they choose to maintain an affiliation. No infighting is allowed, so if the Conclave decides to officially call out Lindmark for the attack, we'll suffer enormous sanctions at the least and ejection from the Conclave at worst."

That sounded rather dire. "Why would your family risk it, then?"

Callista's lips curved in a humorless smile. "It's probably less of a risk than you're imagining. Everyone knows who's responsible for the attack, but the Conclave still hasn't made a public statement. Why do you think that is?"

"Negotiating behind the scenes?"

"On the money." She nodded in what looked like approval. "The fact that Hastings and Korchek haven't condemned the attack suggests they're hoping Lindmark will grant them concessions in exchange for their support. But there's still a chance all four corporations will form an alliance against Lindmark, which means Grandfather must be truly desperate to silence me."

"Why?"

Her smile grew more genuine, and more predatory. "Because I threatened him. Told him I was coming for him. Practically dared him to stop me if he could." She glanced over at Killian. "Right before you blew my plans all to hell and back, I might add."

Killian shrugged and leaned back in his seat, keeping his pose casual. "I've always had impeccable timing. But what does this mean for our endeavor today?"

"Officially, not much. I can still get us in. But a majority of the rumors seem to be claiming that I'm dead as the result of an attempted corporate coup. As long as Grandfather believes his mercenaries actually managed to kill me, he might not go after my people, but I doubt he'll buy it without some kind of proof. Not after what happened with Phillip."

"And will your people believe the gossip?"

"Unlikely. They'll be worried, but they know me well enough to wait before making assumptions."

The outskirts of Haven now loomed ahead of them, but instead of slowing down, Callista picked up speed and swung out at an angle to the city.

Killian shot her a sideways look. "Do I get to hear your plan, or do you intend to test my ability to play along?"

Her only answer was to wink and fly faster. When they were close enough to make out a few of the vehicles patrolling the outskirts of the city, Callista took a hard left. After a complete three-sixty, she hung a right and gunned it straight for the nearest towers.

A tangled heap of metal suddenly loomed up in their path, but she didn't slow, and Killian had to force himself not to react.

She wasn't going to crash, but his body didn't quite believe it. They were so close to the debris he could make out the remains of a burned-out fusion drive before she suddenly aimed the nose of the skimmer... *down*?

Straight into the ground, where nothing awaited them but rocks and tangled metal...

Somehow, they didn't go *splat*, and even more surprising, Killian managed not to sag in his seat after he realized they were in some sort of tunnel. One that had been concealed by the apparently unremarkable wreckage.

"It's okay if you want to kill me." Callista threw him an unrepentant grin as she piloted carefully down the dimly lit underground road. "It's just often easier to show than it is to explain."

As he'd subjected her to a similar shock when revealing his true form, he couldn't exactly contradict her. "I couldn't agree more," he rejoined instead. "But I was under the impression you humans favored a quaint little custom referred to as 'show-*and*-tell.'"

"But my way is so much more fun." She guided the skimmer around a few seemingly random pieces of debris. "I will tell you this much—there are energy weapon turrets under that mess back there. If I didn't have a beacon that indicated my right to be here, it would've blown us to shreds." Callista shot him a glance that was probably meant as a warning. "So I don't suggest coming back here on your own."

"Who claims ownership?"

"Smuggling tunnel." They came to a crossroads, and Callista took a left. "Neutral cities are where the Conclave elite come to indulge their vices, so there's a lot of illegal cargo that comes and goes. The corporations get to keep their own territory clean, while turning a blind eye to whatever their people get up to in cities like Haven Two."

"So you have connections with the black market?" He could admit to some surprise on that front. Considering her crusade against her grandfather, he'd have expected her to keep her business exclusively above board.

"Callista Linden doesn't," she informed him. "But I've spent a lot of time on the underground racing circuit, so anybody I meet down here knows me as Diamondback."

The tunnel system proved extensive, and Killian had to work to keep track of Callista's twists and turns. He quickly realized she was attempting to confuse him so he would be unable to retrace her path, and barely suppressed a grin. Somehow, he guessed she would be more amused than alarmed to learn that she'd failed.

Eventually, she slid into a side tunnel that came to a dead-end, and parked her skimmer. "This is where we get off," she announced, shutting down the thrusters and sliding back the cockpit door. "Time to see what kind of messes Grandpa left me to clean up."

She was more nervous than she wanted to admit. Killian could see it in the carefully controlled way she checked her weapons and tied her hair back. Callista Linden was going to war, and she wasn't sure what she was going to find.

But if he hadn't known her, all he would have noticed was cool determination as she led the way up a ladder to an access hatch that opened after she punched a numeric code into the old-fashioned security pad.

"Believe it or not, in some circles, these codes are safer than prints," she murmured. "You wouldn't believe how many smugglers around here are missing their fingers."

Killian couldn't quite hold back his amusement. "Have you ever chopped off any fingers, Miss Linden?"

"Of course not." She sounded almost offended. "That's for amateurs. If I felt the need to chop something off, I would choose a far more vital piece than a finger."

They emerged from the hatch into a dark, filthy alleyway, in a corner protected by piles of trash. After what Killian had seen of the rest of the city—which was quite clean for the most part—he suspected the trash was deliberate.

As they strolled past the debris towards the entrance to the alley, three forms emerged from the shadows—two men and one woman, all wearing what appeared to be stripped-down combat armor and carrying multiple weapons. The hilt peering over the woman's shoulder... Was that an *energy blade*?

They were even more illegal than the nerve disruptor one of the men was twirling between his fingers. And the second man? Well, he was probably the most dangerous of all, as his hands appeared to be completely empty.

Callista didn't even pause, just nodded, and went on her way until the woman blocked her path.

"Fancy seeing that face coming out of the Warren," the woman said, a lazy smile playing across her lips. "Been seeing it a lot since last night. Mostly on the news vids. They seem to think you're dead. You got a pass, Corpse Lady?"

Killian was watching closely, and he still almost missed the moment when Callista sidestepped, turned, flipped her armored assailant over her shoulder, and ended up with one knee on the woman's chest.

"*This* is my pass, Philene," she said contemptuously. "We both know the rules of the Warren. The only pass I need, I've already proven, so if you want to stop me, it starts getting personal. Do you want to make this personal?"

The woman bared her teeth. "How do you know me, Conclave bitch?"

Callista just smiled in answer.

The empty-handed man glanced at Killian, in no noticeable hurry to reach for his weapons. "You just going to stand there and let your boss do all the work?"

"No idea what you're talking about," Killian returned

smoothly, unable to resist the temptation that presented itself. "She's *my* bodyguard."

The two men exchanged glances and shifted their positions. When the empty-handed one's fingers twitched in the direction of his hip, Killian lifted his hand slightly and fired.

He hadn't used his energy weapon since coming to Earth, so he suspected he was in for a lot of awkward questions from his "bodyguard." But he knew men like these. Knew they spoke the language of power and brutality, and the only way to prevent worse violence was to leave no doubt you meant business.

His first shot blew up the stunner on the first man's hip, and his second knocked the nerve disruptor out of the second man's hand.

"Next one goes right between the eyes," he said softly, noting that the woman on the ground was now holding *very* still.

And all of them were dying of curiosity because they couldn't figure out where he was hiding his weapon.

"Looks like they have a pass," the still empty-handed man said, his eyes hard but cautious.

"And I also have a long memory." Callista rose to her feet. "Any fingerprints on my ride, and you'll be hearing from me."

She turned and walked out the alley without a backward glance, leaving Killian no choice but to follow, with the beginnings of a laugh threatening to erupt.

End of the world be hanged. He wasn't sure he'd ever had quite this much fun.

———

THEY EMERGED into the street and fell in with the flow of traffic, and as she walked, Callista activated her aural implant and scanned for her personal channels.

She also kept an eye out for anyone who seemed to recognize her.

Not that she was trying to be completely incognito. But no one in Haven Two would expect to see spoiled corporate heiress Callista Linden strolling along in her present getup, particularly not after she'd reportedly been attacked in her own home.

Anyone who spotted her would either consider her a doppel-gänger or run off to gossip about her, which could only help her primary cause—making her grandfather as nervous as possible.

Once she confirmed that her team was not currently attempting to contact her, she threw a sideways glance at her companion, who ambled down the streets of Haven Two as comfortably as if he owned them.

She wasn't sure what demon prompted her to continue testing him. But he was so quick to follow her lead—so ready to play whatever game she started. Claiming she was his body-guard? *After* she'd been recognized? She'd almost laughed right in the middle of trying to intimidate those idiots guarding the Warren.

So this time, she slowed down, took his arm, and shot him a wide-eyed look of fabricated adoration. Just an average woman out for a stroll with the object of her affections.

If only she were certain he had a conscience, that look might not be entirely faked.

"Interesting weapon you have there," she murmured in a low voice. "Considering how little we actually trust one another, I'm sure you can understand why it might make me reluctant to let you walk behind me."

Killian cocked an eyebrow and kept walking, placing one hand over hers where it rested on his arm. "As I said once before, I could've shot you in the back a thousand times."

"And still might, the moment you're finished with me."

His smirk grew. "But that's part of why you like me. Because you can't predict what I'm going to do next."

Sadly, he wasn't wrong. Killian Avalar made life a great deal more interesting. But right now, *interesting* wasn't what she needed.

She did like the fact that their relationship was as unpredictable as a skimmer race—that it had tested her and forced her to take risks. She liked it a lot. But in that moment, her needs were more important than her wants.

She needed a shield at her back. Someone she trusted implicitly, but also someone who didn't look to her for commands. Someone who could fly the course at her side.

And she wasn't sure Killian would do it.

Could he? She was almost certain of it. But until she understood what drove him—until she could dive deeper into his complex layers of ambition, betrayal, bitterness, and regret—she couldn't risk letting down her guard.

So she continued down the pedestrian throughway and kept her expression as sappy as she knew how. "Tell me how you shot those sentries."

Killian just smirked and kept walking. "I'm tempted to tell you that I have no idea what you're talking about. But mostly because I want to know what you'll say next."

Callista managed to swallow her retort—not because she didn't intend to question him further about his invisible weapon, but because she'd just spotted a man in a nondescript jumpsuit tailing them through the sparse but more flashily dressed crowd.

He wasn't one of hers. Unlike many of her peers, she knew all of her people by sight.

"Would you care to have a conversation with our stealthy friend back there?" Killian asked, in much the same tone as he might have asked her to go out for drinks.

Oh, but she did love a man who didn't need her to point out the obvious.

"First, I'd like to know whether his goal is to tail me or capture me."

"Your wish is my command, my lady."

He dropped her arm and disappeared into the crowd, and Callista wondered whether she ought to be concerned about safety. Not for Killian—he seemed more than capable of handling himself—but for those who might happen to cross his path. Given his general disdain for humans, he might not be terribly conscientious about leaving bodies in his wake.

Her aural implant suddenly crackled to life.

"Boss?" It was Xavier's voice, and Callista nearly melted into the polycrete throughway in relief.

But she didn't use her wrist-comm to respond. Instead, she activated the encrypted locator beacon in one of her earrings.

"I've got you on the grid." Xavier sounded like he was ready to chew hull-metal. He and Alli took their jobs very seriously, and Callista didn't doubt the past day had been difficult for them. "Base One was compromised, so we're set up at Base Two. Surveillance sweeps are happening every few hours, so we're using intermittent comms only. I can pick you up, but with the increased security, chances are high that we'd be followed."

Whose surveillance? She needed to find out. Was it Conclave peacekeepers? Their presence was tiny and limited to ground troops only, but they were reserved for just such moments as this —when tensions were running high between Conclave members.

Or could all of this be traced back to Lindmark? Hoping she would stick her head out of her burrow so they could cut it off?

"Keep your locator on if you require an escort," Xavier continued. "Otherwise, I'll transmit the surveillance schedule, and we'll get set to receive you at our location."

Callista reached up and switched off the locator. It would be far easier for her and Killian to sneak into her base than to arrange for a clandestine pickup by skimmer.

Killian... Both he and her tail had disappeared. Callista strolled to the end of the block, paused for a mag-train, then crossed to one of the tiny green spaces that dotted the interior of Haven Two. They were too perfectly manicured to feel much like "nature" but better than unbroken acres of polycrete and steel.

To disguise her impatience, she bought a coffee from one of the floating vendor carts on the edge of the throughway and took a deep swallow of the dark, sugary goodness. When there was still no sign of Killian, Callista took a reluctant seat on the edge of the synth-marble fountain at the center of the green space and continued to sip at her drink.

What was Killian doing? Interrogating her tail in the middle of a public street? Or had he dragged the unfortunate spy into an alley for a little clandestine torture?

After a few more minutes of waiting, she heard a loud *pop* coming from the area she'd just walked through moments ago. The sound was followed by the wail of security alarms and wafting clouds of black smoke.

It probably indicated something about her bizarre relationship with Killian that she immediately assumed he was responsible.

It said something even more uncomfortable about *her* that her first response was a quiet chuckle and a resigned eye roll. An alien was running around destroying her city, and the best she could manage was an eye roll?

Perhaps her judgment was impaired by the impending apocalypse. She'd heard that stress could cause people to act in unpredictable ways.

"Ready to go, love?"

It took nearly every scrap of her self-control not to show how startled she was by Killian's sudden appearance behind her. And then it took every remaining scrap not to push him into the fountain.

"That depends, *darling.*" She took a deliberately slow sip of her coffee. "Do you have any news for me? Or did you happen to get a look at whatever dastardly villain was responsible for all that smoke?"

"I do, and I did," he responded, offering her his arm again with a charming smile. "Shall we stroll on while I tell you all about it?"

She stood up but didn't immediately move on. "Did you hurt anyone?" she asked in a low voice.

His smile turned faintly mocking. "Whatever happened to not being a saint?"

"No bystanders, Killian. The gloves are off with my family because they took them off first, but I won't condone collateral damage."

"Will it make you feel better if I tell you the man tailing you was a Lindmark operative?"

"Freelancer or family man?"

"Mercenary, which is the only reason you have not yet been returned to your family's loving embrace. He had your picture but wasn't entirely certain the faces matched."

At least her people weren't the target. Yet.

Callista took Killian's arm and began sauntering down one of the paths towards the far side of the green space. Once again, just an ordinary couple out for a stroll on a fine afternoon. And for now, the ruse seemed like a wise precaution. No one looking for her would be paying much attention to clearly attached couples.

"And just how did you convince him to part with this information?" she asked, painting on a flirtatious smile.

"By being my charming self, of course."

Never mind. She didn't want to know. If the man was genuinely a bounty hunter in her family's employ, she also didn't really care.

"And the smoke?"

"As it turns out, automated recyclers don't handle organic material particularly well."

He hadn't. Callista stared straight ahead and tried not to envision what he was suggesting. Tried not to… Oh, gods above. She was going to have to fix this. Going to have to make sure Killian was never turned loose on an unsuspecting populace again…

"Your tail was wearing real leather boots."

Oh.

"And then some nefarious, shifty-eyed saboteur must have poured something unsavory into the recycler's hydraulics, because they exploded. A terrible mystery. I do hope the city authorities can get to the bottom of it."

"You certainly know how to show a girl a good time," Callista murmured, checking once more for tails as they crossed another throughway and continued deeper into the city.

"Only for you, love," the pirate responded with an exaggerated wink. He was playing up their "couple out for a stroll" ruse with everything he had. "Now, where would you like to go next? To the moon? You know I can arrange that. Concord Five? I hear it's particularly charming this time of year."

Callista leaned in closer. "You say such romantic things. But I have something a little more adventurous in mind."

"Like risking being shot, tortured, and left for dead by your overzealous bodyguards?"

"Why, darling"—Callista bared her teeth in an insincere smile —"I thought you might enjoy it. But if that sounds like too much for you, I'm sure we can arrange for a nice family dinner with my grandfather instead."

Killian turned and met her eyes, and suddenly, his focus seemed far more intense than it had only a moment before.

Callista's heart beat faster as he leaned closer, and his expression made her breath catch in her throat.

"Shall we?" His dark eyes glittered dangerously. "I find myself unexpectedly intrigued by the idea."

Callista was intrigued too, and not just by the thought of Killian in the same room with Eustacius and Satrina Linden.

As entertaining as that would be, it was the man himself who fascinated her, and every moment she spent in his company only deepened her desire to know more of him.

But right now, they had a shield to build and humanity to save.

Her curiosity would have to wait.

TWELVE

THEIR WELCOME by Callista's team was very much as Killian had expected. She was snatched away by a small army of worried people in suits, while her bodyguards—Alli and Xavier—hovered and glared at him threateningly.

Their base of operations was in a sub-level of a public parking hangar, where the constant traffic effectively concealed their comings and goings. Killian suspected few people knew the hangar extended below ground—unless you knew the correct access points, the entire level was designed to appear abandoned.

Inside, however, was a hive of activity, with several rooms dedicated to computer terminals, surveillance equipment, and multiple teams working feverishly on he had no idea what.

The only one who seemed genuinely glad to see him? Katsi. The dark-furred feline padded into the room where he waited, put her paws on his knee, and purred at him insistently until he gave in and scratched under her chin.

The two bodyguards exchanged glances, and Killian couldn't help feeling slightly smug.

He also felt incredibly tempted to call Errol out from his

extra-dimensional world for some playtime, but that would probably be a good way to get them both shot.

After a handful of incredibly boring minutes, Callista poked her head back into the room where he waited.

"You're cleared," she announced. "Come with me."

She started with what felt like an endless round of introductions, after which Killian ended up seated across a table from a woman with a steely stare and impeccably correct posture.

"This is Jocasta," Callista informed him, "my primary business manager."

The woman's white hair and furrowed brow suggested she was old enough to be Callista's mother, but it was her eyes that Killian ended up watching more carefully. Age had clearly not slowed her down a bit, and if he was not mistaken, she was as protective of her employer as any mother would be.

"She's also been in charge of my acquisition of a biotech company called Seren. I believe they may be our best candidate for developing the technology needed for your proposed planetary shield."

What Callista didn't say was how much she'd shared with her people about his true identity.

"Before we begin"—Jocasta addressed him directly—"I'll need some assurances that you're sufficiently qualified in the field of biotech to risk shifting Seren's production on the strength of your word. I've seen the vid from Concord, and I've been briefed on your concerns about future attacks. What I need to know is whether you're just out to gain notoriety, or you genuinely know what you're talking about."

Killian held back a groan and looked at Callista. "Do you have a weapon?" he asked. "Not a stunner. A laser pistol, preferably."

She glanced at one of her people, and the requested weapon

appeared with almost magical speed. Callista accepted it and raised an eyebrow at Killian. "What now?"

He held up one hand as if asking permission. "Shoot me," he said, pointing to his upraised palm. Exactly as he'd once done to Seph in an effort to prove his identity.

Unlike Seph, Callista just shrugged and shot him.

He held back a wince at the pain, but continued to hold his hand where everyone in the room could see the smoking laser burn in the center of his palm.

Several faces paled, but Callista and Jocasta both watched curiously and without flinching as the skin of Killian's hand began to change color. The smoke stopped within the first five seconds, then the burnt edges fell away. New tissue began forming beneath them, and in less than a minute, the hole was filled in by pale, unscarred skin.

He healed faster since his recent infusion of nanotech, but it still stung like all hells, so he hoped they wouldn't ask him to repeat the experiment.

"Interesting," was Jocasta's bland response. "So you're claiming you've achieved this level of tissue repair using biotechnology rather than natural processes?"

He nodded.

"And you believe human manufacturing can duplicate your tech?"

He glanced at Callista, and she grinned wryly. "I didn't tell her who you are," she said. "I said your identity was for you to reveal or not. She just knew you aren't actually my brother."

These humans seemed to be rather quicker to adapt than any he'd known in the past, and the realization gave him hope. If they could accept him and his plans to save Earth without the need for lengthy arguments, perhaps they could still prepare in time.

"Can you duplicate what we use to heal or change shape? No, but I believe you can mimic what's needed to create a shield." Killian leaned forward and met the older woman's piercing gaze with all the confidence he could project. "I have two biotech specialists on my crew, one of whom has spent time studying human technology and its applications. They should be able to bridge the gap between your level of advancement and ours, even if your scientists aren't quite prepared for the complexity of what we're asking."

"Hmm." Jocasta tapped at the screen in front of her. "And have you considered the method of deployment? We know naturally occurring microbes can reach the kind of altitudes this plan requires through normal weather patterns, but I don't believe we're going to want to wait and hope for the best."

"I'm not an expert on Earth's atmospheric conditions," Killian countered, "so I suggest you find one as quickly as possible. I do know our historical records suggest that a combination of ground dispersion and orbital seeding platforms can be effective."

Jocasta nodded briskly. "Noted. When can we expect the arrival of your crew members at the Seren facility to begin the process?"

That fast? Killian was starting to feel dizzy. "As soon as you provide the location."

He'd been expecting more of a fight. It had never occurred to him that it could be this simple. But he'd never counted on an ally like Callista Linden.

She was the one who'd made this possible. Her capability, her charisma, and the groundwork she'd clearly been laying for years as she prepared to take over the corporation her mother and grandfather had nearly destroyed. And it was also possible because of the trust she'd built with the people in her employ. And after what he'd seen of her in action, he couldn't blame them for either their confidence or their devotion. Callista was, in a word, extraordinary.

"Next," Jocasta continued, "we'll need to begin involving the other members of the Conclave in our efforts, and that won't be nearly as simple. Not with all of us in hiding and Eustacius actively campaigning to be allowed to get away with murder."

"Let me handle that," Callista murmured. "Grandfather is my fight."

"This is only the first step," Killian warned. "Even if the shield works, it will only hold the Bhandecki off until we can find a way to destroy them."

"I'll assign a second team to that question," Jocasta assured him. "Lindmark is one of only two corporations to have a division dedicated to developing space-capable armaments. We've yet to crack their security, but as time is short, I believe we can now abandon subtlety." Jocasta eyed Killian closely. "It would aid our efforts immeasurably if we could gain a closer look at the remains of the entity that destroyed Concord Five."

"I don't know if there's enough of it left to help you, let alone enough time to bring it here," he responded bluntly, his heart sinking as he contemplated the delay. "Fireworms often explode when they die, and even if this one didn't, it's two weeks in Earth time to get there and two weeks back. That's if we use my ship and travel at top speed. As quickly as the Bhandecki fleet is moving our way, I might end up trapped on the other side of it. However"—he paused long enough for a quick glance at Callista —"I'm willing to make the attempt once my people have given your specialists what they need to build the shield."

"Then I believe we have enough to go on for now." Jocasta

pushed back from the table and rose to her feet. "With your permission"—she turned to Callista—"I'll start the conversation with Seren immediately."

"Perfect. I'll entrust all the details to you. All I need now is a small team for…"

Killian suddenly stopped listening as his head wrap began to buzz with an emergency comm. He tapped it, but there was no message, only a pre-coded alert.

Ice coursed through his veins as the strident tone of the alert echoed through him. It was unique, and could only be generated by a hidden panel located on the *Fancy's* bridge.

And it was intended to be activated only in the direst of emergencies—only when his ship had been boarded and was about to be under enemy control.

Callista was still deep in discussions of her plans to counter her grandfather's attacks, but she glanced his way and fell silent when she saw him come to his feet.

"I have to go *now*," he told her flatly. "The *Fancy* is under attack."

He turned to leave, planning to make his own way back to the Canyon, but his path was blocked by Alli and Xavier.

He would simply have gone straight through them had Callista not spoken his name.

"Killian."

That stopped him, but not for long. He respected Callista enough not to simply shoot her people, but there was a limit to how long he would wait when his crew was in danger once again.

"Ten seconds," she said, and turned back to Jocasta. "Use our newest cipher for communications. I'll leave my tertiary channel open at all times. Keep me updated on Seren, and let me know when Patrick and Harvey arrive safely. You know what to do if security is compromised."

He could tell she had no doubt whatsoever that her people would handle any threat that materialized, and watched with surprise as her eyes suddenly glistened with tears.

"You all have worked miracles," she told the room as a whole. "I counted on you, and you've never let me down. Thank you."

Then she darted forward to hug Jocasta before moving around the table to where Killian stood.

"Let's go," she said.

He stared at her blankly for a moment, unable to process her intentions. Did she expect him to accompany her somewhere else when his ship—his home and his only way back to his own people—was in danger of being lost? "Go where?"

"Back to the *Fancy*," she said. "Killian, I'm not about to let anyone take your ship."

"Too dangerous," he said, almost automatically. Did she really intend to risk herself fighting for his ship?

"I'm going to pretend you didn't say that," she murmured softly, eyes narrowed in irritation. "Now, are you coming with me or not?"

He'd thought he was beginning to understand her. He knew she wasn't in this for the power or the money—rather, she fought for her people, just as he did.

But he'd been wrong in one very important way, and he began to suspect that even Callista might not understand her own motivations as well as she thought she did.

Yes, she was a high flyer. A risk-taker. An adventure seeker. She sought out challenges to her territory, and she defeated them.

But it was not simply her own territory she was concerned about. Not just her own people.

155

Callista was a protector at heart. And so, he realized suddenly, was her brother.

The impulse that had driven Phillip Linden from his self-imposed exile had not been some possessive desire to take back his family's corporation. He'd known all along that he could have done so and refused.

The one thing that had changed? Seph. Phillip had changed his mind in order to protect the woman he loved.

Similarly, the focus that drove Callista was not merely possessive. It was the instinct to protect everything and everyone in her power—from the strangers living in her apartment building to the dying citizens of a faraway planet she could never hope to save.

And now? She would even protect the ship and crew of a bitter, evasive alien she wasn't entirely certain she could trust.

The Lindens had done their best to raise a new generation of sociopaths. Instead, they'd given Earth its greatest defenders.

Paradoxically, Killian felt some of the icy regret around his own heart ease as he recognized Callista's impatience to defend *his* people and *his* ship.

If bitter experience had made Phillip and Callista into the people they needed to be, what did that mean for his own past? Could he justify letting go of his anger—at his brother *and* the humans who killed his people—and search instead for a new purpose here?

Was it possible to not only take back the past but to imagine a different future?

All of it swirled in a heady cocktail of fear, hope, and anticipation, so without really thinking about the consequences, Killian nodded to the woman beside him—the woman whose determination forced him to see the world differently than he'd ever imagined.

"After you," he said.

————

CALLISTA COULD SENSE Killian's urgency and fear, so she didn't even suggest they return the way they'd come. Instead, they took a nondescript skimmer from the hangar above her people's hideout and merged into the everyday traffic leaving Haven Two.

Fortunately, the surveillance teams (both official and unofficial) were still watching for her to *arrive* in the city and didn't seem to notice when they slipped out instead.

Once they passed the outskirts, she chose a circuitous route to throw off pursuit before entering the Canyon and heading for the *Fancy's* location.

The moment the ship came into view, some of the tension seemed to leave Killian's wiry frame. At least it was still in one piece. But Callista could also tell he'd heard nothing from his crew, and the suspense of wondering whether they were alive or dead had him balanced on a razor edge.

"No charging in without me," she warned him as she settled the skimmer to the ground near the boarding ramp. "If hostile forces have taken the ship, chances are they're my enemies, not yours. We're going to have to play this carefully if we're going to get your ship back without damaging it."

He turned to face her for a moment, eyes bleak and icy cold.

"I don't care who they are. If they've injured my people or damaged my ship, I won't be withholding judgment. I will shoot them, and I won't sit around asking questions first."

"I have no problem with you defending yourself or your

people," Callista rejoined sternly, "but I do have a problem with you getting yourself killed. There's only the two of us, so we're going to have to communicate and not charge off half-cocked."

Killian's sudden grin was more than a little terrifying.

"Actually," he said, leaping out of the cockpit, "there are three of us."

Where had he been hiding another ally? Callista shut down the thrusters, clambered out, and sealed the cockpit, just in time to see Killian reach up and twist the small blue hoop in his ear.

And that's when things got really weird.

A tangle of blue lights spiraled out of the earring, widening and brightening as they streaked towards the ground. When they hit, they bounced off and swirled around until they suddenly coalesced into...

Holy crap.

For a few uncertain moments, Callista thought it might be a projection or a holographic simulation. The alien beast that confronted her was huge—its shoulders possibly higher than hers. Like a cat, but not, it was covered in purple-blue fur that rippled and seemed to almost change color in the evening sun. The fur was longer over its back and down the length of its long, flexible tail, and shorter on its sides and legs.

Around its neck was what she might have called a mane, except that it was made of broad, sinuous tentacles that waved and tangled and moved independently of the breeze—like a forest of eyeless snakes.

And then its broad head turned to look at her out of golden, slit-pupiled eyes, while its forked ears swiveled in interest... and Callista took one very large step back.

The creature was real, and as it opened its jaws in a mighty yawn, it revealed a mouthful of long, needle-sharp teeth that sent her hand in the direction of her stunner almost without conscious thought.

"Killian." She didn't take her eyes from the thing in front of her. "What in the actual hells is that, and where did it come from?"

The beast flopped onto its rump in the dirt, lifted an enormous furred paw, and waved all seven of its silver-clawed toes.

"This is Errol," Killian informed her. "He's been with me a long time, and he protects the ship. I don't have time to explain his living arrangements, but yes, he's real, he's quite intelligent, and he's dangerous unless he knows you're a friend."

He stepped to the creature's side and rubbed under its chin, just as he'd done to Katsi. Maybe that was how he'd made friends with the phantom cat so quickly—he had experience with... cat-things.

"This is Callista," he said, a bit sternly. "She's with me, so don't scare her, and no, she doesn't want to play. There are intruders on the ship, but I don't want them dead until I have a chance to talk to them, so no killing."

Callista could have sworn the cat rolled its eyes, but it rose onto all four paws and padded after Killian as he jogged up the ramp to the weapons bay door. It was closed, but Killian swore under his breath as it opened at the first touch of his palm to the lock.

"Unlocked," he muttered viciously. "But that's impossible. None of my people would have left it unsecured, and no one on Earth should have the ability to hack our systems."

Callista lifted her palm stunner as they paused outside the door, only to have Killian shoot her a warning look.

"Be careful what you hit with that. If you miss, it could damage the ship's systems."

"I'll be careful," she responded coolly. "But I think I would feel better about this if I wasn't the only one going in armed."

"I'm armed," Killian said briefly, all his teasing humor now gone. "My crew all have a form of energy weapon incorporated into our shifted forms. I can choose the intensity of my shots, and the energy is calibrated so as not to damage the ship."

So that's how he'd shot the guards in the alley. Good to know. Even when he appeared to be unarmed, Killian was anything but.

Errol entered first, and when he drew no fire, Killian followed, allowing Callista to bring up the rear. The door shut automatically behind them, just as Errol's approach triggered the door on the other side of the weapons bay.

"Whoever they are, they seem confident enough not to post guards," Callista murmured. "Any ideas?"

Killian just shook his head and followed Errol deeper into the ship, pausing before each cross corridor and tapping his comm-band occasionally as if hoping for a message that never came.

The ship seemed eerily empty and silent, and Callista watched as Killian's expression grew grimmer by the moment.

"Is there a way up other than the lift?" she finally asked.

"There's a separate lift system that leads directly from my quarters to the bridge," he told her. "But I'll have to send Errol up to second first, to clear out any ambush they may have waiting for us."

Somehow, the creature seemed to know what was expected. He entered the lift alone and waited patiently while Killian activated it. The door closed on Errol's blue-furred form, and then they waited, still hearing nothing.

After two or three minutes, Killian activated the lift doors again and stepped inside. "Wait here. If it's safe, I'll come back down for you."

"I thought I was clear on you telling me what I'm allowed to do," Callista returned icily. "If there's an ambush, we'll have a better shot at survival if we stick together."

He whirled to face her, anger evident in his narrowed eyes and clenched jaw. "If they hit you, can you heal laser burns and keep going?"

So he *did* want to protect her, even in the midst of his fear for his crew, and the thought almost warmed her heart a little.

"You know I can't," she said calmly. "But you also know I'm a deadly shot. I can cover you from the lift."

"Right," he said sarcastically, "and if they're too much for me? Can your people hold Lindmark together without you? If you fall here, what chance does Earth have?"

Ah. He wasn't so much concerned for *her* safety as he was for the safety of Earth. For the future of his plan. That information should have simply been filed away as a clue to his behavior, but instead, it stung in a way Callista was not prepared for.

Still, she held his gaze steadily. "And if they attack me here once you're gone? I think it's better for us to stay together."

He didn't like it. She could see his frustration written across his face, but he waited for her to enter the lift before he activated the door and started up. And even then, he didn't give her condescending instructions, just stood silently until the lift came to a stop.

"Don't get yourself killed," he said shortly, and triggered the door.

It opened to reveal Errol, sprawled in the middle of the corridor on his back, licking one of his front paws.

Callista would have chuckled had the whole situation not been so bizarre.

"Not on this level either," she noted.

Killian took off at a jog, suddenly not seeming very concerned about looking around corners or checking for intruders, leaving Callista racing to catch up.

"The alert came from the bridge," he flung back over his shoulder, "so they may have barricaded themselves in."

"Are you sending Errol in first this time?"

"No." He paused to press his hand to a square of blinking blue and orange lights on the curved wall of the corridor. "He's too startling for anyone who hasn't seen him before, and I don't want them firing indiscriminately on the bridge. Too much chance they'll damage something I won't have enough nanotech to repair."

The wall vanished, and as they walked through what Callista assumed were the Captain's quarters, she noted that they were spare and utilitarian, unlike the dashing image Killian went to so much effort to project.

The area just inside the door was arranged very like a human conference room, with a long table surrounded by chairs. Killian led her past the table, through another opening in the far wall, into what appeared to be a bedroom with an adjoining washroom.

But there were no comforts in evidence. No personal possessions. No decor, nothing soft or inviting, and nothing in bright colors. The deck was hard and bare, the chairs seemed to flow from the same material as the deck, and what little light there was came from hidden recesses in the walls.

Bleak, was Callista's first thought, and it made her wonder why a man with such a sharp and vivid personality would live in such a stark environment.

Punishment, perhaps? A reminder of what he'd lost? Or a motivation to never give up on returning home?

But Killian didn't pause to gaze at the surroundings, only crossed to the wall beside the bed and reached into one of the light sources. The wall vanished, to reveal a space not much bigger than a coffin.

"You still want to stick together?" Killian asked a bit acidly. "This goes straight to the bridge. When the door opens, we'll be in full view of whoever has taken over my ship. This is your last chance to back out and wait here until I assess the situation."

She didn't need to think about it. "I'm going." Callista stepped inside and pressed herself as far against the wall as possible. "But you can stand in front of me if it makes you feel better."

He cocked his head at her, then reached out and took her by the shoulders. Her eyes flew wide as he held her that way for a moment, his hands firm even through the bulk of her jacket and his eyes steady on hers, as if asking a question he couldn't quite put words to.

But he didn't tell her to be careful. Didn't say he cared about her safety. Instead, he turned her to the side, so her shoulder was facing the door, and entered the lift behind her, putting them back to back.

"This way," he muttered, "we can both see to shoot."

Callista grinned in spite of herself, feeling a spike of elation at this evidence of Killian's trust. Maybe he didn't want to trust her and just didn't feel like he had a choice. But it was a step in the right direction.

Despite their constant testing of one another, and all their arguing and evasions, it seemed they actually made a rather good team.

THIRTEEN

IN THAT TINY SPACE, it was impossible to ignore Callista's presence. Impossible not to feel her pressed against his back, sense the tension in the air, or hear the sound of her breathing

And as the lift began to move upwards towards the bridge, it proved equally impossible for Killian to set aside his growing frustration with his own feelings.

There should have been no room in his heart for anything but fury at the intruders and fear for his crew's life. Yet to Killian's dismay, his heart was proving less discriminatory.

He was afraid for Callista, too. Afraid for a *human*. Afraid for a woman he couldn't trust, who likewise didn't trust him.

Except that was no longer entirely true.

He trusted her enough to have her at his back. To show her the *Fancy's* secrets. He trusted her to help him save his people.

And she, in turn, was willing to risk her life to do so. A woman with everything to lose was ready to confront his enemies with a weapon in her hand, thereby placing her own future and her own plans in grave danger.

But why? Yes, she knew that Earth's future depended on the

knowledge and expertise of his crew members, but Callista Linden had people for this sort of thing. She could have sent her security team. Could have done any number of things that didn't involve her personally risking her neck on this lift.

Killian had no illusions about her willingness to accept risk— the woman practically chased it down and invited it to dinner. But she also had a reason for everything she did.

No, that was unfair. Callista Linden probably had *multiple* reasons for everything she did. And with that thought came an echo of her brother's voice, saying that Killian never did anything for fewer than three reasons.

So what, his skeptical heart demanded to know, were her reasons now?

And why did he keep wanting to shield her from danger she was perfectly capable of handling on her own?

Her voice interrupted his thoughts. "Talk first or shoot first?"

"I won't know until the door opens."

"Any hypotheses?"

He'd only come up with one. "Shortly after the fireworm collided with Concord, we sent a message to my homeworld requesting assistance. It's possible they listened and actually sent someone. I can't imagine anyone else being able to bypass the locks to access the ship's systems."

But as for why they would hold his crew hostage... The possibilities chilled him.

The lift drifted to a stop.

The door opened.

In the space of a moment, Killian took a step out of the lift, dropped to one knee in preparation to fire, swept his gaze across the bridge, and saw them all.

Harvey, Rill, Dinah, and Patrick. Motionless in their chairs, hands taped palm-down to their consoles. Somehow even in that near-instantaneous sweep, it registered that they didn't appear to be afraid.

But they did appear to be watching the man in the captain's chair.

A man Killian recognized at the exact same moment Callista exclaimed in surprise.

"Phillip?"

There was no mistaking that short, sandy-blond hair and familiar, glacial stare. The Lindmark heir had, in fact, made himself at home on Killian's bridge. And now, his ice-blue eyes fixed unerringly on Killian's face while the hand resting on his knee held a decidedly lethal-looking laser pistol.

He looked different, Killian noted—both more relaxed and more focused. But neither of those seemed to have made a notable impact on the pure fury written across his face.

Three questions presented themselves for immediate consideration.

How had Phillip reached Earth so fast?

How had he bypassed the *Fancy's* security?

And where was Seph?

Though perhaps a fourth question was in order—how quickly did Phillip intend to shoot Killian for abandoning him on Concord Five?

"Phil, is that actually you?"

The man currently occupying the captain's chair shifted his gaze to Callista, and Killian thought his eyes narrowed slightly.

"Unless you want me to call you Lissy for the rest of our lives, I suggest you reconsider the nickname."

Callista lowered her weapon and grinned. "Congratulations, you pass. What are you doing here?"

"Confronting a traitor," he said coolly. "What are *you* doing here?"

"The goal was to liberate the crew," she informed him, strolling over to Rill and starting to pry up the tape that imprisoned the pilot's hands. "Really, Phillip? Duct tape?"

He shrugged. "Why not? It's been working for hundreds of years. And I'd really rather you leave that where it is. I have no desire to be shot in the back."

Killian strode away from the lift to stand beside Callista. "You have no argument with my crew," he said briefly. "Harvey and Patrick are needed to begin work on Earth's atmospheric shield. Allow them to leave, and you and I can sort out our differences."

Phillip raised an eyebrow at Callista, who pinned her brother with an assessing gaze in return.

"He's telling the truth," she said finally. "My people are waiting for them at Seren Biotech."

"*Your* people? Or Lindmark's people?"

Callista sighed. "It's a long story, Phillip, and I'll tell you everything, but we don't have time for the two of you to fight it out."

"We're not going to fight it out," Phillip said softly. "I'm going to kill him."

"No, you're not." Callista's voice was just as low and dangerous as her brother's. "There's a lot more at stake here than your personal vendettas. Lindmark is imploding, and Earth is about to be crushed. We need everyone, which means you're going to have to live out your revenge fantasy later."

"He shot Seph!"

"I stunned her," Killian snapped.

"Yes," a new voice interjected mildly, "you did, but I've decided to forgive you."

The bridge door was now open, and leaning against the wall just inside it was a tall woman with warm brown skin and curling light brown hair. Her hazel eyes assessed him, but without animosity, and the corners of her lips were curled up in an almost-smile.

"Hello, Killian," she said. "Strangely enough, I'm actually glad to see you. And Phillip will be too, once he's gotten this out of his system."

Seph. Killian struggled not to let his emotions show on his face. She was fine. And somehow, she didn't hate him for what he'd done.

It was a relief. Almost as great a relief as finally facing Phillip after the way they'd parted.

"I don't expect him to forget or forgive," Killian said coolly. "I did what was needed, just as he did."

"Needed?" Phillip stood and stalked across the bridge to stand eye to eye with Killian, jamming the tip of his laser pistol between two of Killian's ribs as he came to a stop. "I made it clear that I wanted her safe, and you left her to die."

"I left her to save *you*!"

Everyone froze.

Damn. Killian hadn't meant to ever say those words out loud. Hadn't meant for anyone to know. He'd spent so many hours since then doubting his own motivation, even *he* wasn't always sure what he'd actually intended.

But his crew all looked as though he'd suddenly attempted to blow up the bridge.

Phillip's brow was furrowed with... anger? Confusion? Surprise? All of the above?

"And that," Seph said, sounding amused, "is why I forgave him. That and the fact that he could very easily have taken his second ship, but he didn't. He didn't even change the security settings."

Change the security settings...

He'd forgotten. Forgotten that desperate moment when the *Fancy* had been locked in a dive towards the surface of a dead moon. He and his crew had been incapacitated by a weapon intended to fry their nanotech. Just before he lost consciousness, he'd given Phillip full access to the *Fancy's* systems. And never rescinded it.

"So that's how you got here so fast," Callista murmured.

Phillip shot her a sharp look. "How much do you know?"

"Enough." She shrugged, holstered her weapon, and folded her arms. "Enough to request that you stop messing around and help us prepare to face the Bhandecki. Lindmark is in full self-destruct mode, and if we can't stop them, our options will be limited."

"We?" His weapon didn't move, so neither did Killian.

In truth, he found himself quite curious to see how this part of the confrontation would play out.

From his conversations with Callista, he doubted the two siblings had ever been close. But had they been rivals? Or had Phillip known no more of her ambitions than Callista had chosen to show the rest of the world?

And if Phillip decided not to cooperate—if he chose to screw with their plans and take Lindmark for himself—what was Killian prepared to do in response?

As a potential leader for Lindmark, Phillip made the most sense. He had the necessary knowledge and experience, and with the truth about his relative innocence even now being publicly debated, returning him to the top of Lindmark's power structure should be a relatively short and easy path.

But Callista had earned this. She'd fought for it, and what was more, she could do it. If the other corporations could get past her personal history and the lie of her public persona, she had the charisma and the capability to lead them in their efforts to survive the Bhandecki.

Would either of them be able to trust the other enough to work together?

Callista didn't waste time with long-winded explanations. She walked over, shouldered Killian aside, and stepped between him and her brother's weapon.

"We," she said firmly. "You. Me. Killian. His crew. And everyone else we can convince to join us. In case you missed it, Galloway has been destroyed, just like Vadim. There's no more time for power plays or political games. I know you want Grandfather gone, and so do I. But that's not the end goal anymore—survival is. We have one chance to get this right. So are you going to be a part of it, or are you going to make me prove just how badly you've underestimated me all these years?"

Tension filled the bridge, thick and heavy, accompanied by silence.

The two Lindens could not have looked more different—Phillip's light hair, muscular build, and stoic demeanor contrasted against Callista's dark hair, slender form, and seemingly mercurial temperament.

Phillip's gun hand twitched upward, and Killian reacted before he had time to think about the consequences.

He reacted with the speed, reflexes, and strength of his nanotech-enhanced form, advantages he rarely used and always took care to hide from humans. But when Phillip moved, there had been room for only one thought—he couldn't let Callista be hurt.

Phillip's gun flew across the deck with the force of Killian's strike, and the Linden heir's body followed with an audible grunt. By the time he landed, Killian was crouching over him, hand on his throat and murder in his eyes.

"You have every right to point that at me," he said in a low, dangerous tone, "but never point it at her again."

Phillip looked up from where he lay on the deck, stunned surprise registering in his blue eyes before he shocked everyone by suddenly beginning to laugh.

It took him a few moments to gain control, but when he did, he met Killian's murderous gaze with wry resignation.

"So now you know how it feels," he said.

The reality of what he'd done sank in, and Killian rose to his feet, feeling as unsteady as if he'd been punched in the face. He hadn't thought about it—he'd just reacted to defend Callista. Who didn't need defending in the slightest.

But why had he done it? From Phillip's statement and the amused look he wore…

No. That was impossible.

Like they were drawn by a magnet, Killian's eyes moved slowly to meet Callista's. Hers were dark and anxious, and—he was relieved to see—completely confused. Maybe she hadn't realized what had just happened. Maybe only Phillip had figured it out. Which was embarrassing enough, but not as terrifying as allowing Callista to see the truth.

"Well," Seph said cheerfully into the awkward silence, "I don't know about the rest of you, but I never expected the end of the world to be quite this entertaining."

———

THEY ADJOURNED to Killian's quarters after that—all except for Rill, Harvey, and Patrick. The three of them left almost immediately, taking the jump-ship that had brought Phillip and Seph to Earth and heading for Seren Biotech, which was located on an island in Korchek territory.

Callista remained serene and focused on the outside, but couldn't stop replaying the startling memory of Killian's reaction when he thought she'd been threatened.

She knew he respected her abilities and was well aware that she could handle herself in a fight. She also guessed he liked Phillip far more than he cared for anyone to know. So he should have understood that Phillip would never hurt her.

Unless he hadn't been thinking very clearly. Unless his emotions had triggered a reaction before his brain could remind him that she wasn't in any danger.

But what did that mean? How should she interpret the stricken expression he'd worn afterward, and his refusal to look at her ever since? And what on Earth was with Phillip's sudden change of heart?

They all took seats at the table, and Phillip was the first to speak.

"I'm going to assume we're all up to speed on what we're facing, so why don't one of you fill me in on the current plan?"

"Which plan?" Callista answered dryly, refocusing on the problem at hand. "Before your pirate friend here showed up, I had a perfectly good plan to take Lindmark from Mother and Grandfather and fix it before they destroyed everything."

Phillip actually chuckled, and Callista's jaw nearly dropped at the difference between this man and the brother she remembered. So much of the ice was gone, and the wall around his feelings seemed nonexistent. He'd even remembered how to smile.

Probably thanks to the woman at the opposite end of the table, who leaned back in her chair, looking entirely at ease.

"So Phillip was right about you," the woman noted with a grin. "Hi. Sorry for the lack of introduction. I'm Seph."

"Callista." She offered the woman a friendly nod. "Phillip was right about what?"

"He told me you'd eat Killian alive."

Callista switched her gaze to her brother, who was looking at Seph with amused affection. Not an emotion she'd ever thought to see on his face.

"So you knew?" she asked curiously. "You knew I was hiding behind my public facade?"

"You've always been the smartest of the three of us," Phillip said without any noticeable bitterness. "You avoided the traps Mother set for you, while I walked right in. Tell me"—he fixed her with an intent, serious gaze—"do you *want* it? Is running Lindmark something you would want to do for its own sake?"

And to Callista's surprise, she had to stop and consider it for a moment. She loved Lindmark, but she'd always believed she would be happier if the corporation were safe and she could just walk away. If she could only make a life for herself based on nothing but her own skills and abilities. But now that she was confronted with that question somewhere other than the privacy of her own head, it suddenly became complicated.

Could she really set aside this goal and these ambitions she'd been working towards for so long?

What would she choose if she felt like a choice were possible?

"I've spent years with the knowledge that if anyone was going to save the people of Lindmark, it would have to be me," she acknowledged, and Phillip winced visibly at her words. "I started laying the groundwork while I was still in my teens. I have the ability and the resources to make it work—to make Lindmark better and stronger than it has ever been. To make our people safer than they've ever dreamed of being. But do I need to be in charge?"

She shook her head, relieved by the realization that her answer hadn't changed. "No. Not unless that's still the best option for Lindmark. I want Grandfather out, I want Lindmark to be what it was meant to be, and I want our people to be safe. But I'll do whatever is necessary, play whatever part is needed, to make them that way."

Phillip nodded. "And what about you, Avalar?"

Callista risked a glance at Killian, where he lounged in his chair, looking every inch the care-for-nothing rogue.

"You know what I want, Phillip Linden. My people and I want to go home, and we'll do what we have to to get there."

Sometimes, she had to work to remind herself that he wasn't human. That this wasn't his home, and he would eventually leave. Assuming they all survived.

The thought left her feeling strangely empty, but she couldn't allow it to distract her now.

"Phillip"—she leaned forward and put her elbows on the conference table—"you've asked us what we want, but what about you? We saw your transmission. But like me, you probably thought you would be alone in your efforts. What do you truly want, besides humanity's survival?"

"You're assuming I want *that*," he said dryly, with an enigmatic glance at Seph. "Truthfully, I no longer know exactly what to hope for. As you said, I expected to find myself alone in this endeavor." He nodded to Killian. "Not to mention, it seems I owe you both a measure of thanks. From what I've seen since we arrived, it seems you've done a remarkable job of rehabilitating my image."

"I suspect you can thank Grandfather for part of that," Callista reminded him. "His attack on me has done him no favors, especially not with so much damning intel currently in circulation. After what he did to you, it will look like an attempt to cut our generation out of the succession and maintain power."

Phillip cocked his head. "Do you suppose Carolus…"

"No." She wished their oldest brother could have been an ally. "I'm afraid Carolus is exactly as he appears. I've tried connecting with him, hoping that he was hiding much the same as I've always done, but there's too much evidence to the contrary." Her lips curved sadly. "And believe me, I know what to look for. The truth is, he and Father both prefer not to acknowledge anything that might interfere with their comfort."

"Then what do you recommend as our next step?" Phillip looked as if he genuinely wanted her opinion—as if what she thought really mattered to him—so Callista took a moment before answering.

Ever since Killian revealed the truth of the alien threat, a part of her had continued to cling to her plans to take Lindmark for herself. She'd justified it with the undeniable truth that it would allow them to face the Bhandecki from a position of strength. And by reminding herself that she was still the only one with both the right and the ability to do the job—and do it well.

But what if that was no longer the case? What if it was not even the best way to ensure victory?

It might mean scrapping all of her carefully laid plans. Throwing aside everything she'd fought for over the past ten years. It would mean explaining to her teams that they may not ever see the fruition of all their work. The positions she'd planned for them to take might never materialize.

But if it was the right thing to do?

She looked her brother dead in the eye. "Tell me this first. I've seen the evidence, Phillip. I know that Mother and Grandfather were responsible for everything they blamed on you. I'm well aware that Daragh wasn't your fault. But I need you to tell me how much you knew."

She couldn't give up her ambitions if it meant handing the corporation over to someone else just like Eustacius. "I get that you didn't give the orders. But if you knew everything and still chose to do nothing, that's not really much better."

Her brother didn't appear angry or embarrassed by her question. He just nodded. "That's fair. And I wish I could give you a better answer. The truth is, I didn't know everything that was happening." He leaned back in his chair and closed his eyes for a moment before continuing. "But I don't think I wanted to know. I convinced myself that whatever they'd done was necessary. That those who lead must make hard decisions that won't be popular with everyone. But I never let myself wonder whether those decisions were *right*. And for that, perhaps I am as culpable as anyone else."

It wasn't a perfect answer, but it was better than she'd dared hope for. And he might still be lying, but once again, Callista knew it was time to trust her instincts.

She believed she could trust Phillip. And so help her, she also believed she could trust Killian to have her back when it counted. But would they be willing to trust *her* once they knew what she had in mind?

"Then I believe our next move must be a decisive one," she said firmly. "We don't have time to do this the polite way. We need to step up, remove Mother and Grandfather, and take over from the top down."

Phillip's eyebrows shot up. "Won't the Conclave object?"

She shook her head. "I don't think they will. All of them know Grandfather attacked my home in Haven Two. They know he's unstable and feeling threatened, and while Hastings and Korcheck are still holding out for a possible alliance, I think they'll work with us. Sarat and Olaje will back anyone who's willing to take Grandfather to task for his crimes.

"What's more," she continued, "I have good relationships with almost everyone in the younger generation. They might not think I can run a corporation, but they don't dislike me."

"Except Maxim?" Killian murmured from his side of the table.

She grinned and shrugged. "Except Maxim. But he's only a second son, and his father doesn't take him seriously."

"And what about the current family heads?" Phillip asked.

"They don't know me," Callista admitted, "but they are all at least familiar with you. Your press is good at the moment, thanks to Killian's public appearances, and combined with the uncertainty caused by the transmissions from Vadim and Galloway, I believe we can build on that momentum. Give the people someone who has already faced this danger and survived. Someone who wants to see change rather than someone who continues to indulge in internal politics while we're facing an external threat."

Phillip nodded slowly. "You're suggesting a literal coup. But do we have the numbers for that? LSF won't be sitting on their hands."

"No, we don't have the numbers for a straight frontal assault." And she wouldn't vote for that approach even if they did. The casualties would be unthinkable. "But neither will anyone expect us to go about this the old-fashioned way, because no one even realizes we're a threat. Grandfather might know, but he won't have told anyone. It would be too embarrassing to admit that he underestimated me, and anyway, who would believe him?"

Phillip's eyes began to gleam with amusement. "So you're planning to waltz into the tower, point a stunner at his head, and demand that he step down?"

She laughed. "As fun as that would be, I do have a slightly more sophisticated plan in mind. If everyone is on board, of course."

She took a deep breath, looked over at Killian, and flashed him a wry grin. "How do you feel about going to dinner at Lindmark Tower after all?"

FOURTEEN

IT TOOK two precious days to set up what was needed and make contact with Callista's agents inside Lindmark's upper echelons. Two days of meetings and plans that Killian was largely not a part of, despite the fact that his ship seemed to have become their default headquarters. Those two days seemed impossibly long, and gave him ample time in which to wonder what was happening to him.

Something had changed when he attacked Phillip on the bridge of the *Fancy*. Not just in his own heart, but between him and the man he'd once considered a friend. After that moment, Phillip had never again brought up what had occurred on Concord Five and seemed to accept Killian as a committed ally.

Though that was no doubt due in part to Seph's genuine forgiveness. She was either a greater actress than Callista or a saint, and Killian was mostly convinced it was the latter. She and Phillip were clearly devoted to one another, so if she'd decided to believe Killian's story, perhaps Phillip had simply decided to follow her lead.

Even if he didn't believe in Killian's reason for leaving Seph there in the first place.

That reason had been true—he'd hoped she could save Phillip from himself. But it wasn't as if he'd ever wanted credit for any form of altruism. No matter what he did, altruism was never his only motivation. Even now, he'd agreed to help with Callista's plan for no fewer than four reasons.

First, he'd agreed because this was the quickest path to getting what they needed—every member of the Conclave on board with their efforts to repel the Bhandecki.

Second, because Eustacius Linden was no better than the pirate scum now infesting Concord Five. The current head of Lindmark would never act in a way that might diminish his own wealth or power, and so would never agree to the cooperative effort that would be necessary to save Earth.

Third, he'd agreed because the entire plan appealed to him. It was sneaky, outrageous, and unlikely to succeed, and as such, exactly his style of crazy.

And fourth…

He'd agreed to help because Callista asked him to. And that was the part that was currently driving him to re-evaluate his own sanity.

Along with the nature of his humanity.

It wasn't something he'd given much thought to over the years he'd worn human form, but he was forced to think about it now. Forced to confront the uncomfortable feelings of worry, anxiety, happiness, excitement, and even despair that seemed to assail him on a daily basis—all of them dependent on Callista's mood and proximity.

Was he losing his mind?

Phillip didn't seem to think so. *So now you know…*

It continued to trouble him, even as he sat beside Callista on their way to Markheim. So much so that he could sense her shooting him a series of worried sideways glances.

"You've been a ghost of yourself ever since Phillip showed up," she said finally. "Are you still worried about what happened on Concord? Or is something else bothering you?"

A ghost of himself…

No, he'd been a ghost of himself ever since his brother betrayed him. That ghost had merely been wearing Killian Avalar's face. But at some point, Killian had become the reality, and he wasn't sure he still remembered who he used to be.

Not this bitter, angry shell. Carefree laughter had characterized his early years, along with the certainty that he knew what he was meant to do. He'd always had a gift for getting people to like him and follow his lead, and had dared to believe that he would be a fair and decent ruler. He genuinely loved his people, so it was no hardship. His life had seemed a golden road, stretched out before him into an unending future.

But with every day he spent among humans, that future—that self—had seemed farther and farther away.

What if that future was gone for good? What if…

What if it was no longer the only thing he wanted?

It felt like treason even to *think* it.

And Callista was still waiting for his answer.

"Phillip," he said with a shrug, "has apparently let it go. Not that I would have recommended it. But I suspect he would do whatever Seph asks, and sadly, she seems to trust me."

"Sadly?" Callista raised a mocking eyebrow. "Do tell why her inexplicable willingness to believe in you somehow brings you grief."

"A terrible blow to my ego," he replied smoothly. "A man of my reputation can't afford for people to go around *trusting* him."

"Well, then I suppose I ought to apologize for *entrusting* you with a part of our plan this evening," she said dryly. "But I think you're avoiding the issue. Just like you've been avoiding *me*. Is there something you're not telling me?"

So many things he wasn't telling her. So many things he couldn't even put words to. Until Callista, he'd never had a problem finding the words he needed.

"Only that I hope you won't forget yourself and shoot me in the head before the night is over."

"I'm already tempted," she murmured as she merged her skimmer into the approach lanes for Lindmark Tower. "But I have a feeling it wouldn't inconvenience you all that much."

"I can't decide whether I should feel flattered or insulted," he noted, keeping a careful eye out for any hint that Lindmark security had been given orders other than what Eustacius and Satrina had claimed. He wouldn't put it past them to attempt an assassination, in spite of the carrot that had been dangled in front of them tonight.

They might see it as a bigger win to rid themselves of two problems at once.

But contrary to his pessimistic expectations, they arrived unscathed and parked in what was obviously a prime spot in the Tower hangar.

"Surprised they haven't rescinded your privileges yet," Killian noted as they exited the skimmer.

"Phillip wasn't wrong about who built Lindmark." Callista smoothed her dark brown curls and played with her bracelets as they walked. "Grandfather knows security is important, but he's never dealt with the day-to-day demands of keeping his empire secure. He has people for that. And he's probably too embarrassed to tell those people that he lost control of his last potential heir, so he can't have them rescind my security clearance.

"And besides, have you forgotten?" She shot him a wicked glance from under lowered lashes. "We're here by invitation… Phil, darling."

They made their way to the tube, and despite the nature of their errand, Killian did not detect any particular degree of scrutiny from Lindmark staff. There were a fair number of security officers in evidence, but he had no way of knowing whether it was more than usual. Callista didn't seem outwardly concerned, but then, did she ever?

Once they entered the tube, Callista placed her hand in a strange little metal box. A light flashed, and they were off, moving swiftly and without interruption on their way to the top —a landing three floors below the tower's peak.

The moment they stepped off the tube into what appeared to be a secretary's office, two security officers searched them both for weapons, to which indignity Callista submitted only after a great deal of pouting and loud protestation.

The woman behind the desk watched Callista's performance with inscrutable calm. She had smooth, medium brown skin, short white hair, and dark eyes that proclaimed she'd already seen everything and wasn't likely to be impressed by whatever you had to offer.

But when she caught Killian watching her, she dipped her chin for a moment and winked.

Good grief. Was there anyone Callista was incapable of winning over?

Once the security officers finished reassuring themselves that neither of their guests were armed, they were allowed to enter the private tube system that led to the topmost floors of the Tower. There was only one way up, which seemed incredibly shortsighted to Killian.

Even if it was likely to work in his favor tonight.

After the tube came to a stop at the topmost floor and the door slid open, Callista gestured for Killian to precede her as they stepped out onto a gleaming marble floor. With a tiny jerk of her head, she directed him to the right, towards a pair of double doors that opened on an opulent conference room.

Two people stood behind the table, watching them with undisguised animosity.

One was a woman—presumably Callista's mother. She was pale and icy, with blonde hair and a brittle, precise sort of beauty, marred only by the hatred she exuded as she glanced between her "children."

The other, he assumed, was Eustacius.

The man had to be over eighty but appeared much younger. He'd allowed his hair to gray, but kept it ruthlessly tamed in a side-swept style that didn't entirely suit his age. His hands were still strong, and his dark eyes did not waver as they swept across Callista to land on Killian.

Or rather, on the man he assumed was his grandson.

"So." The old man's voice betrayed no emotion. It was cold, flat, and uncompromising. "This was your plan from the beginning. Not to sacrifice yourself to save Lindmark, but to hide in a hole like a rat until you saw an opportunity."

Better a rat than a bloodsucking tick like Eustacius, but Killian just shrugged and tried to maintain Phillip's icy detachment. "Rats are adaptable," he said. "But it took me two years too long to realize that leaving Lindmark in your hands wasn't the way to save it."

"So you and your sister came up with some asinine plot to take it for yourselves?"

Callista laughed musically and strolled forward to sit on the edge of the table. "You *did* teach us everything we know about asinine plots, Grandfather. But I confess, I'm mostly flattered that you think it was our genius plan to have hostile aliens attack right when we needed them the most."

"Yes, genius." Eustacius's sneering response suggested he was not overly familiar with sarcasm. "You are both so staggeringly intelligent that you strolled right into my office and handed yourselves over like the spineless idiots you are."

"Oh, come now, Grandfather." Callista's eyes were dark and mocking. "I thought we were having a friendly family dinner. You did invite us to discuss the future of the corporation. Shouldn't we at least pretend to get along until after the fish course?"

"Family?" Satrina burst in, her shrill voice at odds with her icy exterior. "You were the one who came here and threatened *us*. Don't act as though you are any daughter of mine. You have ignored everything I have ever taught you and betrayed the very name you were born to. The best thing you could have done for this family and this corporation is *die* when you were supposed to."

Killian had thought himself immune to the cruelties one person could inflict on another. He'd seen too many to allow himself to feel them too deeply. Had experienced his own share of betrayals.

But this? Her own mother wishing she were dead? It stabbed so deeply, the pain nearly took his breath away, and it wasn't even aimed at him.

Callista...

Her beautiful face was a blank mask as she returned her mother's regard. Perhaps no one else in that room could see past it, but he could.

Callista Linden still had a heart, and her mother had just broken it.

After the life she'd led, the truths she'd been forced to face, she might have believed herself incapable of being surprised by her family's cruelty.

But he'd seen how she surrounded herself with people who cared for and fought for one another. She'd no doubt learned early what her family was, and had somehow dedicated herself to fighting it with love, protectiveness, and dauntless courage.

Her love for the people of Lindmark and for the people who followed her was what made her stronger than her grandfather. It was what would enable her to win against his cruel, self-interested tactics.

But that same love left a weak spot in her armor. Love would always be a vulnerability. It always left a place for an enemy to strike and wound when you least expected it.

That was why Killian had chosen to shield himself so fiercely after his exile. To never again let himself love what could be so easily taken away.

But the pirates who slaughtered his people had still taken him by surprise. And it hurt, so he'd locked himself away even more deeply, to the point where his remaining crew was no longer certain they could trust him.

He and Callista had chosen different paths, and Killian couldn't help but wonder... Would he come to regret his choice? Or would she?

Callista's dark eyes never wavered as she looked at her mother. The only outward sign of her pain was the rigid set of her shoulders where she perched on the edge of the conference table.

"I wish I could say I'm sorry," she said. "But I won't lie about this. The greatest honor of my life is to know that I've disappointed all your expectations for me."

Satrina's wrist comm buzzed, but she ignored it. "I hope you're satisfied with honor," she hissed, "because it's all you will ever have after today."

The door burst open. Yolande, the secretary, stood in the doorway, rigidly upright but with a slight frown on her stern features. "Sir, you will want to see this," she said, and gestured to the viewscreen on the wall behind the conference table.

Eustacius swore under his breath but activated the screen and took a step back as the room was suddenly filled with the noise and the flashing lights of a news conference.

Drones swarmed, and all sounds suddenly died as a man stepped to the forefront of the crowd.

A blond man who looked an awful lot like Phillip Linden. And who stood on the steps of a terribly familiar building.

"I am here today," he said, "to address the rumors and mysteries surrounding the destruction of Concord Five. The truth is being hidden by the Conclave in pursuit of economic advantages, but after I've shared my personal experiences, I will answer whatever questions you may have regarding what I know, what I don't know, and the plans I have to counter the threat we are all about to face."

Eustacius roared in outrage, picked up a chair, and threw it at the screen, but Phillip's face still filled the view.

"When did this take place?" he snarled.

Callista pointed at the flashing red letters in the upper right-hand corner of the screen. "It's live, Grandfather," she said

187

politely. "If you only look out the window, I'm sure you'll be able to see the crowd forming below us."

"Then it can damn well stop now!" He slapped the top of the table with an open hand, and a hidden screen appeared beneath his palm. A green light flashed as it read his palm print and connected.

"Connect me directly to Commander Jennings," he growled. "And open a line to request a Convocation with the other Conclave heads. This is an emergency."

He looked up at Killian as if suddenly realizing that he had more than one problem on his hands.

"I don't know if you're the real Phillip or the imposter, but both of you can die today."

Killian's only response was to shift his gaze to Callista.

She nodded.

He lifted an empty hand and shot Eustacius Linden in the chest.

———

HER GRANDFATHER WENT DOWN, and Callista told herself it was normal that she felt nothing but the rush of adrenaline.

Nothing but determination, as Killian shifted his aim and stunned Satrina less than half a second later. Neither had time to cry out. They could only lie on the floor and watch as their world fell apart around them.

"Are you ready?" she asked Killian, her voice tight and strained, even to her own ears.

He nodded, but instead of stepping around the table, he took two steps closer and grasped her shoulders gently. "Are you all right?"

Callista sucked in a quick, startled breath, and her eyes jerked to his. "What do you mean? I'm fine."

"You don't have to lie."

No, she was not all right. This was the moment she'd spent more than ten years planning for, but she felt no thrill of victory —only the cold emptiness of wondering how it had come to this. Wondering whether she was as monstrous as her mother and grandfather.

She'd truly felt nothing when they fell. No sadness, no remorse, not even exultation. Only purpose. Shouldn't the blood ties of family mean something more than this?

And how had Killian seen the truth she'd been so careful to conceal even from herself?

"I will probably never be all right." The truth burst out of her despite her determination to carry on. "This family is twisted and broken, and I never really escaped, even though I thought I did." The words cut her on their way out, but she couldn't hide now that she'd seen what was in her own heart. "I've lived my life believing I was acting in spite of them, when in reality, that life was always leading up to this moment. When I would become exactly the monster they always hoped I would be."

"You are *not* a monster," Killian said fiercely. "I've seen how you fight for what you love. I've seen you take the harder path for the sake of what you believe in. So don't listen to their voices in your head. Don't believe what they say about you, because all they know how to do is lie."

She nodded, not trusting her voice. He sounded so sincere. And even knowing him as she did... she believed him. She had to. They had a world to save, and she could not afford to lose her focus in the middle of it.

"You should change," she said, and almost without thought,

reached up and squeezed his hand where it rested on her shoulder. "Don't worry. I won't throw up or make you catch me when I faint."

His smile caught her completely off guard. It wasn't mocking or sarcastic, or even flirtatious. It was warm, genuine, and a little rueful.

"Good, because I was hoping you'd be there to catch *me*. Just in case."

And then he shifted. Faster this time than the last—a swift transition through his natural form to a taller, human one.

When he finished, Callista almost took a step back. "I don't like it," she told him frankly. "So let's finish this so you can get back to normal as quickly as possible."

He nodded and stepped around to the other side of the conference table, where the hidden viewscreen was just connecting to Commander Jennings, the highest-ranking officer in the Lindmark Security Forces.

"Sir," the commander said briskly. "What are your orders? We've surrounded the crowd on the front steps, and we're awaiting your command."

"You are commanded to stand down," Killian growled back in a passable imitation of her grandfather's raspy voice. "The news conference is moving forward on my orders. You will also alter the security protocols for the Tower immediately, to allow entrance and highest security privileges to my grandson, Phillip. He will be resuming oversight of all on- and off-planet operations as soon as possible, and his access must not be hindered in any way."

Commander Jennings was as stone-faced as they came, but Callista almost laughed behind her hand as he floundered in the face of his orders.

"I… Yes, sir, I understand," he stammered. "But, sir…"

"Now!"

Jennings disappeared, and Killian glanced up at Callista.

"Before I do this," he said, "are you sure this is what you want?"

She'd thought almost too long about the implications of what they were about to do, and in the end, there had been only one possible conclusion. "I'm sure," she said. "We don't have time for me to convince the other Conclave members to trust me. I intended to take over Lindmark from within and prove myself over time, but right now, all they understand is the Callista they see at social functions. The reckless driver and the relentless partier. They know Phillip, and they'll listen to him, even if they don't like him."

It hurt far more than she'd anticipated, having to say it aloud. But while it was undeniably painful, she also knew it was right. No matter how hard it was to relinquish her ambitions, it mattered more that they bring the Conclave together. And whether it made sense or not, she trusted Phillip not to misuse her people.

So she stood back and listened as Killian, wearing Eustacius's face, engaged in a brief emergency conference with the heads of Hastings, Korcheck, Sarat, and Olaje.

It was almost overwhelming to realize that their "asinine plot" had actually worked. They'd needed to gain control of the LSF and manage the perceptions of the rest of the Conclave at the same time if they were to succeed, and they'd done it—thanks to her grandfather's predictable response to any perceived threat. Due to the executive comm connection hardwired into this room —and his palm print identity verification—none of these transactions would ever be questioned.

And from the expression on his face where he still lay stunned on the floor, Eustacius knew it.

With a grave dignity that looked entirely wrong on her grandfather's face, Killian explained his change of heart to the other Conclave leaders. He informed them that Phillip would be taking on the public duties of leading Lindmark from that time forward, and—most important of all—he laid the groundwork for the partnership that would be needed if they were to counter the Bhandecki threat.

Timed as it was to coincide with Phillip's news conference on the steps of Lindmark Tower, the other corporations would have no reason to disbelieve his word.

Callista doubted the other Conclave members would abandon their efforts to gain an advantage by studying the fireworm that had crashed into Concord Five. That would be asking too much of the cutthroat world of corporate politics. But by the time their ships returned to Earth and they were able to mobilize science teams in response, they would no doubt have bigger things to worry about. The truth of Phillip's claims was rapidly becoming clearer, and eventually, all of Earth would have no choice but to believe him.

She only hoped their belief wouldn't come too late.

When the call was over and the connection terminated, Killian met her gaze across the table.

"It's done," he said softly.

"Not yet," she reminded him. "As soon as the press conference is over, you have to change back, and then we have some acting to do." Thankfully it was Killian in here with her and not the real Phillip. Her brother was crap at acting.

"Acting?" Killian raised an eyebrow. "I thought Yolande was in your pocket?"

"Of course she is." Callista had been Yolande's favorite since she was five. Not that Eustacius had ever realized it. "How else do you think I got a sample of Grandfather's DNA? She's got our back, but there are security feeds everywhere but here and the executive office. We still have to convince everyone of our version of what happened in here and get out before anyone realizes there were two Phillips at the Tower today."

And then? The real work would begin.

FIFTEEN

IN THE DAYS after the surprisingly simple coup, Phillip Linden was all the world wanted to talk about—his unexpected return, his terrifying warnings, his past history, and his present ambitions. The public was particularly charmed by the news of his surprising romance with former Lindmark Security officer Persephone Katsaros. If the celebrity gossip feeds were any indication, many even seemed to see it as proof that he had changed.

A fair number of news outlets also publicized the shocking evidence of Eustacius Linden's sudden mental health crisis. After taking the unprecedented step of removing himself from the leadership of Lindmark and handing power over to his grandson, he'd reversed course, denied the action, and made multiple wild claims about a shapeshifting assassin who appeared in his office, shot him, and then stole his corporation.

The gossip tabloids were delighted to have a story they didn't need to lie about to make sensational. They even published feature articles about the former chief executive's retirement to an exclusive private retreat, from which he was never expected to emerge.

Satrina Linden had yet to speak publicly about her father's decline, but she, too, stepped down from her position within hours after his first announcement. Her few friends said she was grieving her loss, and confided in reporters that she might never be able to resume her public life.

Killian half expected that Callista would disappear as thoroughly as her grandfather, buried under the tidal wave of responsibilities that came with the change in power. But despite the burdens of restructuring an entire corporation, she continued to reappear at the *Fancy* each night. She even seemed to have adopted one of his passenger cabins as a temporary home.

Which probably explained why he walked into the mess one night, unable to sleep, and found her at a table. Her jacket lay across the bench, her head was pillowed on her arm, and she had no fewer than three handhelds scattered around her. There were two comms by her elbow, a plate full of crumbs beside her face, and a stack of ancient paper with barely readable printing under her arm.

Fortunately, Killian had been around humans long enough to know what the situation required, and only shook her awake after he'd brewed a cup of dark, fragrant coffee. Disgusting stuff, but every human he knew seemed to live on it.

Callista picked up her head, blinked at him with red, bleary eyes, and then snatched the offered coffee with a groan.

"What time is it?"

"Either too late or too early, depending on how you look at it," he responded, telling himself he wasn't worried at all by how exhausted she looked.

"Sorry," she muttered, taking a gulp of the coffee. "After I finished going over everything, I was too tired to get up and go to bed."

Once, Killian would have taken advantage of this situation to make some kind of joke and flirt outrageously. And maybe he would again, but some instinct told him that was not what Callista needed.

"Have they not made much progress on your apartment?" He tried to ask casually, but she still shot him a look of embarrassed chagrin.

"I never meant to take such shameless advantage of your hospitality," she assured him, sitting upright while beginning to straighten her papers and gather her devices. "It was just that..."

Killian reached out and grabbed her hand before he thought better of it. "I'm not complaining," he said firmly. "But the *Fancy* doesn't exactly live up to her name. It can't be convenient or comfortable to stay here when you're coordinating with teams in Markheim."

She shrugged but didn't look at him. "My apartment won't be ready for a few days yet. My team is transitioning out of the safe house and back to their own living spaces while they get settled in their new positions, and I couldn't stomach the idea of living in Lindmark Tower."

He probably should have let go of her hand, but she wasn't pulling away and... he didn't want to. "Isn't there anywhere else that feels like home?"

Callista shook her head. "The apartment was just for show. Part of that life I was living and the facade I was putting on. Now that all that is over..."

She'd been cast adrift in more ways than one, he realized. Robbed of purpose, when it was purpose that drove her. All she needed was a reason, and she could conquer anything, but all of her reasons had changed. Lindmark was safe. Her people were safe. The plan to save Earth had been set in motion, and she probably wasn't certain where she fit anymore.

"You're welcome to stay," he said suddenly. "For as long as you want. With Rill, Patrick, and Harvey gone, it's not like there isn't enough space."

She finally met his eyes and nodded once. "Thank you. But I know it has to be irritating to have me constantly underfoot."

"You *know*?" he echoed, feeling irrationally frustrated by her assumptions. "Shouldn't you ask me before you decide for yourself how irritated I am?"

Her eyes dropped to where his hand rested on hers, and her head tilted as if she were genuinely confused by something. "Then why don't you tell me," she said in a strangely serious voice. "Do I irritate you, Killian Avalar?"

He didn't look away, and his heart... Whatever his heart was doing, it was terribly uncomfortable. And yet, for whatever incomprehensible reason, he didn't want it to stop.

"You did," he admitted, and he could see her surprise at his honesty. "When we first met, I was sure you could not possibly have irritated me more."

She laughed quietly. "I can't even be mad because that was exactly the effect I was going for. And now?"

"Now? You're only slightly irritating." She laughed again, until he continued. "But when I'm not irritated, I still find myself intrigued. Challenged. And occasionally terrified."

Her expression suddenly shifted, and he could swear he'd disappointed her.

"Yes, I do seem to be terrifying a lot of people lately," she said, offering him a twisted smile as she pulled away from his touch.

But Killian wasn't backing down. Maybe he shouldn't be

having such an important conversation in the middle of the night, but he suddenly wanted her to know the truth.

"Yes, but unlike Maxim, I'm not terrified *of* you," he continued, holding her gaze and wondering whether he'd lost his mind. What he was about to say would make him vulnerable, and he hated feeling vulnerable. And yet, he felt as if the words needed to be said. As if he didn't dare miss this moment to tell her something true about himself. "I'm terrified by what you do to me."

She sucked in a quick, startled breath and froze where she sat.

"And," he added, "I would be even more irritated if you stopped."

Her eyes flew wide. Not startled, exactly, but more as if she were seeing him for the first time. "What does that mean?"

He shrugged, because damned if he knew either. "I supposed it means that I..."

An alarm suddenly blared through the ship, loud and strident, interrupting his thoughts and leaving him frozen for a handful of seconds.

Until Dinah's voice came over the internal comms.

"Captain! Bridge, now!" Her typically calm, stoic voice was tense with panic, and Dinah did not panic. Ever.

He knew what this was.

Killian leaped to his feet before grasping Callista's hand again. "Get to your skimmer and wait until you hear from me," he said urgently. "I want you ready to fly in case we need a scout."

For an instant, he was sure she would see straight through him, but she accepted his orders and jogged out of the mess, pulling on her flight jacket as she ran.

The moment she was out of sight, he bolted for the bridge, pulling up Dinah on the comm as he went.

"How far out are they?" he snapped.

"There's just one so far," she reported. "But it popped out of a new rift that puts it only six hours out of attack range."

A new rift. Killian swore viciously as he realized what that likely meant.

An alpha fireworm was only six hours from Earth.

And Earth was nowhere near ready.

"I want the drives hot," he told Dinah. "We're going to have to manage this on our own, so I'll need you to prep the weapons bays while we're waiting to take off."

He switched channels and commed Patrick.

"How close are you to being ready?" he demanded without preamble.

"We still have a few tests to run, but I anticipate we'll have the first batch prepped for deployment in… two days, give or take a few hours."

"Not fast enough," Killian responded tersely. "Any chance you can speed that up?"

Patrick went silent for a moment. "How far out are they?"

"Six hours."

"Not a chance." Patrick sounded grim, no doubt because he knew exactly what was at stake. If he didn't think it was possible, then that was that.

"Understood." Killian cut the connection and commed Callista. She would probably never forgive him for what he was about to do, but there was no way in hell he was dragging her into this with him.

"I'll open the cargo bay," he told her. "Need you to fly the perimeter of the Canyon and look for anything out of the ordinary. Our security got pinged, and I'm thinking it could be someone out there trying to get a closer look at our tech."

"Done," she said, and Killian winced.

Every bit of trust she'd granted him over these past few days, he'd just shredded beyond repair, but he would do it all over again. Now he just had to get her away from the ship before they took off. And before any of Earth's technology got a look at what was coming for them. Should the public realize how close they were to destruction, the resulting panic would completely destroy their preliminary efforts to build a cooperative defense.

A few moments later, he entered the bridge and slid into his chair, powering up his control screen with a few taps. The cargo bay doors opened at his command, and he called up a view of the bay just in time to see Callista's skimmer rise smoothly into the air and float slowly out into the night.

Only once the doors were closed and she'd sped away did he open a comm channel.

"Callista."

"What is it?" He could hear suspicion in her question. She could already tell something wasn't quite right. "Do you need me to come back?"

"No. I need you to keep going. I need you to get to Phillip. Warn your people. Pull together everything you can in case I don't succeed."

"Killian"—her voice was dangerously soft—"what are you talking about?"

"An alpha worm has just entered the system, and it's only six hours from Earth, at your ships' speeds," he told her bluntly. "The shield isn't ready. I added missile bays to the *Fancy* a long time ago, so Dinah and I are going to head out there and find out whether missiles really do work. I'll be counting on you and Phillip to prepare whatever you can scrape together to back me up."

"You lied to me."

"I did."

"I could have helped you."

"Earth needs you." He almost added "more than I do," but that would have been another lie, and he'd lied to her enough.

"It needs you too, Killian Avalar." Callista was audibly furious.

Hang Earth. What he wanted to know was whether *she* needed him, but it was far too soon to ask. "Then go find some more ships and come save me," he said flatly. "But I'm the only one with a shot at stopping this, and you know it as well as I do."

"If that fireworm doesn't kill you..." Her voice broke off.

It sounded as if she were genuinely upset by the prospect, and Killian couldn't help being a little bit happy about it. "I know," he said, with a tiny smile on his lips. "*You* will. And maybe I'm crazy, but... I hope you get a chance to try."

He heard swearing and then silence, followed by a few deep, deliberate breaths.

"I hate you," she said finally. "Don't die."

"Don't worry," he said softly. "I'm not done letting you irritate me yet."

He looked up at Dinah—who was watching him with eyes wide and mouth slightly open—and nodded.

"Take us up there," he said soberly. "Time to find out whether any of us are getting out of this alive."

———

SUDDENLY THERE WERE tears streaming down her face, and Callista had no idea how to fix it. She hadn't cried this hard in years. So many years. And she really had no idea why she was crying now.

The man was an idiot. And he'd lied to her, right after making her *feel* things. She didn't even know exactly what she was feeling, only that... He made her want to find out. Made her want more of whatever it was.

So now here she was wasting time crying when she should have been calling Phillip and making a plan.

Stabbing angrily at the skimmer's internal comm screen, she entered the security code that would send her straight to Phillip's personal device.

The connection buzzed uselessly for a few moments. Most likely, he was asleep. She hoped he was asleep.

But when he finally answered, he sounded fully awake. "What's wrong?"

"Your stupid pirate friend is what's wrong!" she snapped.

"What did he do?" Phillip's voice went low and dangerous, and Callista realized how her words had probably sounded.

"He tricked me into leaving the *Fancy* so he could fly off and face an alpha fireworm. *Alone*."

Phillip fell silent for a few moments. "Where?"

"He said it's only six hours out. He knows the shield isn't ready, so he's going to try missiles. But he and Dinah are the only ones aboard. They can't possibly take on this enemy without backup!"

Her brother swore, quietly, viciously, and with feelings that seemed to echo her own. "How fast can you get here?"

"Maybe an hour if I push it. What do we have that we can send?"

He went silent, probably searching the Lindmark databases. "It's not good news," he said finally. "We've been working on space-capable missiles for years, but haven't spent much time testing them on board ship. It was too hard to hide, and the Conclave never technically signed off on making them legal.

Grandfather didn't want anyone to know how far we'd gotten with them, let alone that they were already available on the black market. There's one more file here I haven't been able to access yet..." His voice trailed off.

Callista tried not to think about anything except flying faster. Her prototype was already past what anyone else would consider safe speeds, but if she could find just a little more...

"Holy mother of..." Phillip sounded halfway between fury and awe. "I may have something. Can you meet me outside Markheim? There's an abandoned manufacturing complex about ninety miles northwest of here. I'll comm you a more precise location when you get closer."

———

IT TOOK TOO LONG. Everything took too long, but eventually, Callista touched down between a pair of towering smokestacks in the shadows of factories long since left empty. Phillip emerged from the darkness shortly thereafter, with Seph close behind.

"No guards?" Callista queried. "You're both a bit too valuable to be running around in the dark without anyone to watch your backs."

"I don't trust any of the LSF not to shoot me yet," Phillip countered, and it wasn't as if Callista could blame him for that.

Seph lifted a hand to reveal that she was carrying a compact, high-powered laser pistol. "We're both armed if it makes you feel any better." She held the weapon as if she knew how to use it, and Callista recalled that Seph had trained with the LSF before leaving Earth for Daragh.

"That is," Seph added with a touch of wry amusement, "if you trust me not to shoot *you*."

"I trust you more than I trust my brother," Callista returned, sharing a quick grin with the other woman. She still couldn't believe Phillip had possessed enough good sense to fall in love with someone like Seph—capable, level-headed, funny, and entirely unpretentious.

"If the two of you are finished, I'm going to find out if these codes are still good," Phillip muttered, glaring a little at both of them before leading the way towards one of the apparently empty buildings.

At an unmarked side door, he pulled the cover off the entry keypad, which lit green the moment he touched it.

"Still has power," Callista noted. "Must be something here."

Phillip punched in a code, and the door opened soundlessly to reveal the blank but gleaming steel walls of a lift. Once they were all on board, the door closed, and the lift moved down. It was impossible to judge their speed, but Callista thought they were at least ten floors below ground when the lift stopped, and another door opened, on the opposite side from where they'd entered.

Lights flicked on as they exited the lift, revealing a long hallway with offices on either side.

"It's going to take years to unravel all of Grandfather's plots and side projects," Phillip muttered. "I thought I knew how deep he'd gone, but this has been here for years, and I never knew about it."

"What is it?" Callista couldn't imagine how this underground complex was going to help them defeat the Bhandecki.

"This," Phillip said, pushing open the double doors at the far end of the hallway, "was the start of Lindmark's plans to take more territory by force."

The doors opened on a vast room, high and wide—a room filled with sleek metal shapes unlike any Callista had ever seen.

Some were in various stages of assembly, but most appeared more complete. They looked like skimmers but much larger, with... were those miniature *fusion* drives?

"Yes," Phillip said, "it's exactly what it looks like. You're looking at the beginning stages of the Lindmark War Fleet. Fully space-capable and heavily armed with not-yet-legal technology, from disruptor cannons to missiles."

Callista felt the blood drain from her face. "If the rest of the Conclave ever learns about this..."

"They won't believe we truly want to build an alliance," Phillip said softly. "They'll know Grandfather was preparing for war behind their backs, using technology none of them knew about or had ever been asked to approve. That's why it's just the three of us tonight. I needed to know what we would find. And I needed to decide whether to wait and see if Killian is successful, or send one of these up now and risk destroying all our efforts."

Callista experienced a brief moment of pure rage before she recalled who she was talking to.

Phillip. Her brother had changed a lot, but not *that* much. And he would always consider the bigger picture before he made any decisions. He'd spent so long believing he didn't have a heart, it would not be the first thing he consulted when making a decision of this magnitude. He would have assessed the situation and weighed Killian and Dinah's lives against the probability of their future success.

It made her furious, even while she understood it.

"Send me," Callista said.

Phillip raised an eyebrow and waited for her to explain.

"If any of these are fueled and flight-ready, I'll take it. No one else needs to know what we found here."

"You really think the other corporations won't notice a new type of space-capable ship jumping out of atmosphere?"

"The mercenaries that attacked my apartment had space-capable ships," Callista argued. "There's no reason for anyone to suspect this is related to Lindmark. And if by chance they do find out, you can blame it on me. Tell them this whole facility is mine —as a part of my plan to take Lindmark for myself. Hell, tell them the reason Grandfather tried to kill me in Haven Two is that he found out about it."

"No." Phillip's voice had turned to ice. "I won't be a part of throwing you to the wolves, Callista. Not even for this."

She'd trod on a nerve, apparently. Perhaps taking the blame for Eustacius's crimes had been harder on him than he'd yet admitted.

"It's not a bad plan," Seph broke in, her gaze warm and compassionate, as if she, too, had realized what was behind Phillip's protest. "And this is not the same as what they did to you. She has a choice, and it's not up to us to take it away from her."

Even in the dim light of the underground hangar, Callista could see emotions flickering across her brother's face as he locked eyes with the woman he loved. Somehow, they were speaking to one another without any need for words, and Callista suddenly felt as if she were intruding on something intimate and precious.

Even in the relatively short time they'd been together, Phillip and Seph seemed to have come to know one another deeply and fully. Seph had seen Phillip's scars and was probably the only one he would ever allow close enough to touch them—the only one who could reach the deeply damaged heart he tried so hard to hide.

That kind of closeness… Callista had only ever dared to dream of finding it for herself. She had people she trusted with her safety and who trusted her in return. People she cared about, and people she would sacrifice her life for. But no one she dared entrust with her whole heart.

She should certainly not entrust it to the one man who actually seemed to understand her—who respected her choices and made her *feel* things, drat him.

Why on Earth did the one man who had ever been able to keep up with her have to be a lying, secretive, impossible alien rogue?

Phillip finally groaned and ran one hand through his hair in exasperation. "I'm not going to win this, am I?" he muttered, turning to Callista. "Look, I know perfectly well you were never the helpless, wide-eyed socialite you pretended to be, but can you fly?"

She stared at him for a moment. Had he really never known?

"How familiar are you with the underground racing circuit?"

Phillip snorted. "Not that it was ever very far underground. Back before I left Earth, everyone knew the big names."

"Ever heard of Diamondback?" she asked.

He nodded. "Who hasn't? Diamondback is the most freakishly talented pilot to ever fly the circuit. Couldn't get very many races there at the end, because no one else could measure up, and they knew it."

Callista let the corner of her mouth curl up in a smirk. Then she unzipped her flight jacket, took it off, and threw it at her brother's face. He'd seen her wear it, but somehow he'd never seen her back. Or maybe he'd just never made the connection because it seemed so impossible.

"Take a good look," she said. "And then tell me if you still want to quibble about my piloting skills."

He looked at the jacket in his hands with a puzzled frown. Turned it over. Saw the diamond pattern on the back and jerked his eyes to hers with a stunned expression.

Her lips twisted apologetically. "When you said you knew I wasn't who I pretended to be all those years, I guess I assumed you knew about this too."

"I wish I had," he said, a touch of bitterness in his voice. "I wish I hadn't been so blind. So busy trying to meet their expectations that I became this…"

He didn't say it, but she heard it anyway.

"We aren't monsters, Phillip."

Killian's voice echoed in her head, telling her the same thing. And suddenly… she believed it. Not just because he'd said it, not just because she needed to, but because it was *true*.

She and Phillip were nothing like the rest of their family. They both fought for what they loved. They took the harder path because it was the right one. And they were doing their damnedest to fix the mess their mother and grandfather had left behind.

"We aren't what they tried to make of us," she said fiercely. "And this is our chance to prove it. Let me do this. Let me do the one thing I'm best at, while you do what you're best at."

The ghost of some distant agony haunted his eyes as he stared back at her. "And what am I best at, besides being a Linden? Besides hurting people and breaking things out of arrogance and hubris?"

"You're a leader," Seph broke in, echoing Callista's own thoughts. "Both of you are. Not simply because you have a position someone gave you, but because you see where we need to go, and you find a way to get there. You take responsibility for those around you and bear the weight of decisions that affect us all. And you never ask for anything in return. If that's what it means to be a Linden..."

"We should all be proud to bear that name," Callista finished the thought quietly. "Let's not allow those who came before us to define the Linden legacy. Let's make it what it ought to have been all along."

Phillip stood unmoving, pain warring with hope on his face.

"Promise me," he said finally. "Promise me you won't die out there."

Callista nodded. "I promise I'll do everything I can to come back in one piece. And bring the *Fancy* with me."

Phillip grunted. "Good. Because I have words for that pirate."

Seph propped her hands on her hips and subjected him to an exasperated glare. "When are you two going to admit that you care about each other?"

"We don't," Phillip growled. "I fully intend to kill him."

"Get in line," Callista grumbled. "Because I get to be first. *After* I save him. Now. Which of these birds is flight-ready? And if they aren't, why isn't anyone down here working on them?"

"From what I could discover, Grandfather was worried you'd track his people and find this facility, so he pulled everyone off once he realized you were serious about taking over. He was planning to resume work after he dealt with you."

"Aw, I think I'm a little flattered," she murmured.

"But most of them have at least been tested, and a few have space-capable missile launchers ready to go."

"There." Once she knew what to look for, it was clear which of the small ships were already carrying a payload. Jogging over to the nearest docking station, Callista booted up the diagnostics and ran down the list.

"This one looks good. It's had a hundred and fifty hours of flight testing, and it's all fueled up." She held out a hand, and Phillip tossed back her jacket. "Any last-minute warnings? Sage brotherly advice?"

"Just stay alive," Phillip said, meeting her eyes with more sincerity than she'd ever seen from him. "I'm beginning to think you and I have a lot to catch up on."

Sudden tears burned her eyes as it finally hit her.

She had a brother—a brother who cared about her and had her back.

No matter what happened after this, they were family, and they would continue to fight, not just for their family legacy but for each other.

"We do," she said softly. "And I will."

Phillip nodded once before turning and making his way to the nearest control terminal. He input his security codes while Callista opened the hatch, entered the tiny ship, and sealed it behind her.

It was really not much more than a cockpit and a weapons bay, arranged around a tiny fusion drive and atmospheric thrusters. Easy enough, she decided, as she strapped herself into the pilot's spot and punched up the computers. Everything came online swiftly, and Callista found her way into the system with relative ease.

She opened a comm connection. "Ready when you are," she said.

"Bay doors are coming online," Phillip returned. "The tunnel is to your right."

Flashing yellow lights indicated the exit, and as Callista eased power to the thrusters, the lights turned green.

"You have energy weapons, but they won't help," Phillip reminded her as she headed for the tunnel. "These birds are meant for speed and maneuverability, so their payload is only two missiles. You'll need to make your shots count, assuming they're effective."

"Understood."

As she floated through the bay doors and into the exit tunnel, the reality of the moment finally hit home. She was headed for space. Headed into a fight with an alien creature no human had ever encountered before.

No previous battle she'd fought could prepare her for this. No race could compare to this race for her life and for every other life on Earth.

This was for real, and she couldn't afford to lose.

The familiar buzz of adrenaline rushed down her limbs as the tunnel took a sharp curve and headed for the surface. When she saw the end of the tunnel ahead, Callista began to accelerate.

In some ways, she'd been preparing for this her entire life. Now was the moment when she would finally find out whether it was enough... whether *she* was enough.

Or whether their efforts to save Earth were doomed before they'd even truly begun.

SIXTEEN

AS THE *FANCY* accelerated past Earth's atmosphere on a trajectory to intercept the incoming threat, Killian couldn't help but question his sanity.

He was only trying to save Earth in the first place so that he and his people could go home.

So what sense did it make for him to be throwing himself in the path of this fireworm, risking both his life and the only ship that could take all five of them back through the Rift together?

No sense at all.

He glanced over at Dinah, whom he'd dragged into this without a second thought because that's what he'd always done. Why hadn't she questioned his decision? Protested his intention to gamble with both their lives?

"For what it's worth, I'm sorry for this," he said.

"Sorry?" She regarded him quizzically from her seat at the pilot's station. "Captain, I'm not aware of anything that requires your apology. You made a decision to engage, and I followed."

"I'm risking our ability to return home, right when it seems we might actually have a chance."

She let out an aggravated sigh and propped her hands on the edge of her console. "Captain, perhaps it is past time we made you aware of this, but when we followed you into exile, we all accepted that it was likely the last time we would ever see our home."

"Yes, we all knew that was possible," he argued. "But that didn't mean we gave up hope."

She shrugged. "Perhaps you didn't. But the rest of us have always known we were sent to do the impossible. Why not choose to forget and make a new life here?"

Killian stared at her, stunned by her implication.

"Then why follow me into this madness? Why let me risk all your lives for a dream you never believed in?"

"Because *you* believed in it. Because it was better than no dream at all. It is your own hope that's driven you, and all of us, as far as we've come."

He could have wept. Was this genuinely how they all felt? Had none of them ever believed him capable of ending their exile? "Why didn't you tell me?"

"Because even when you wouldn't admit you still had hope, we knew it was the only thing keeping you alive," Dinah said bluntly. "And as you fell deeper and deeper into despair, we watched you become a shadow of yourself. Mocking the things you once stood for and drifting through life like one who was already dead. If we told you we'd given up on the dream of going home, what might you have become then?"

He didn't know the answer to that, but Patrick's words returned to his mind like an echo. He *was* more dangerous and more willing to cross lines than he ever had been before. And for what? What was it he was really chasing? He told himself he wanted justice, but it had been years since he believed such a thing was possible. Was it restoration? Revenge? Or had it simply been too painful to consider giving up on the future he'd always thought would be his?

"You all should have left me," he said, and his words echoed across the nearly empty bridge. "Years ago. Why didn't you?"

"Because our loyalty never depended on your perfection," Dinah said tartly. "You earned it by always trying to do the right thing for those you were responsible for. Did you expect us to run and leave you alone when you were broken and betrayed?"

"If you had, more of you might still be alive," he muttered.

"And if we had, we would not now be in a position to save these humans from a threat they don't understand. Stop trying to tell yourself you don't care! You do, or you wouldn't be the man we've believed in all these years."

"You don't even like humans," he reminded her.

"Perhaps not," Dinah admitted. "But you do. And you care what happens to them, even if you don't want to admit it. That's what makes you a captain worthy of our loyalty."

He wanted to laugh. He wanted to cry. He could feel pieces of the wall he'd hidden behind breaking off and falling away to reveal his pain and uncertainty, and he wanted it to stop.

Dinah was wrong in some ways. Perhaps he'd never completely given up hope of returning home, but he'd been relatively happy as a care-for-nothing pirate captain. Happy to hide behind the impossibility of his task and go on his way, pretending nothing really mattered. Building walls around his shattered dreams and pretending they no longer existed.

But his task wasn't impossible anymore. And humanity's survival mattered more than he'd ever dared admit to himself.

So here he was, on a possibly doomed mission, ready to face

down an enemy he wasn't sure he could defeat, for a planet full of humans who might never even know he'd tried.

And it felt right. As few things had felt right since the day their exile had been enacted.

"Then you're with me?"

Dinah nodded. "We're with you. We've all been drifting. In need of a purpose. If defending this planet can restore that purpose, then that's reason enough."

It was enough. Enough for Dinah. Maybe enough for Rill, Patrick, and Harvey.

And while that was an immense relief, it wasn't enough for *him*.

He'd finally realized he had bigger dreams.

"Bring the missile launchers online," he said abruptly. "And let's see how many shots we'll have. Pilot or gunner?"

Dinah huffed as if in offense. "How many years has it been since you attempted any kind of evasive maneuver?"

He grinned at her. "I evade serious questions every day. But in a ship? It's been a while."

"Then you handle targeting. If I might dare to suggest, your history proves you possess greater talent in that area."

Killian abandoned the captain's chair for the weapons station and felt his blood begin to pound with the certain knowledge that battle was coming. A battle he wasn't sure he could win.

"We're dealing with an alpha," Dinah reminded him, "which means our main target needs to be the control pod." Where the Bhandecki pilots would be directing the worm's actions and trajectory using a magnetic field emitter. "If we can remove their means of direction, we might be able to lure it away from Earth, even if the missiles don't prove effective against its armor.

"And we have to avoid its line of fire. One hit and…"

They might be called "fireworms," but they didn't really breathe fire. Rather, they emitted a chemical compound that could burn through a metal hull in two minutes or less. Even a single hit from the worm's primary weapon could result in a hull breach.

"So you're saying if we can't kill it," Killian mused, "our first objective has to be distracting them from their destination. But the pilots might be too focused on reaching Earth to consider stopping for a single ship."

Dinah shrugged. "Then we'll have to force them to treat us as a threat."

They discussed potential strategies for nearly an hour as their course took them nearer and nearer to intercepting the worm, but in the end, all they had was conjecture. No one had engaged the Bhandecki at close range in living memory—at least, if they had, they hadn't lived to tell about it.

"Activating viewscreen now," Dinah announced. "The worm should be in view shortly."

Killian clutched the armrests of his chair as tension gripped his body. They were about to come face-to-face with his people's fabled enemy. About to confront the bogey that had terrified Wyrdane children for centuries. And...

"There!"

A silver blip appeared on the screen, seemingly tiny and insignificant—until Dinah magnified it, and the creature filled the forward viewscreen.

It was not exactly as he'd imagined it.

In his nightmares, the alpha worms were long, smooth cylinders with rippling frills, crowned by the gleaming silver of the spaceship parts the Bhandecki integrated into their bodies—each piece made of a metal that deflected energy weapons as easily as the worm's hide seemed to do. Like cyborgs, they were seamless, malevolent, and terrifying.

The reality filled him with a different kind of horror.

The creature before him was scarred and broken, with wounds both old and new. Perhaps Killian had never really considered how the Bhandecki might go about fusing ship parts to a living body, but it had clearly been done without care for what would become of the fireworm.

Like the surface of an asteroid, its dull gray skin was scarred and pitted, covered in ramshackle metal structures like it had been afflicted by some bizarre industrial disease. The worm's flesh had been carved out in chunks to make room for the unnatural additions—not composed of gleaming metal, but of patched and rusted pieces held together by prayer and cosmic duct tape. Gaping holes loomed where the integration had failed, or perhaps where the pieces had finally fallen apart. It could have been a ghost ship, drifting derelict through space, but for the rippling of its frills that marked its progress.

The frills, at least, were undamaged, or it would have been unable to move. No one understood exactly how, but somehow the frills absorbed energy, propelled the fireworm through space, and aided in navigation.

But how was it even still flying? How could that colossal hulk still be alive beneath the weight of the cruelties inflicted by its Bhandecki masters? And how could Killian be feeling sorrow for a creature that had probably participated in the loss of millions of lives?

"Gods," Dinah breathed. "What have they done? Death might even be a kindness."

"We don't dare change our plans," Killian said, as much for himself as for Dinah. "If we don't stop them, this worm can still destroy an entire city if they choose to sacrifice it. But maybe…"

The worm's frills rippled faster. Its body curved like a giant fish, and its trajectory shifted… towards the *Fancy*.

"Captain, I believe we've been spotted."

"Good," Killian returned grimly. "We should be more maneuverable than they are, so let's see how far they'll follow us."

If he could lead the creature farther away from Earth, it would only be to his advantage. And to the advantage of everyone he'd left behind, as they prepared for the possibility of his failure.

But it took only minutes to realize that their distraction wasn't going to work. The moment they accelerated away from Earth, the fireworm changed course again and resumed its original heading.

Time to see if missiles really could be the answer.

"Dinah, see if you can get us closer to its flank."

The *Fancy* accelerated towards the fireworm, swerving smoothly aside at the last moment to fly parallel to its body.

"Targeting is online," he announced, keeping a close eye on their range. "I'm going to aim for one of the metal constructs and hope to take out the pilots."

Hope. That was the tricky part, wasn't it? He'd never fired one of the missile launchers before and felt almost reluctant to do so. After all, what if it didn't work? What if this last, theoretical hope proved worthless and left them with no way to destroy the Bhandecki fleet, even if they could get the shield particles ready in time?

And who even knew where in that vast bulk the pilots might be lurking? What if he expended all of his missiles and hit nothing vital?

His finger hovered over the screen as he wavered, until Dinah suddenly jerked the controls and veered away from the worm.

"Captain, look at its side. Just behind the frill."

She shifted the view and zoomed in, where the gray hide of the fireworm had begun to glow green in a row of perfectly circular spots...

"Get us further away," he barked, but it was too late. The glowing spots opened and spat puffs of... something. Something that swarmed and expanded and then suddenly exploded into a rapidly widening cloud.

"What is it?"

"Hells if I know," Dinah snapped. "There's no record of this, but maybe no one ever engaged an alpha this close before."

"Can we capture it? Get a closer look?"

"You sure you want to risk that?" Dinah's eyebrow shot up. "We have no idea what it might do. Could be a poison. Might be nanotech."

"Take us right to the edge of it, and let's see what happens."

She grumbled under her breath, but they swooped back around until the *Fancy* flew right on the trailing edge of the strange, slightly luminescent cloud.

It was definitely particulate. Definitely unnatural.

"Captain, one of the thrusters has just gone offline!"

"Damn." He was no engineer, but Dinah was. "I'll fly while you run down and check it out."

Killian slid into the pilot's chair as Dinah ran for the lift. He cut power to the drive while splitting the screen between flight controls and weapons arrays.

The fireworm continued on its way, even as the *Fancy* fell further behind.

After a few anxious minutes, Dinah commed up from engineering. "Captain, it's not good news. Those particles..." He heard a decidedly frustrated huff. "They're definitely some kind of nanotech, and they work similarly to what we know of the fireworm's primary weapon. They seem to be attracted to metal, and once they attach, they eat right through it like an acid. Out of the six aft thrusters, we've lost two. I think I can repair the shielding on one, but the other is down until I can find replacement parts. We absolutely must stay away from that cloud."

"Understood. We'll have to try targeting the integrated parts from farther out."

His targeting systems had never been tested with projectile weapons, an oversight he now regretted as he pulled up the image of the fireworm on his screen. While the launch tubes were fully integrated into the ship's systems, the energy cannons had always proven sufficient for encounters with overenthusiastic pirates. Besides, he hadn't wanted to waste any of the few missiles he'd been able to acquire.

Fortunately, the integration seemed fairly intuitive. Killian selected the largest of the metal additions visible on the worm's forward section, narrowed the focus, chose a missile bay, and...

Fired.

The missile sped away, arrowing through the distance between him and his target until... it connected. But where? And had it done any damage?

There was no explosion, but Killian hadn't expected one. Realigning the viewscreen, he focused in on the section of the worm he'd targeted... and clearly missed. The metallic hull panels were intact. But there was a gaping hole in the fireworm's side, rapidly venting liquid and debris into the void of space.

"Missile hit and did some damage," he reported to Dinah. "But not enough, and targeting is going to be a problem."

"Damn." He heard Dinah muttering over the comm. "I should have known. The only models we were able to purchase use pretty ancient infrared targeting systems. The fireworm itself is probably emitting more infrared than the segments we need to hit, so we're either going to need to upgrade to a system based on visual imaging, or bypass it entirely."

Obviously, they were past the point of a system upgrade. And if they bypassed the targeting system, they would have to rely solely on the instincts of the pilot and the gunner working in tandem. It would be virtually impossible to target precisely enough to take out the Bhandecki's additions without getting in a lucky hit. And they didn't have enough missiles to just chip away and hope they hit something vital.

Not without a steadier hand at the helm than his. If Rill were here, perhaps she could find a way to fly them in closer without risking a crash.

Rill... or Callista.

But Callista was safe on Earth. And if he wanted her to stay that way, he needed to come up with a solution—and fast.

———

CALLISTA DIDN'T HAVE the first idea how to track the fireworm, let alone identify the rift it had created in order to enter their system undetected.

But she had other methods—like the locator beacon she'd hidden on board the *Fancy*. Killian would be furious when he found out, but she'd needed some reassurance that he couldn't just fly away and disappear.

Now she could only be thankful for her early suspicions. Her tiny craft's computers were limited, but more than up to the task of homing in on the signal, which left her with six hours in which to distract herself from the fear that she wouldn't make it in time.

She was not very successful.

By the time she was close enough to require a course change, she was drenched in sweat and more than ready for something—anything—to relieve the unrelenting tension.

Were Killian and Dinah still alive? Did their missiles have any chance against the fireworm? Or were they about to see firsthand what the destructive capability of these aliens could do when pitted against a completely unprepared foe?

She began messaging the *Fancy* as soon as she thought she was in range, but silence persisted for far too long. The beacon was still transmitting, though, so unless the ship had somehow been reduced to a derelict hulk...

"Unidentified ship, this is a warning. Do not approach these coordinates, or you will be destroyed."

Dinah's voice.

"Dinah, it's Callista. I'm here to help, so I'm definitely approaching your coordinates. What's happening?"

A burst of static made her wince, just before a new voice came over the comm. "Callista, what the *hell* are you doing?"

It was Killian—very much alive, and clearly furious.

"Exactly what you told me to do, you idiot!" she snarled back at him. "You said to find ships and come save you, and that's exactly what I've done. Except it's just me."

"That," he snapped, "was hypothetical!"

There! Ahead on her viewscreen, Callista saw the tiny, familiar form of the *Fancy*. And not far off, a larger, cylindrical shape...

The fireworm.

She zoomed in, mouth agape as her gaze traveled over its

gargantuan bulk. The mutilated surface of its hide bristled with metallic structures, an obscene hybrid of life and technology. Many of the visible wounds were old, but some were clearly new —evidence of the battle in progress.

"Don't get near the worm," Killian warned her urgently. "We're still learning about its capabilities, but it has two separate defense systems. Watch out for expanding particulate clouds, and do not, whatever you do, approach the leading end."

"Understood. It appears the missiles are effective?"

"In part."

She could hear the strain in his voice and felt her own fear swell in response.

"Several of our maneuvering thrusters are down, so we can't get too close," he said grimly. "We've managed to seal off the hull breaches caused by its defenses, but they've made us about as nimble as an asteroid. The only way to stop it is to target the Bhandecki-made structures—to kill the pilots or knock out the guidance systems—but our systems aren't precise enough."

Callista called up her targeting systems and raced through the diagnostics.

They were fairly high-end, thankfully. The ship was equipped with optical imaging tech, which should enable her to home in on any part of the target she chose.

The catch? Her ship was never meant for long-range battles. Rather, it had been intended for near-point-blank engagement, so the missiles' range was severely limited to cut down on weight. She was going to have to get uncomfortably close in order to lock in on her target.

A distraction was what she needed, but if the *Fancy* was already heavily damaged, she couldn't ask Killian to risk himself and his ship any further.

"I have two missiles," she reported, as casually as she could manage, "and a targeting system that should be able to put those missiles right where we need them. Just tell me where to aim, and I'll do the rest."

She was met with silence.

"Killian, I can do this. Just tell me what to look for." She so desperately wanted him to trust her. Needed him to believe she was capable of this. But could he? They'd established a bizarre sort of partnership since he'd crashed into her life, but could he follow her lead in something this monumental?

"Do you even know what you're asking?" he said finally, his voice strangely soft.

"I'm asking you to believe in me," Callista said simply. "And to trust me to have your back."

More silence. It felt like an eternity, but in reality, it was no more than a handful of seconds while he struggled with her request and finally seemed to reach a decision.

"Your target will be centered somewhere near the leading end," he said, sounding almost defeated. "It probably won't be on the surface, but it will have vents of some sort. If you have radar imaging, look for hull-metal structures with space behind them, not just plating."

"Got it." He trusted her. Maybe not completely, but enough, and he probably had no idea how much it meant to her.

But Killian wasn't done. "Callista, I'm begging you…"

It was his voice, but it didn't sound like him at all.

"Get in, get out, don't linger. Your ship is tiny, and you probably don't have the ability to seal off a hull breach, so don't risk getting hit. We can find another way."

Suddenly, the whole universe seemed a little bit brighter.

"You're cute when you admit that you care," she said, grinning at her comm like an idiot. "But don't worry. I'll be careful."

"I don't think you know how," was his response.

"I guess we're about to find out."

As if sensing the presence of a secondary threat, the fireworm adjusted course, body curving and frills rippling faster as it shifted.

Callista locked her sensors on the leading end and headed in for a closer look.

If only there were some sort of pattern or logic to the Bhandecki's additions, her task might be easier. But they seemed incredibly haphazard. Half of the structures seemed to be falling apart. Many appeared to be riveted on or even strapped in place.

Two proved to have hollow cavities behind them, but only one showed a significantly different infrared signature, suggesting it might go deeper than her sensors could penetrate.

That, then, would be her target. Callista locked the optical sensors on the segment she needed to hit, adjusted her speed, and began a spiraling attack pattern that crossed center and reversed direction at random intervals.

The worm changed its heading again until it loomed in her viewscreen, seemingly aiming for a head-on collision.

"Adjust course!" Killian barked in her ear.

"Trust me," she muttered. "I don't want to die any more than you want to go home and tell Phillip I'm dead."

But she needed whoever was piloting it to believe they could predict her actions. So she held steady, increasing her speed incrementally until she was at the top of what her targeting systems could compensate for.

The narrowed end of the fireworm's cylindrical body began to glow red. At the last moment, Callista twitched the controls, jerking her ship out of the way before the worm spewed a glowing mist into the space directly in front of it. The cloud of mist expanded as it went, but Callista was already past and locked in on her target.

Too close. She had only a split second in which to fire, and she took it, triggering the missile before taking an abrupt turn and darting away at a right angle to the fireworm's length.

"That was a crap shot, and you knew it," she muttered to herself. She should have waited, but it was too late. And now, she only had one shot left.

"Surface impact," Killian reported.

"Shot too fast," she admitted. "Going to have to make the next one count."

"You need a shield," he said flatly. "A distraction so you can hold course long enough for a clear shot."

"You've already admitted you're about as maneuverable as a float-barge," Callista reminded him. "You're not sacrificing yourself or your ship for this."

When he answered, she could almost hear his amusement. Could see him sprawled in his captain's chair, a cocky smile on his lips as he volleyed her own words back at her. "Don't you believe in me, love? Trust me to watch your back?"

"It's not *my* back I'm worried about, you idiot. It's yours!"

"You're cute when you admit you care."

That was it. Killian Avalar was going to die. But at her hands and no one else's.

Callista glared at the comm. "I hope you remember the rules, *darling*," she growled.

"Don't die?"

"Because I'm going to kill you," she agreed.

"I'll hold you to that, Callista," he said softly. "So you'd better stay alive long enough to mean it."

Then he shut off his comm, and it was all Callista could do not to scream into the void between them for him to stop, to rethink this, that they would find another way.

But just as she'd begged him for his trust, she had to respect him enough to offer hers in return. To let him choose his own course and judge for himself what he valued enough to risk his life for.

It was the kind of partnership she'd always wanted, but only now could she see the pain it would bring with it—to watch someone you loved step into hell without questioning their motives or their judgment. To simply stand at their back and trust them to know their own heart.

The *Fancy* came about, limping and bleeding, and appeared to be preparing to fire on the worm. But so suddenly it drew a gasp from Callista, one of the aft sections blew wide open. As debris vented into space, the ship slewed and began to drift, tumbling powerlessly towards the path of the fireworm.

Killian Avalar had been ignoring the odds for probably as long as she'd been flying, so she had to trust that he knew what his ship could do.

Even as the out-of-control vessel tumbled closer to an unavoidable collision, she sent more power to her drives and prepared to fire her second missile.

This time, she approached from the side, arrowing straight towards her target at maximum speed, as if aiming to ram the worm.

But even when proximity alarms began to blare in her ears, Callista held back, ducking down under the fireworm's bulk only an instant before they collided. And the moment her ship darted out from beneath the frill, she switched targeting aft.

The *Fancy* continued on her path, powerless to prevent a collision. Unable to maneuver out of the way of the fireworm's primary weapon…

Callista locked onto the hollow area located about where she imagined an eye might be, reversed the launch tube, and fired.

The fireworm's tapered end began to glow red.

"Killian, go!" she screamed, but she had no idea whether he heard her. Whether he even could.

Impact.

The missile shot straight through the shielding and into the vulnerable hollow beneath.

One second. Two. Three. Each one an eternity.

Callista's heart pounded painfully, and she'd just begun to sag in defeat when every visible metal structure down the length of the worm's bulk suddenly crumpled or exploded into a fountain of metal shards.

They'd done it.

A death like that one should have made a sound, Callista thought, but in space, there was none. The fireworm began to thrash silently, as if in agony, its frills flaring wide before falling still.

And yet, the *Fancy* was still too close. There was no way it could escape the worm's death throes…

But Killian's ship suddenly seemed to shudder and slow, and then, as if pulled by an unseen hand, it turned. Moving much like the float-barge Callista had named it, the once-graceful ship awakened from her death dive, rolled, lurched, and yet still she turned, avoiding the flailing fireworm by a margin that would have made even an experienced racer cry for mercy.

They'd really, actually done it. The *Fancy* was clear, and the fireworm was moving farther and farther off course, falling away from their position and drifting off into the endless darkness of space.

She wasn't going to cry. Not yet. It was too soon. They still had to find a way to return Killian's broken ship to Earth.

And hope he survived the trip, so she could kill him for herself.

SEVENTEEN

THERE HAD BEEN time for one brief, blinding moment of exultation.

One quick snarl of victory. One mental toast with his ally.

They'd done what had perhaps never been done before. And by sheer luck, they'd both survived it.

Killian was less sure the *Fancy* would survive re-entering Earth's atmosphere. Somewhere in the depths of engineering, Dinah was working frantically to restart their thrusters, while countless pieces of his beloved ship remained behind, now in fragments lost to space.

Bringing his ship home would require insane luck and complete concentration, so he could spare only a few thoughts for what this victory would mean for the future. None of those few, however, were encouraging.

It would require a pilot with every ounce of Callista's impossible skill to pull off that move, and even then, she'd needed a second pilot to play his own part. One who was slightly crazy and had nothing to lose. Not to mention, in this case, they'd been facing only a single enemy.

When the Bhandecki fleet arrived, there would be multiple enemies, no room to maneuver, and a decided shortage of suitably insane pilots. They would have to find a new strategy.

But Earth would be safe for a little longer while they figured it out.

His comm buzzed, and he found himself slightly surprised it was still working.

"Still breathing," he said, and wondered whether the sound he heard in response was static or Callista's teeth grinding together in sheer rage. Despite everything, the thought made him smile.

"For how long?"

He could hear her tension in all the yelling she *wasn't* doing. "All seals are currently intact, and environmental systems seem to be holding their own. I'm more worried about breaking up in atmosphere or not being able to slow the ship in time."

"What can I do?" She sounded completely serious. Alone in her tiny fighter craft, she was still looking for a way to save him.

Which forced Killian to consider a new and utterly absorbing question. Why? Why *exactly*?

The answer mattered to him far more than it should.

Up until now, any of her actions could be construed as being in Earth's best interest. She needed him for his knowledge—for his vital contributions to humanity's survival.

But that was no longer true. She had what was necessary to build the planetary shield, and she'd destroyed the alpha worm almost on her own. Callista didn't *need* him anymore—and if anything, she should see him as a threat. With his knowledge and his ability to change shapes, he could easily wait until the power transfer within Lindmark was complete and then take her beloved corporation for himself.

But she'd trusted him to fight beside her. Begged him to trust her at his back.

Did he dare hope that his safety mattered to her in the same way hers had come to matter to him? Did he dare admit to himself that he had come to care—deeply—for a *human,* and hoped she might care for him in return?

When he'd last left Concord and set himself on this path, he'd been finished with humans forever. They'd betrayed and disappointed him too many times, so he'd deliberately cut his last ties to humanity when he shot Seph. He'd even told her he was finished with allowing humans to be his allies.

So why did he now feel as though he could conquer the universe, as long as Callista was willing to fight beside him?

"Either she'll hold together or she won't," he told her, fighting to keep these revelations to himself. "Nothing you can do at this point but get back to Earth and spread the word."

"I'm not leaving you behind," she said fiercely. "Don't you have escape pods or something? This ship might be tiny, but there's room for you and Dinah if it looks like you won't be able to make repairs in time."

"I won't leave the *Fancy,*" he told her, as gently as he was able. He didn't even know why he was trying so hard not to upset her. Callista was smart and capable, so she knew what might be coming. "She's not just a ship—she's all we have of home, and I have to do everything I can to get her down in one piece."

"Even if you die with her?"

"I don't plan to die, and neither does Dinah."

Callista didn't say anything.

"But if we do…"

"Just shut up," she snapped. "If you're not going to die, then get busy figuring out how. I'll follow you and make sure Phillip knows where we are."

Killian smiled again. It was decidedly odd to feel this happy when his ship was in so many pieces. "I'll try to make sure we land in Lindmark territory. Otherwise, someone else might kill me before you do."

Shutting down the comm, he turned his attention to ensuring that Callista would get her chance to kill him. He was looking forward to it far more than was probably healthy or wise.

———

FIVE HOURS LATER, they were as ready as they were going to get.

"Thrusters are up to about fifty percent of normal function," Dinah reported from engineering. "Aside from one that I don't think I could get running again, even with a fully equipped repair facility."

"We're still open to space in at least four places," Killian reported. "Can the seals maintain their integrity at the speeds we're going to be traveling?"

"They weren't meant to," Dinah snapped. "So you'll have to keep our speed down as much as possible. I'll hold things together as best I can from down here, but I don't know how much magic I have left."

"I don't want you down there when we're landing," Killian ordered firmly. "If we crash, engineering will be in shambles."

"I'm going to stay as long as I can," Dinah responded mutinously. "So just you worry about flying this hulk and let me worry about my drives, will you?"

"Aye-aye, Chief Engineer."

He heard Dinah muttering just before she cut off the connection, and grinned a little as he turned his attention to the viewscreen ahead of him.

Earth's atmosphere loomed before them, innocent enough for a ship under full power. Not so for the *Fancy*, and as the gravity well began to tug at them and the friction of the atmosphere began resisting his efforts to maintain course, Killian tried adjusting the thrusters to compensate.

They responded sluggishly and with only partial power, and the *Fancy* began to pick up speed as they fell.

Too fast. They were already moving *much* too fast, and the fluctuations from his sensors suggested he would get only a few brief bursts of full power from the thrusters before they died. He would need them most for the actual landing, so he was going to have to let the atmosphere act as a brake and hope the hull plating would hold, despite all the breaches caused by the fireworm's defenses.

The outlook was not encouraging, but he didn't really have a choice, so he pulled back on the thrusters and let the ship drop.

"Captain, what's happening?" Dinah sounded halfway between fury and panic. "We still have power! Why aren't we using it?"

"Can't talk now," he ground out between gritted teeth. "Just trust me when I say I'm doing the best I can."

Using only minimal power from the thrusters, Killian fought to keep their descent steady. The atmosphere fought back, but he remained focused on the glowing dot that represented their former landing spot.

He wasn't going to make that. But if he were lucky, they wouldn't overshoot by much.

As for where they would end up... The viewscreen couldn't

help him. Half his sensors were offline. He needed someone to guide him.

Taking a precious second to activate the comms, he opened a link to the only person who could help them now.

"Callista, I'm flying blind, and I don't want to crash into a city. Can you follow my trajectory and update possible landing sites?"

"On it." Her voice sounded tight, but she didn't hesitate. "If you were aiming for Haven Two, it looks like you're going to miss to the west. Aim for one of the areas I'm about to send you, and your chances of hitting a populated area should be minimal."

All around the bridge, warnings began to flash. It was getting too hot, in areas of the ship never meant to be open to atmosphere. Would biotech survive? Or would the hull metal buckle under the strain?

Callista's message flashed onto his screen, and Killian swiftly chose his destination. It was farther than he liked, but they might make it if he could engage the thrusters at exactly the right moment...

Suddenly the ship lurched sickeningly beneath him.

"Dinah, what's happening? Are you okay down there?"

"It's not going to hold, Captain!" Static nearly drowned out her words. "I have to abandon engineering. Stay on course. Don't put any unnecessary strain on the thrusters, or we may lose them entirely. You have to save them for the final descent!"

Damn.

He cut power completely, and the *Fancy* dropped towards Earth like a dying bird.

"Killian!" He heard Callista's panicked cry but couldn't spare a moment to answer.

They were falling. Falling too fast. There was just one more thing he could try.

The forward viewscreen finally cleared to show Earth's surface far below but growing closer by the second. They were close enough to see skyscrapers and waterways… "Too close," he muttered, and engaged the drives.

They weren't meant to be used this deep in atmosphere, but as long as they all survived, surely Dinah would forgive him. Surely she would be able to repair the damage, if only his poor, broken ship had enough left for this one last gasp…

The drives fired, and the *Fancy* shuddered beneath him as it shot forward. A groan from somewhere beneath his feet suggested he might have lost another piece of the hull, but he couldn't spare so much as a wince. Their downward trajectory had leveled out, but he was still moving too fast.

So he cut back on the drives, gradually renewing their descent, but losing altitude slower this time.

Maybe even slow enough. The glowing dot of his destination loomed on the horizon, and as it began to grow brighter, Killian activated the landing sensors.

They flashed in warning to announce that his speed was still too high, but they were going to have to deal with it. There was no way the ship could hold through another abrupt shift like the last one.

Closer and closer to the ground… He could make out more details on the surface now. Could see the endless sprawl of city giving way to rocky desert, studded by plateaus and canyons. Running into one of those at the wrong moment would get him just as dead as a failed re-entry.

When Dinah finally messaged him from her quarters to say she was ready for landing, Killian knew it was time to risk the thrusters.

Finding a relatively open stretch, he fired only the left thrusters, hoping to turn the ship.

Nothing.

So he tried the right side, and it answered, but slowly. The *Fancy* banked and leveled out, leaving an ominous-looking range of hills directly in his path. They were just going to have to set down before they got there.

Which wouldn't happen without the left thrusters, so in a split-second decision, he stabbed at the control screen and initiated a reboot of the entire system.

Five seconds till he would need the thrusters online. The screen remained dark. Four. The restart symbol glowed dimly in the corner of his screen… Three. Two. The controls flickered on, then off, sputtered, and went dark again. One. The bridge lights died, and Killian slammed both hands onto his console in desperation.

The screen flared brightly in response, and Killian threw the thruster controls to maximum.

Either this was going to work, or they were about to end up as nothing more than a shiny debris trail scattered across the next mile or so of desert.

A shudder traveled through the ship, and it wobbled on its axis as the thrusters fired at different times. But they came on, and Killian felt a brief, vicious thrill of victory as he adjusted them to equal power and threw everything they had into slowing the ship.

The mountains came closer, but they were almost down… so close… The ground loomed in the viewscreen, rough and uneven, but survivable as long as he could…

The control panel flickered again, the thrusters died, and the

Fancy hit the earth, sliding uncontrollably across the rocky ground.

They were moving too fast, and there was nothing he could do—no way to change their trajectory. Killian clutched the sides of his chair, gritting his teeth against the forces that threw him from side to side, hoping they would come to a stop before they crashed.

If they did crash, he could only pray that Callista would not be the one to find them in the wreckage.

And that they had done enough to save Earth.

This wasn't the way he'd planned to die, but it wasn't like fate had asked him what he wanted. If only…

———

CALLISTA SCREAMED ALOUD when the *Fancy* hit, bounced once, and skidded across the desert floor.

They'd come so far. It couldn't end this way.

But the battered ship continued to slide, leaving a trail of broken pieces behind before coming to a stop only a few hundred yards from a rocky plateau that would have turned it into a heap of spare parts and shattered hull plates.

Callista set down her ship, sent a frantic message to Phillip with their location, and bolted out of the cockpit towards the remains of the *Fancy*.

There wasn't enough left of it to explode, she told herself grimly as she raced around the broken shell, coughing as she breathed in the dust clouds from their landing. There had to be a way in, and as she searched, she could only hope grimly that the inside was in better shape than the hull.

When she reached the aft portion of the ship, she found her

entrance—the weapons bay lay open to the air. Whatever loose items it had once contained were long since lost to space, and as Callista climbed through the opening, she winced at the extent of the damage. This would take months to repair, assuming they could even find compatible parts.

Killian would be devastated. If he'd survived...

But of course he'd survived. He would have been on the bridge. Going down with his ship, like the captain he was.

Stubborn bastard.

Somehow, she had to get up to the bridge level, but there was no way the lifts were functioning, and the *Fancy* had no visible maintenance hatches.

"Hello?" she called. "Dinah?"

The only answer was the hiss of escaping gases from somewhere and the pop and groan of tortured metal.

The doors... At least the doors didn't operate on tracks. An opening appeared in the wall as Callista approached the far side of the weapons bay, allowing her to exit into the corridor beyond.

It was dark, illuminated only by the fitful flickering of the lights set into the floor.

If the doors were still functioning, maybe there was a chance.

Callista ran for the lift, but her first instincts proved correct. No matter how she tried to activate it, the controls remained stubbornly dark.

How else could she get to the bridge?

She was about to start beating on the doors when something brushed against the back of her shoulder.

"Dinah?" she gasped, and whirled around, but it was not Dinah.

She didn't scream, exactly, but an embarrassing whimper

escaped her throat at the sight in front of her.

Golden eyes glowed in the dark. Needle-sharp white teeth gleamed in a threatening smile only an arms-length from her face.

"Errol!" Caught between terror and relief, she almost threw her arms around the neck of Killian's bizarre-looking cat-thing but thought better of it in the face of those strange, sinuous tentacles. Thankfully, he didn't seem inclined to eat her, or he probably would have pounced instead of alerting her.

"Where's Killian?" she asked softly, extending a hand to rub the cat-creature carefully beneath his chin. "Can you take me to him?"

He cocked his head and took off down the corridor. Either he was smarter than the average Earth cat, or she was dumber than the average human to be following him into the dark.

Callista trailed along behind until Errol reached what looked like a blank wall and sat on his haunches, watching her expectantly.

What was she supposed to do? Was there a door here? And even if there were, it wasn't likely to open for her.

But the cat seemed to want her to try, so she ran her hands across the wall, feeling for any surface that might be a little different than those around it.

At about shoulder height, she found it—a circular patch that felt warmer to the touch—so she pressed her palm tightly against the wall. Lights began to flash beneath her hand, just before a narrow opening appeared soundlessly in front of her.

Had Killian given her security access and never told her?

Slipping inside the tiny space, she glanced around until she found what she was looking for—handholds cut into the wall as it curved up and out of sight. A maintenance tunnel—and a way around the ship in case it lost power. Callista smiled grimly as she reminded herself there was no way Killian wouldn't have prepared for a moment like this one.

Tucking her fingers into the first notch in the wall, she began to climb. When she reached the top of the tunnel, she clung with one hand while repeating the process from two levels below. This time she found the access pad more quickly and pulled herself through the open door with a sigh of relief.

She only yelped a little when she realized Errol had followed her.

The cat leaped up and through the doorway, shaking its head a few times before stalking off down the corridor—towards the bridge.

Callista broke into a run, brushing past Errol when he paused in front of the open bridge door. Inside, she could see more flickering lights, primarily from the forward viewscreen as it flashed occasionally with lines of characters in an alien script.

"Killian!"

The answering silence brought a lump to her throat, but she wasn't ready to give in to despair just yet.

Instead, she made her way to the captain's chair, only stubbing her toes twice in the darkness.

It was empty.

Where was he? She would have sworn he would be here until the last...

Something grabbed her ankle. She hissed and reached for her weapon on instinct, but ended up flailing and falling onto something soft that grunted when she landed.

"Killian?" she gasped. That was certainly *someone's* chest beneath her hands...

The lights brightened momentarily, and relief flooded

through her as she caught a quick glimpse of the face beneath her.

Killian was alive. A trickle of blood ran from his forehead to his chin, and his eyes were wide, probably with shock. A sound escaped him—not quite a sob, but a sound of desperate relief—and then he moved. His arms came around her, and he held on as if she were the only thing that mattered. As if he couldn't go another moment without reminding himself that they'd both survived.

He must not be too severely injured if he could move that fast, but she had to know. "Killian, how badly are you hurt? If you're still bleeding, we need to get you out of here."

He didn't answer, but his hold on her grew even tighter, as if he were trying to convince himself that she was real. And after the terror of the past few hours, Callista suddenly realized that she needed that reassurance too. So she didn't try to pull away—just took a deep, shuddering breath, relaxed into the comforting rise and fall of his chest, and told herself that everything was going to be okay.

And strangely, it was. Somehow, as long as Killian was still alive to make a total mess of her mind, her heart, and her plans… everything else could be fixed.

Without warning, his arms flexed, and he rolled—until she was the one lying on the floor, with his hand beneath her head and his weight braced on his elbow.

She didn't need light to feel the intensity of his gaze. Didn't need to see to know that he was trembling. She could feel it as his other hand crept up to touch her hair, her cheek, and finally cup her jaw.

"I'm so glad you're alive," she breathed. "I thought…"

That was as far as she got before he kissed her.

EIGHTEEN

HE WAS ALIVE.

Callista was alive.

Kissing her seemed like the most rational thing he could do.

Until his brain seemed to restart itself, and Killian abruptly realized that she was kissing him back and none of it was rational but he didn't care.

He'd kissed women a few times since becoming a human. It seemed like an important part of fully inhabiting this life, but it had never affected him like this. He'd never *felt* anything before.

Now, he felt everything. He felt his own perplexing desire to touch her, taste her, know her. His strange longing for her to trust him with her secrets.

Her lips were soft and warm, and they opened to his as if she welcomed his touch, but there was nothing else soft about Callista. She rose beneath him, tangled her fingers in his hair, and pulled him closer.

And in that fierce response, he felt her passion, her terror, and her determination. Her willingness to embrace whatever came and face it head-on.

This. This was how she would kill him. Had she planned it on purpose? Or had she been as surprised as he to discover that this was the only place he wanted to be?

She pulled back suddenly, breathing hard and still framing his face with her hands. "Killian, is Dinah all right?"

Trust Callista to be true to her protective instincts, even in a moment like this.

"She made it to her cabin before we hit, so hopefully, she was able to strap down. Did the second level look intact?"

"I didn't stop there to find out. Errol led me straight here."

He gritted his teeth as the ugly reality of the crash intruded on the moment. "Then we should go back down and see what's still in one piece. But Dinah is tough. I'm sure she's fine."

She had to be okay. Biotech and medical—those had to be okay too. They could find a way to rebuild almost anything else, but their supplies of nanotech were irreplaceable.

Without them? He and his crew were neither more nor less than human. Stuck in these forms, stuck in this part of the galaxy, for the rest of their lives, however long those might be.

And yet, that thought didn't sting quite as badly as it once might have. What if he *were* forced to remain a human? What if he never went home and stayed here on Earth with Callista?

"I'm still going to kill you," she said softly, from where she lay beneath him on the deck. She sounded amused, and slightly perplexed.

That made two of them.

"Only if Dinah doesn't kill me first," he acknowledged, rolling to the side and collapsing to the deck beside her. "She may never forgive me for crashing her ship."

"*I* may never forgive you for lying to get me off this ship you just crashed."

He didn't have the energy for flippancy—just enough to prop himself up on one elbow and gaze at her in the darkness. "I won't apologize for it. I didn't have time to convince you, and I didn't know if you would trust me enough to just do what I asked if I told you the truth."

"Don't lie to me again," Callista said seriously. "I won't tolerate people who kiss me and then lie to me."

He wondered how many men had done that to her. Had Maxim Korchek been one of them? And why did the thought make him want to go back in time and beat the man to a bloody pulp?

"I thought you were going to kill me anyway."

"I didn't say *when* I was going to kill you." She sounded almost happy about it. "I think I'm going to have to kiss you again before I decide."

That idea definitely appealed to him, but she wasn't finished.

"There's just one thing I need to know first…"

"I'm fine," Dinah said from behind them. "Didn't need to be rescued. Thanks so much for asking."

Killian groaned and flopped back onto the deck. What had Callista been about to say? And how long would it be before he could ask her?

Now he was going to have to get up. Figure out how bad the damage was and how guilty he was going to feel over it. But he didn't want to think at all. He'd rather lie here next to Callista and pretend…

Pretend what, exactly? Even if there were no Bhandecki, even if he hadn't just crashed his ship, what did he expect to happen next? That they would engage in some kind of normal human relationship? That Callista would be happy with him or he with her? Bending their schedules around one another's lives?

Changing everything to make this more than a spontaneous kiss in the aftermath of a traumatic event?

"How bad is it?" Callista asked.

"Bad enough." Dinah's tone was tight and clipped. She was worried.

Killian rolled to his feet and pushed his hand through his hair before looking around his once immaculate bridge. What he could see of it was... bad enough.

On the other hand... "We defeated an alpha fireworm," he reminded Dinah. "That's not a small thing. There is no record of anyone among our people having accomplished that before."

"No record," she growled, "because how many of our people sent out to face these things ever return home?"

None, that's how many.

"Someone had to be first," he said, forcing himself to project a jaunty confidence he wasn't even close to feeling.

"I hate to break up the party," Callista announced, pushing herself off the floor, "but I've just heard from Phillip. Sounds like our ride is here."

Their moment, it seemed, was over.

But had it just been a moment? Or had it been something more? Something bigger? He had so many questions. So many... feelings. Absurd, irrational, uncomfortable feelings.

But then they left the bridge, and even the chaos in his heart was drowned out by a numb feeling of shock as they made their way out of the wreck.

It was worse than he'd imagined. Every fresh bit of damage they encountered should have hurt, but the pain remained distant. He couldn't really wrap his head around the implications, so he disconnected himself completely. Otherwise... how could he grapple with the reality that his ship might never fly again? That he and his crew no longer had a home?

At least the drives appeared to be intact, and the heart of the ship remained untouched, but the rest?

He remained distracted even when they met up with Phillip, who looked over the wreckage grimly before announcing that he'd commandeered a flying garbage hauler. They were able to float the *Fancy* carefully back to the Canyon and set her down as gently as possible near the outskirts of Haven Two.

Afterward, they gathered in Callista's nearly restored apartment. Phillip, Seph, Callista, Killian, Dinah, and a handful of Callista's staff—the few who knew of the fireworm and would now be forced to confront the implications of the recent battle.

While Xavier and Jocasta cornered Callista—from the sound of things to give her a stern lecture about endangering herself without telling them first—Killian found himself in front of one of the brand new windows, unable to stand still. The view was spectacular, but he barely saw it. His people were fine, and the progress on the atmospheric shield was moving quickly, but he found no consolation in remembering those facts.

"Don't make me throw you out that window, Avalar."

Phillip came over to stand next to him, forcing Killian to stop his incessant pacing.

"What's bothering you?" Phillip was watching him with a keen, piercing expression. "We're going to expedite the work on your ship—just as soon as you figure out what you need—and everything else is going according to plan."

Killian didn't really have a coherent answer. True, he didn't share Phillip's faith that the *Fancy* could be restored, but he knew things about his ship that he wasn't ready to explain. And the crash wasn't the only thing troubling him, but he didn't think he could describe the feeling of discontent that had seized him, or the anxious need to be *doing* something.

Phillip, however, seemed to take Killian's silence as sufficient reason to question him further. "Is there something going on between you and my sister?" Phillip said it in a low voice that no one else in the room could have heard, but Killian's gaze shot straight to Callista.

"Ah." Phillip didn't sound angry or happy, just aggravatingly sure. "Does she know?"

"Does she know what?" Killian didn't even try to contain his irritation with this line of inquiry.

"That you're in so deep, you might never get out, but damned if you care because she's the only one who has ever made you feel as if this life is worth what it costs you?"

Killian's head jerked around in spite of his frustration, and he met Phillip's knowing gaze with curiosity.

"I assume that's how you feel about Seph?"

Phillip nodded. "It is. And because that's the case, allow me to give you a piece of advice. Make sure she knows. Don't wait, don't guess, don't hope, just make sure. Because nothing will ever hurt as much as believing you missed your chance to tell her."

Tell her what? How could he tell her anything when he didn't understand himself?

———

CALLISTA ACCEPTED Xavier's chastisement as meekly as possible —not that she'd ever been very successful at meekness. Both Xavier and Jocasta were fully aware she would do the same thing again. They understood and respected her decisions, or neither of them would have as close a relationship with her as they did.

But it seemed to make them feel better to fuss, so Callista let them, while internally stewing over something completely different.

She couldn't tell what Killian was thinking, and it was driving her mad.

And she'd never had a chance to ask her question.

Why had he kissed her?

It had been one simple kiss, and far from her first. So why had this one thrown her off her stride?

More than that… It felt like the first real kiss she'd ever had—real, honest, and therefore unexpectedly complicated.

Conclave heirs were always falling in and out of relationships, but they were rarely serious, because most Conclave families brokered marriages as they did business deals—with the good of the corporation in mind. Satrina had attempted once or twice to steer her daughter in that direction, but Callista had never entertained even the smallest thought about cooperating. She'd seen what such a mercenary system did to her peers and wanted none of it for herself.

So she'd flitted around, dated a few times, and flirted incessantly as a part of her public persona.

But it had always been an act, on both sides. She'd never kissed someone just because she wanted to. Never kissed a man she actually liked enough to leave her wondering about the consequences to her heart.

Not until Killian. Not until this smirking, sarcastic, spiky-haired pirate had somehow sneaked past her defenses. And he'd done it by being a better man than most of the humans she knew.

He protected the people entrusted to his care. Acted instead of waiting for others to fix problems. And yet, he also trusted her to do what she did best and watched her back without needing any glory for himself.

Callista might have been able to resist even that potent combination, but Killian was also the only man she knew whose mind was twisty enough to follow where she led without having to ask too many questions. If only for that, she ought to at least hire him, but a working relationship wasn't the only thing she wanted. Or was it?

And how could she know the answer unless she first knew why he'd kissed her?

But she couldn't ask him, because Killian and Phillip were standing together by the window, talking too quietly for her to overhear. She couldn't help but wonder if the two had decided to fully bury their differences. Or maybe they'd just agreed to get along until the Bhandecki threat was dealt with.

"Callista, you need to see this." Priya strode into the room, her dark eyes bright with excitement. "We're receiving another transmission from a colony planet!"

She placed a reader on the table that was currently the only furniture in Callista's sitting area. When everyone had gathered around, she began playing back the transmission.

Unlike the previous messages from besieged planets, this one was crystal clear. There were no screams, no flames, no visible destruction—just a face.

But it was a face Callista remembered, dimly, even though she had never met the woman.

"Hello to whoever might be receiving this message," the woman said. Her pale blonde hair was gathered in a braid, and her dark blue eyes stared into the camera with a relaxed sort of confidence. "My name is Emma Forester, and I'm transmitting this from the independent colony world of Daragh, hoping there is still someone out there to receive it."

Callista's eyes flew to her brother. He'd gone slightly ashen, his jaw tense as he stared at the woman on the screen.

Daragh had been the Linden family's greatest crime—the one Phillip had eventually been exiled for. But even beyond that, he had a history with this woman, and from his expression, it wasn't a part of the past he was anxious to relive.

Seph moved quietly to stand beside him, slipping her hand into his without saying anything.

"The alien fleet that destroyed Vadim and Galloway arrived here two days ago."

Callista's breath froze. How was the woman still alive to send this message? Had Killian's hasty explanation of the biotech shield been enough to protect them?

"We lack the technology or the materials to construct a shield as instructed, but Daragh has her own defenses."

So it did. The entire planet was a sort of sentient life form—one that had proven more than willing to protect the living creatures that called it home. From the way Phillip was rubbing his neck, Callista suspected he knew more about Daragh's capabilities than he'd ever let on.

"After studying other segments of the data we received"—Emma glanced down as if to check her sources—"we've been able to keep the Bhandecki at bay, and we believe this information could prove vital to humanity's efforts in the future."

She looked straight into the camera. "We've discovered that the fireworms are individual entities, but they are intimately connected with one another through a telepathic net. I realize this concept may be met with skepticism, but if you have followed any of our work at the Daraghn Institute of Psionic Research, you'll know that such connections are not as rare as many people believe."

Killian's mouth dropped open. "We knew the alpha worms could control the smaller ones, but telepathy?"

"Daragh has similar abilities," Emma continued. "She has been able to use those to establish a link with individual fireworms and has confirmed that they are not only fully sapient, but are unwilling participants in this war."

More jaws were dropping all around.

"How did we not know this?" Killian murmured.

But even if they had known, could they have done anything about it?

"In battle," Emma was saying, "the worms are directed using magnetic field generators, but the alphas are previously subjected to extensive mental conditioning that prevents them from realizing they have a choice. However, we've discovered that it is possible to break this conditioning using Daragh's telepathic connection."

The seed of hope took root in Callista's heart. Was this the breakthrough they so desperately needed?

"So far, Daragh has successfully freed two alphas from Bhan-decki control. In the process, she was able to convince them—and the sections of the fleet under their direction—to act in our defense. But it won't last long. The Bhandecki are growing increasingly desperate and will probably destroy the alphas rather than allow this to continue."

"Daragh will be safe," Emma said, and the steely look in her blue eyes suggested she would take on the fireworms with her bare hands to make that a reality. "But we have been working to determine how this information can be used to protect other planets. We believe that certain frequencies of brain waves can either connect with the alpha worms or potentially confuse them, to the point they are unable to link with the remainder of the fleet. But the gamma frequencies required are high, and rarely seen in anyone without psionic training."

"Do we know anyone who's been to the Institute?" Callista murmured to Priya.

She shook her head. "We have two people there now, but no one who's completed their study and returned. It hasn't been that long since the program was up and running, and the travel time is three months."

Three months in a *human* ship...

"It would take too long for any of us to reach Earth," Emma said, with evident regret, "so we are sending our best guesses now, in hopes that it will help with Earth's defenses. You will need someone with psionic talent, capable of producing gamma waves of—"

The screen abruptly went dark.

"What happened?" Phillip's gaze was intense, his blue eyes like chips of ice in his frozen face.

Priya snatched up the reader and tapped the screen a few times before looking up. "That was all," she said. "The transmission died. Likely the beacon was destroyed before it finished sending."

What had Emma Forester been about to say?

Between shock and stunned disbelief, it was a handful of seconds before anyone else spoke.

"We need to know what they discovered," Phillip said finally.

"Even if the shield is deployed in time, we need all the weapons we can find to deal with the fleet afterward."

"Six months is too long," Jocasta insisted. "We can't afford to focus any of our efforts on such a long shot."

Emma's revelations offered so much hope, but it remained just out of reach. Unless they were willing to gamble everything…

Callista found her gaze wandering to Killian and discovered him watching her as well. Their eyes locked, and in his, she saw the glimmer of something that was far from despair. He was obviously considering something reckless. Something all but impossible. Something no sane person would ever attempt.

"Whatever it is," she said quietly, "I'm in."

He cocked an eyebrow. "How did you know I was thinking about doing something crazy?"

"I guess I just know what crazy looks like."

His smirk warned her what was coming. "I didn't realize you spent that much time in front of mirrors."

"Where are we going?"

He regarded her more seriously. "Someplace no human has gone before. Someplace we may not come back from. You still interested?"

Interested? "You clearly know the way to my heart, Captain Avalar."

His eyes flared wide, as if she'd actually surprised him with that one.

Phillip turned to glare at them both. "Something you'd like to share with the class?"

"Killian has an idea."

"How interesting." Phillip's sour expression indicated that he might have forgiven the pirate for their past history, but he still wasn't exactly a fan. "Is this going to be as half-assed and ridiculous as the 'plan' that nearly got me and Seph killed last time?"

"Worse," Killian said coolly. "Are you willing to trust me?"

Phillip laughed harshly. "That's bold, coming from you, Avalar."

"I can see why you'd be shocked. Normally, I'm so humble and retiring."

Clearly, someone was going to have to interrupt them before they declared their undying love. "You two can flirt later," Callista said firmly. "Killian, what's this plan of yours?"

He locked eyes with her. "I still have the jump-ship. It's big enough, and hopefully fast enough, for two, maybe three of us to fly to Daragh and ask our questions."

Callista crossed her arms and let her mind race ahead. Was it possible? Could they afford to send the jump-ship on such an errand when the *Fancy* was lying in pieces? "How long would it take?"

Killian's gaze darted away. "A little under two weeks. That is if we go the normal way."

Everyone exchanged glances, but it was Seph who seemed to realize what he meant. "You have no idea where that will lead. No way to tell whether it's a permanent one."

Killian cocked his head to the side. "No, but I'm fairly certain. Given the timing of the transmission we just saw and the recent scarring on that fireworm we destroyed, I believe it most likely came straight from the siege of Daragh. And it was definitely an alpha. Maybe they were trying to get away before the planet claimed another one."

"You'd better not be suggesting what I think you are." Phillip looked as if he were considering throwing Killian out the window.

"Why not?" Killian, for once, did not joke or evade. He faced Phillip coolly, refusing to give an inch. "I've already given you everything I know. I've done my part, and from here on out, Earth doesn't need me. Why not take a chance on this and hope it's the breakthrough we've been looking for?"

A strange tension stretched between the two of them, and Callista longed to shatter it. But this… They needed to solve this for themselves.

"Because you have no idea what we may need when the Bhandecki arrive," Phillip countered. "You're one of the best pilots we have, and you've proven you know how to defeat the worms. Not to mention, your ship is more capable than any we can boast. Why would we throw away that resource in a vain attempt to gain information we may not be able to take advantage of?"

"Dinah is a better pilot than me," Killian responded flatly. "And it was your ship that defeated the worm. I was only the decoy. We haven't had a chance to discuss it yet, but the strategy we used out there won't work in a full-scale battle. We *have* to find some other advantage, and this could be it."

Finally, slowly, reluctantly, Phillip nodded. "I can't pretend I don't know why you're doing this. But if you think it might work…"

"Excuse me?" Callista broke in, glaring first at her brother, then at Killian. "Would someone please tell the rest of us exactly what you're contemplating?"

"The rift," Killian said simply. "The fireworm we fought came through a newly formed rift, and I believe it came straight from the siege at Daragh. Maybe they're thinking about giving up and moving on and sent that alpha as a scout to scope out their next target. Or maybe it was just trying to escape. Either way, I plan to take my jump-ship through the rift and try to reach Daragh in time."

And what if the rift didn't lead where he thought? What if it proved unstable and collapsed before he reached the other side? Or what if they reached the other side only to encounter the entire Bhandecki fleet?

"I'm going with you," Callista announced.

The room went dead, as if no one dared to be the first to voice their objections.

"I'm the best pilot we have." It wasn't bragging—it simply *was*. She'd known she had a gift since the first time she piloted a skimmer, and she'd spent thousands of hours honing that gift to a razor edge. The cockpit was the one place she felt whole, at peace, and entirely at home in her own skin. "If we're going to fly through a potentially unstable rift and attempt to break through a siege, I'm the best person for the job, and you know it.

"And besides." She looked over at her brother. "Lindmark doesn't need *me* anymore either, Phillip. I might have gotten us this far, but you're the best person to lead this corporation, both now"—she took a deep breath—"*and* in the future."

She heard a quiet gasp from Jocasta, and Priya looked a little shell-shocked, but Callista knew her words were true.

"I didn't come here to take anything from you," Phillip said quietly. "And I won't be a part of any plan that devalues your abilities or your right to a say in Lindmark's future course. I want you with me."

It meant a lot to hear him say it. To know that he was not the man their grandfather had tried to make him. But Callista remained convinced she was on the right course. Believed wholeheartedly that this was the best way forward—for herself, for Phillip, and for Lindmark.

"You're not taking anything," she said firmly. "I'm choosing to step aside. And I won't devalue myself or my people. We've worked damned hard to get this far, and they are fully capable of taking you wherever you want to go. But it isn't my skills that Lindmark needs now—it's yours. I have my own path to walk, and I don't think it's in a corporate boardroom."

Callista wasn't sure what exactly that path would end up looking like, but even as she said the words, they felt right.

"How can you trust me that much?" Phillip betrayed a rare vulnerability in even asking the question, and she could do no less than honor it by telling the truth.

"We both survived this world in our own way," she told him. "But just because we did it differently doesn't mean I don't know —intimately—what you had to do to survive. You came out with scars, but you came out better and stronger, with a compassionate heart that wants better for the people our grandfather betrayed. You knew coming home was going to hurt, but you decided to come back and try anyway. You're a man worth trusting, and I have no doubts about your ability to lead both Lindmark *and* the Conclave through this crisis."

She'd stunned him. She could see him wanting to believe her, but the scars of his past ran deep.

"I'm not sure you couldn't do it better," he admitted.

She shook her head. "I used to think it was what I wanted. But the truth is, I'm a fighter. I want to win. I want to see justice done, and I want to save Lindmark. But a fighter is not necessarily the same as a leader. Once the battle is won, I would probably get bored with the day-to-day duties and go looking for a new challenge."

Phillip, on the other hand, had always thrived on duty—on

fulfilling those day-to-day responsibilities that made the corporation work.

This was the right thing to do, and she knew, with time, she could convince even her most dedicated staff to support Phillip in the future.

"So." She looked around with a bright smile and let her gaze land on Killian's apprehensive-looking face. "When do we leave?"

NINETEEN

TWENTY-FOUR HOURS LATER, they were ready to go.

Rill brought the jump-ship from Seren, while Killian salvaged what he thought he might need from the wreck of the *Fancy* and left its repairs in Dinah's hands.

He knew she would be an even more exacting taskmaster than he, but it still stung to leave the *Fancy* behind while it lay crushed and broken. It felt like abandoning a friend, even while he knew the idea to be ridiculous.

As ridiculous as his plan to sail through a rift and hope he knew what was on the other side. Was he crazy to think that this plan might work? Historically, his plans weren't exactly known for being effective. But he'd failed so badly in his attempts to prepare humanity for this attack, he felt he had to continue to try.

As he checked over the jump-ship's systems, double-checked her drives, and calculated supplies, he found himself with a growing reluctance to take anyone with him into this unknown. How could he accept their trust, knowing full well he might be about to betray it again? Not by any choice of his own, but by the very nature of the risk.

He should tell Callista to stay. Should tell her he didn't need her, didn't want her with him.

But if he lied to her again, even for what he could claim was her own good, she would hate him, and he couldn't bring himself to let that happen.

What she thought of him *mattered*. Not letting her down *mattered*. And in the end, Callista didn't want his protection. What she wanted—the one thing she'd pleaded for him to grant her—was his trust. For him to trust her judgment and her abilities.

To trust a human at his back.

And strangely, the thought no longer repulsed him as it once had. Which was fortunate, because he was about to break that rule twice over. *Two* humans were about to be crowded into the tiny space of his jump-ship for this last-ditch attempt to save their species.

And if either one of them died, Phillip Linden would tear him limb from limb.

"We're here," Callista called out before ducking her head through the hatch and peering around the tiny bay that was the center of the jump-ship's design.

It had never been meant for long journeys—more for short hops between planets. Aside from the main bay that featured cargo clamps, mounts for their energy weapons, and a tiny but functional mess, there were two small cabins, a washroom, and the cockpit, with seats for four.

There would be no avoiding each other, for however long this journey ended up lasting.

"It's just as spacious as I remember," Seph said dryly as she followed Callista into the bay. "Maybe more, since Phillip won't be here to take up half the ship with his cheery personality."

The man in question somehow managed not to crack a smile from his position behind her right shoulder. He also hadn't threatened to shoot Killian yet, so perhaps he would be permitted to launch without collecting any more scars.

"I can't imagine why I let myself be talked into this," Phillip growled, glowering in Killian's direction.

Scars were apparently still on the table. "Not my idea," Killian replied with perfect honesty. "If you recall, Linden, I planned to go alone."

"You could have said no!"

Killian cocked an eyebrow at the man he'd often wished to consider a friend. "And how does that typically work out for you?"

Phillip didn't bother to answer, because they both knew the truth.

"I wouldn't risk this unless I thought it had a chance," Killian said more seriously. "And I won't endanger us any more than necessary."

"Last time, necessary meant leaving Seph to die."

Their gazes locked. "If you think I'm still that man, then convince her not to go."

Time seemed to stretch as they stared one another down, until Phillip finally grunted and gave in. "If I thought you were still that man, I would have killed you already, Avalar. But we both have things we'd rather not relive. And Callista trusts you. She doesn't trust easily, so if she matters to you at all, try not to ruin it."

Killian had no idea what might have led someone like Callista to trust him, considering everything she knew about his past *and* his present. But he didn't intend to ruin it—he intended to…

Perhaps he should set out to prove that trusting him was the right decision. But the truth was, he would let her down somehow, someday. That was inevitable. The one thing he *could* do was prove that he trusted her in return.

"I think we're ready to leave as soon as the diagnostics are complete," Callista told him. "How about we go and check over the computers?"

She jerked her head in the direction of the cockpit, and he suddenly understood—she wanted to give Phillip and Seph a moment to say goodbye in private. With a final nod at Phillip, he followed her into the front compartment of the ship and settled into the pilot's chair, gesturing for her to take the co-pilot spot.

"Why is Seph coming with us?" he asked, quietly enough that the pair on the other side of the door would be unable to hear. "I wouldn't have thought they'd be willing to spend that much time apart."

"It was Seph's idea, but she finally managed to talk Phillip into it. Said something about it finally being spring," Callista said with a shrug. "I don't know if I've ever seen him look so grim, but he seemed to understand. And the truth is, they both think we'll need an ambassador on Daragh. My family isn't exactly popular there, and without someone they know to vouch for our identities and intentions, they might not be willing to trust us. Plus, she's had medical training that might come in handy if we end up in a fight."

The reasoning made sense, but still… Killian suddenly realized he'd been looking forward to those uninterrupted hours with Callista. Time to talk over what had happened between them, and maybe time for a repeat…

But that probably wasn't a very helpful thing to be focusing on when they were trying to save the world.

So he remained silent while he checked all the flight and nav systems, ensuring they were in perfect working order. He could feel Callista's curious gaze flicking his way multiple times but was oddly unsure how to engage in casual conversation.

What could he say? Should he mention the kiss first? Pretend it hadn't happened? Talk about the weather?

Had he ever felt this awkward before in his life?

How was he supposed to take Phillip's advice and tell her how he felt when all of his glib sarcasm and flair for flirtation seemed to have deserted him entirely?

He was about to call up the command screen for testing the internal comm system when Callista's hand suddenly landed on his arm.

"Killian, there's something I need to ask you." Her dark eyes held an unfamiliar vulnerability, so he had a quick moment to prepare himself for whatever question was troubling her.

"I don't know what you're thinking," she said. "I don't know what you're feeling, and I especially don't know why you kissed me. But before we fly off into the unknown, and before I let myself wonder whether I want my heart to be involved, there's one thing I need to know."

He braced himself.

"What will you do if we win?"

Okay, that was not the question he'd expected. It was also not a question he was at all prepared for.

He probably would have preferred she ask about the kiss, because his answer wouldn't have involved digging up old wounds and exposing them to the light.

"I…" What *would* he do? He hadn't dared think that far ahead since the day the fireworm crashed into Concord Five.

In the past, he'd always thought that if he had the chance, he would go racing home, eager to clear his name and return to the life he'd once loved. But was that even possible now?

Even his happy memories of home had been broken and stained by his brother's betrayal. Despite all the years of longing for justice, he'd never really stopped to consider whether those wounds would ever heal. Whether he could ever feel the same way about the life he'd once taken for granted.

Would it even be possible for him to start a new life amid the ashes of the old? Could he really just go back and pretend these years of exile meant nothing?

But what if he decided that the answer was no? Would he be able to move on? Accept the reality that his exile was permanent?

"I don't know," he said finally. "I've spent so long dreaming of returning to my world—of taking back what was stolen from me and picking up where I left off—that I've never moved past my thoughts of revenge. I've never stopped to think about what would happen afterward."

"What was stolen?"

What had his brother *not* stolen? Was he really ready for Callista to know the whole truth about him?

"My life," he said simply. "As best I can translate it, my title was once First Prince of the Northern Wyrdane Protectorate. I was intended to lead my people after my mother. It was never a sure thing—some of us live for a very long time—but I never questioned my destiny. I looked forward to it."

"What happened?"

He didn't need to see Callista's face to hear her compassion. Would she still feel so much if she knew what he'd been accused of? And given what she knew of him, would she hesitate to believe the charges? There was only one way to find out.

"My brother convinced everyone that I killed our mother. He stole the loyalty of my people and drove me and anyone who challenged him into exile as punishment."

She didn't move. "And did you kill your mother?"

Finally, he lifted his eyes to hers and held her gaze without wavering.

"Yes," he said quietly. "I did."

————

EVEN AS THE shock of that confession reverberated through her, Callista knew there was more to it. Whatever drove Killian, he was not a murderer.

"Why?"

"Why?" Killian's brow arched at her question. "Will knowing my reasons make it any better?"

"I don't believe you killed your mother on purpose," she told him calmly.

"My own people believed it, so why shouldn't you?"

She could hear the pain in his flippancy. "Maybe I know you better. Or maybe I know how easy it is to make fiction into reality, after what my family did to Phillip."

He tried to hide it, but she could see his relief.

"I still don't know what happened," Killian admitted. "We were together that day, and she'd been experimenting with new nanotech that was meant to be more permanent—able to store multiple DNA samples. She tested them on herself, as she'd done many times before, but something went wrong. She lost form almost immediately, and I... I froze. I didn't know what to do, couldn't open my mouth to call for help, and she died in front of me."

"So your brother blamed you."

"I was the only one with her. He claimed I'd been dissatisfied with waiting for her to vacate the throne, so I tampered with the nanoplasm and killed her. And even if that wasn't true, I was already angry with myself for not reacting faster. For not stopping her or finding a way to save her."

The parallels between Killian and Phillip ran deeper than she'd ever guessed.

"And if you went home now?"

"Among the Wyrdane, my return after a successful mission would be seen as evidence that I am innocent. Or at least as proof that I have paid the full price for my crimes. We believe in the idea of destiny, and that fate has a way of working things out as they are meant to be."

"Do you still believe that?"

Even as she asked, she thought she knew the answer. How could he go on believing in destiny when so many lives had been lost? How could he be willing to accept all of the pain he'd endured, just because it meant he was now in a place to save humanity?

"Not so very long ago, I would have said no," Killian replied slowly. "I could see nothing good coming of my exile. Only pain, death, and bitterness. How could that be my destiny when I'd done nothing wrong? How could my people's suffering be their destiny when they'd committed no crime?"

"But?"

His hands dropped to his knees and clenched there. "Evil is still evil. I will never call it necessary, and I will never stop grieving for the lives that were lost. But perhaps"—he seemed to be grappling with the words, even as he spoke them—"it is possible that something good can be found on the other side.

"I've watched Phillip become the man he is," Killian went on, "in contrast to the one I first met. I've watched you defend your people, and I've seen some of the forces that made you who you are. Without the pain you've both been through, Earth would be left defenseless. Without the betrayal that sent me here, humanity would already be dead. And while there was a time when humanity's destruction would not have been of great concern to me, I can no longer say that. I can't pretend that the loss of human life does not cause me deep and unimaginable pain."

His gaze lifted, and Callista found herself facing a man stripped of all pretense. She could see the heart he tried so hard to hide and wished she could share the burdens he clearly still carried.

"What changed?" she asked gently, hearing the tremor of tears in her own voice.

Slowly—ever so slowly—Killian reached across the space between them and took her hand, closing his fingers around it with a gentleness she would not have expected him to possess. "I met someone," he said. "Someone who irritates, terrifies, and enthralls me. Someone who reminds me of how much I used to love life. Someone who makes me wonder whether a different future is possible."

Callista reminded herself to breathe. It wasn't like she'd never had a man say romantic things to her before. It was more that she'd never been convinced any of them *meant* it. Killian... Well, she thought he meant every word, and it terrified her. Thrilled her. Sent a spike of adrenaline straight to her heart and left it racing. But what if she were wrong?

As if he'd heard her thoughts, Killian shot her a crooked grin.

"Don't think I'm not aware that my reputation is standing in my own way right now. How can you be sure a man like me means what he says? What if I say this to all the pretty girls?"

"A girl does occasionally wonder where the flirting stops and the sincerity begins," Callista admitted.

"I've flirted a fair bit," Killian acknowledged. "And I've kissed women before, without ever promising anything. But I've never been in one place long enough for a relationship, so kissing is all that's ever happened."

"Is that all that's going to happen between us?" she challenged him quietly. "Did you kiss me because it was convenient? Because we'd both survived the battle, and you couldn't think of anything better to do?"

He regarded her without a trace of flippancy or flirtation. "Is that what you want me to say, Callista? That it was a passing impulse—something I now regret?"

"What I want…"

What she wanted was the same thing she'd always wanted. Someone to share her crazy life. Someone dangerous. Slightly mysterious. A rogue with a conscience, who loved speed as much as she did. Someone who wasn't afraid of risks, because Callista's entire life was a risk.

And Killian… He was all of those things.

The truth hit her with the force and brilliance of a meteor strike—she wanted him to be all hers. She wanted all of his razor-edged daring, his raffish reputation, his irreverent humor, and even the broken pieces of his heart. She wanted his willingness to spit in the eye of his enemies and charge into the heart of battle with a grin and a wink.

Her heart had been so set on Lindmark, she'd never taken time to even consider romance, but now that her heart was free?

She'd picked the most impossible man in the galaxy.

Who was still waiting for her answer.

"What I want," she repeated, "is…"

The door at the back of the cockpit opened.

"Ready when you are," Seph announced, sounding subdued but resolute. "Phillip is getting ready to head back to Markheim."

Callista's heart sank. She'd lost her chance. Or, perhaps more accurately, she'd been saved from stammering her way through a confession of feelings that might end up being unwelcome.

She wasn't afraid of being the first one to say the words. But she would prefer to feel a bit more certain of how they would be received.

So she turned back to the console in front of her and pretended her heart wasn't pounding in her chest as she fastened her flight harness and made ready for launch.

"Are we ready?" Killian's hand was already poised to activate the thrusters when the jump-ship's comm buzzed with an incoming message.

She opened a channel.

"Abort launch, Captain!"

At almost the same moment, Callista's aural implant crackled to life.

"Callista." It was Jocasta. "Can you do a long-range scan and tell me if you're seeing the same thing we're seeing?"

A chill of dread shot through her as she leaned towards Killian. "Long-range scanners!" she demanded urgently.

He brought up the forward viewscreen. Extended his search farther and farther…

A sea of bright red dots blossomed across the screen.

So many. Callista's mouth went dry, and her hands shook where they gripped the edge of the console.

And they were still coming.

"How far?"

Killian's lips thinned, but his hands flew faster than ever. "Eight hours, if our estimates of their speed are correct. That's if they head for Earth immediately, but they may be waiting for more of their fleet to arrive."

There wasn't enough time.

They could never get to Daragh and back in time to stop the invasion.

For the first time, Callista wondered whether she ought to begin believing in the impossible.

Was it better to give up now, or to spend the last hours of her life in the futile pursuit of a victory that would always be just out of reach?

"Callista?" Jocasta was still waiting.

"I'm seeing it," she responded, forcing the words out between frozen lips. "Do you have a count?"

"They're still coming." Jocasta's voice sounded hollow with disbelief. "There are over a thousand already."

Killian activated his head wrap. "I'm connecting with Patrick," he murmured. "They have to be getting close."

Even if they were close to being ready, how could they deploy the shield in time? They had mere hours.

Hours in which to inform the people of Earth that the threat was not only real, it was here.

Hours in which to keep the masses from panicking and find a way to protect them.

Hours in which to shield the planet from a merciless enemy.

"Patrick?" Killian patched his comm call into the jump-ship's systems. "Give me some good news. Tell me the shield is ready."

"The first batch of particles will be finished in two hours,"

Patrick responded grimly. "But that's left us no time for final testing. We'll have to send them up and hope none of our shortcuts failed."

Killian glanced at Callista. "Do your people have a deployment plan?"

She opened a voice channel with Jocasta. "What's the status on shield deployment?"

"Orbital platforms won't be ready for weeks," the older woman replied, her voice tight with worry. "But we can repurpose the ground dispersion canisters for use by small craft. If we can find enough ships and pilots, we could use them to seed the upper atmosphere and hope the wind currents are in our favor."

Ships and pilots...

And suddenly, Callista knew what she had to do.

"Get on it," Callista told her firmly. "I want as many of those canisters as we can find, on the ground at Seren by the time the shield particles are ready." She unfastened her flight harness and rose from her chair. "I'll be headed that way as soon as I can raise a fleet."

Killian was out of his seat before she could take a single step.

"What are you planning?" His dark eyes were focused intently on hers.

"I have to stay," she said quietly. "Phillip is the right man to lead Lindmark, but he's the wrong man to lead a life or death charge where split-second decisions mean the difference between victory and defeat. This is my fight. Getting through to Daragh and coming back with a solution is yours."

She didn't know what she expected him to do in response. If he'd been any other man, he might have begged her to reconsider. Demanded that she rescind her resolution. Pleaded with her to be safe.

But because he was Killian, he kept on surprising her.

He crossed the distance between them, took her face between his hands, and claimed her lips in a scorching kiss.

It wasn't possessive or demanding. Nor was it a desperate attempt to make her stay. It was a simple statement, made without the need for words.

It held his unwavering belief in her abilities. His trust in her judgment. And his heart. Every broken, patched together corner of it was in that kiss, with no walls or reservations.

There should have been no room in her own heart for joy at that moment, but for a brief instant, it was all she could feel—joy, and the rush of adrenaline that told her she was alive. Hope was not dead. And this race was just beginning.

Killian pulled back and rested his forehead on hers. "We don't have to talk about it now," he murmured quietly, "or ever. But no matter what happens, I wanted you to have that."

"We will most definitely be talking about this, Killian Avalar," she said fiercely. "So go. Come back. And I'll make sure Earth is here waiting for you."

She forced herself to step away from him and glanced at Seph, who offered her a single, sympathetic nod.

"We'll be fine," she said. "Now go save the planet."

Callista's lips twisted into a reluctant grin. "I'll do my best," she said.

TWENTY

IT WAS a tense but quiet flight to the rift. Killian couldn't seem to stop checking and rechecking the systems, and even the typically unruffled Seph kept glancing at her comm as if waiting for a call.

But when he caught her yawning for the fifth time, Killian jerked his head towards the back of the ship.

"Not much you can do while we're en route. Why don't you see if you can catch some sleep."

Seph didn't hesitate—she freed herself from her flight harness and headed for the door. "Thanks," she said gratefully. "I haven't slept much since we arrived, so maybe a nap will help settle my nerves. Just promise to wake me before we go through the rift."

Once she extracted his promise, Seph disappeared, leaving Killian alone with his thoughts.

He didn't care for most of them.

No matter how firmly he told himself that this was the only way, it felt as if he were abandoning Earth. Felt as if he were running away, leaving the burden of Earth's defense resting on Callista's shoulders. As much as he trusted in her abilities, she was one woman against a potential tsunami of destruction. If even one thing went wrong, even one part of their plans went awry, Earth might no longer exist by the time he and Seph returned.

But he was committed, and he couldn't turn back now—not without all but ensuring failure and defeat.

He knew it, but he didn't have to like it.

When the long hours between Earth and the rift eventually drew to a close, Killian sent an alert to Seph's comm. She appeared in the cockpit a few moments later, bleary-eyed but resolute, and sat in the co-pilot's chair, gazing at the viewscreen with unmistakable apprehension.

"Tell me honestly," she said, finally breaking the silence. "What chance do we have?"

Killian looked across the cockpit and saw the fear she didn't want to voice—that she might never see Phillip again. That even if they survived and made it to Daragh in time, it wouldn't be enough to save their loved ones back on Earth.

But if there was anyone in the universe he owed absolute honesty to, it was Seph.

"I don't know."

"Can you at least tell me a convenient lie?" she asked, sounding a little wistful.

"I could," he acknowledged. "If that's really what you wanted. I could tell you this rift will be a permanent one, and it will take us exactly where we need to go. I could even assure you that the shield will work exactly as we planned, and that we will arrive in time to divert the fleet and end the Bhandecki threat forever."

"But?" She sounded gently amused.

"But you'd probably shoot me," he responded dryly.

"As I recall, that doesn't do much good."

He almost chuckled at the memory. "I'm guessing you've wished a time or two that you'd missed and shot me in the head."

"Don't think I haven't considered it," she warned him. "But I don't know how to fly this ship, so your life is safe for now."

She gazed at the emptiness around them and suddenly changed the subject, as if unable to continue bearing the weight of the world's desperate need. "So where is this rift? I keep picturing a crack in space filled with gases and flashy lights and weird magical woo-woo."

"I think every astronomer in history just died a little," he muttered. "But if you recall, we sent drones through a rift on our last flight together. This one won't be much different."

"Yes, but I didn't get to see that one because *someone* didn't wake me up."

He almost laughed. At least she wasn't talking about *him* this time. The last time they'd been on the same ship, he'd stuck Seph and Phillip in the same cabin in a last-ditch attempt to convince them to help with his plan.

Now that he thought about it... that plan had actually worked. Sort of.

"Sorry to say, you're in for a huge disappointment," he told her. "Rifts aren't actually visible. They're like a hole or a fold in space. The ship's scanners can detect the endpoint, but you won't be able to see it when we fly into it."

Seph frowned. "Then why did Dinah tell me that human ships wouldn't be able to survive rift travel?"

"There are some fairly complex things going on within the rift that completely scramble human computer technology. As a result, your spaceship drives don't seem to work once they get inside."

Her eyes suddenly widened as though she remembered something important.

"Killian, what *did* end up happening with those drones you sent through the Rift before? Did no one from your homeworld ever answer? Or is it still possible that they'll send help?"

His lips twisted bitterly. "No one answered. But truthfully, I didn't really expect them to. There's no reason for any of them to risk themselves. They might send out scouts, like me, but over the years, we've become more of a warning system than anything. Also a way of getting rid of anyone who becomes inconvenient. If they choose, the Wyrdane can sit on their planet forever and watch while the rest of the universe is overrun."

He slowed their speed, preparing to pinpoint the entrance to the rift, hoping with every bit of optimism he still possessed that it would, indeed, lead to Daragh.

Suddenly Seph turned to face him. "What would *you* have done? If you were still there, on your home planet, and those drones had arrived begging for help to save a species you'd never met, would you have done anything?"

"No," he answered without hesitation. His past life was mostly hazy now, but he did recall that much. "My people are long-lived, curious, and playful. We grieve lightly, sometimes fight among ourselves, and we can be generous when it suits us, but we have no sense of altruism. It would have made no sense to me to risk my long life to save beings that had nothing to do with me."

"And yet here you are," Seph said, eyeing him knowingly. "Saving humanity. Trusting a human to have your back."

As if he hadn't noticed.

"What's your point?"

"Has it occurred to you," she asked, "that you might be more like us now than you want to admit?"

Well, now it had.

He'd wondered whether his life among the Wyrdane was truly over. He'd wondered whether Killian Avalar might have somehow become his true self. But he'd never considered those questions without an underlying sense of hopelessness or defeat.

And yet, what would he choose if he believed it was possible to live out his future like any other human?

What if he had already chosen, by virtue of the decisions he'd made and the actions he'd taken up to this point?

He'd learned to care about human life. Learned to make judgments based on whether a thing was right or wrong, whether it would hurt or heal. Learned to fear death, to alleviate pain, and to seek companionship.

Even more so than the shape he chose to wear, did those things make him human?

And if he chose to fully embrace his humanity, what would it mean for his future with Callista?

His sensors flashed in warning, ejecting him from his thoughts as the jump-ship closed in on the entry point to the rift.

"Strap in," he told Seph. "Not sure what we're going to find on the other side, but I'd rather we be prepared."

The rift itself was incredibly anticlimactic. The viewscreen went dark, the ship's systems flashed a few times, and then it felt as if some unseen force was squeezing them tightly as they passed from one point to the next. He heard Seph take in a few labored breaths as the pressure increased almost to the point of pain… and then it was over. The pressure eased, the systems came back online, and the utter darkness was replaced with a new starscape.

At least the rift had not collapsed. If nothing else, they could always fly right back through it. But he was still hoping…

Killian's hands flew over the console as he brought up scanners and charts. Searching for something familiar. Trusting that his gamble hadn't led them to a distant, unexplored corner of the galaxy...

There.

"We did it," he whispered in awe, as much to himself as to Seph.

"Daragh?" she exclaimed, jerking against her harness as she attempted to lean forward far enough to see his console.

"We're just a few hours out," he said, feeling a grin spread across his face. A grin that died as he continued to adjust his scanners and realized what was missing.

He'd thought to find at least part of the Bhandecki fleet. But according to his sensors, there were no fireworms anywhere in that sector of space.

Not that he had *wanted* to fight his way through to Daragh, but what was good news for him and Seph was bad news for those they'd left behind.

If the entire fleet had moved on, they were probably even now preparing to attack Earth.

Anxiety surged beneath his skin, demanding that they turn around. Go back. Join the fight. But that was exactly what they couldn't do. He had to trust that Callista and Phillip and Dinah and Rill and everyone else he cared about would do their parts, while he and Seph continued on, hoping for a miracle.

He was still gritting his teeth against the urge to run when the ship's comm buzzed with an incoming transmission.

He opened a channel.

"Welcome to Daragh." The voice was young, female, and entirely businesslike. "If your intent is to land, please identify your ship and your affiliation."

Killian nodded to Seph. It was her turn to forge the way.

"Hi there, Daragh." She smiled ruefully at the screen, no doubt assailed by memories. "It's been a while. This is Persephone Katsaros. I'm a passenger on an unnamed ship, and our affiliation…" She paused and bit her lip for a moment. "I guess you could say we're affiliated with the last defense of Earth."

"Seph?" A new and slightly shocked-sounding voice came over the comm. "Is it really you? This is Emma! Emma Forester. Do you remember me?"

Seph's lips quirked at the corners. "I tend not to forget the people I share life and death experiences with. Can you clear us to land? We got part of your message about how to deal with the fireworms, but it cut off before the end."

"Of course!" There was a quiet rustling in the background. "I'd ask how you got here this fast, but that's probably not the most important thing right now." They heard the quiet buzz of a transmission. "I've just sent landing coordinates, so if you can make your way there, I'll meet you groundside. You may have a little difficulty on landing—Seph, I'm sure you remember how Daragh feels about strangers—but I promise you'll be cleared once I arrive."

What did that mean?

"Can you swear the ship will not be damaged?" Killian demanded. "I won't risk landing if your planet can't be trusted to keep her paws off my ship."

He heard quiet laughter. "She'd be flattered by your concern, but I'll have words with her, I promise."

He'd heard rumors about Daragh, but now that he was here… It was easier to contemplate the idea of a sentient planet from far, far away.

———

THEY TOUCHED down on a landing pad surrounded by a deep, shaggy carpet of vegetation in shades of brown, yellow, and orange. There were tall brown grasses and yellow-gray trees with nearly transparent leaves, all lying undisturbed beneath a pale violet sky.

If the Bhandecki had done any damage to the planet's surface, it wasn't immediately apparent, so Killian was feeling cautiously optimistic as he and Seph left the ship and took their first breaths of crisp, cool Daraghn air.

But no sooner did his foot hit the landing pad than the ground suddenly heaved beneath them, causing the ship to groan in protest.

Killian nearly lost his balance and was about to drag himself back up the ramp and attempt to take off when a skimmer raced into view. It slewed to a stop beside the ship, and two people jumped out—a slender blonde woman and a much taller dark-haired man wearing combat armor and carrying a laser rifle.

"It's ok," the woman shouted, "just give me a second!"

She ran to the edge of the landing pad, placed her bare hands on the ground, and shut her eyes.

Killian wasn't sure what to make of her odd behavior, but Seph seemed undisturbed. She ignored the tremors, smiled, and approached the man as if they knew each other.

"Hey, Rybeck," she said, and shook his offered hand.

His answering smile was warm and genuine. "Good to see you, Seph, even if the circumstances are less than ideal. How long did you end up staying on Concord?"

She laughed. "That is a very long, very complicated story, and you probably wouldn't believe more than half of it."

The ground finally stopped shaking, and as the tremors eased, the blonde woman rose to her feet and approached Killian with a serene smile. "I think Daragh is willing to accept you now, as long as you behave yourselves." She winked. "Welcome. I'm guessing you must be Killian Avalar."

"I am," he admitted. "But how did you know?"

"Daragh told me." She reached up and collected her hair into a loose tail before continuing. "She said you aren't the same as the rest of us, and your name was on that message about the Bhandecki, so I made the connection. Thank you for that, by the way. I don't think any of us would still be here if you hadn't reached out when you did."

Killian experienced an unwelcome stab of shame. That had technically been none of his doing. If he hadn't listened to Callista…

Thankfully, Emma interrupted his thoughts. "So you said you're here for the rest of my message."

He nodded. "It cut off before the end. We were hoping you might have information that can help us, because otherwise, we're out of ideas. The fleet that just left here is only hours from attacking Earth."

Emma blanched. "And have you managed to prepare the shield you mentioned?"

"It's hopefully being deployed as we speak, but even if it works, we have no way to evict them from Earth's system. We've tried missiles, and they work to a point, but there just aren't enough pilots with the necessary skills. Not to mention…" he paused as the ground began to rumble underfoot once more.

"Go ahead," Emma encouraged. "It's fine."

"I'd rather not kill the fireworms if I don't have to."

The rumbling stopped abruptly, and Emma began to laugh.

"Daragh approves of your reluctance," she told him.

He couldn't help glancing around nervously. "And the planet just *told* you this? How?"

"I've gotten rather good at communicating with her." She glanced over at her companion, who appeared relaxed but was clearly keeping a close eye on the newcomers. "And we can usually tell whether she likes someone or not."

Killian took a deep breath and tried not to show how uneasy that made him. "Look, we really don't have time to spare. What can you tell us about how to deal with the fireworms?"

Emma bit her lip. "It's probably not as simple a solution as you're hoping. The only way we've managed to make contact is through amplified gamma waves of a hundred and twenty hertz or higher. Easy for Daragh, not so much for the average human."

"What does that mean for someone who has no idea what you're talking about?"

"Sorry," Emma apologized. "Essentially, you'll need someone with both a significant mental talent and some degree of serious psionic training."

"Is that a problem?"

"It means," she said with a wince, "under the circumstances, I'm not sure how you might go about finding candidates. Even at our institute, very few are capable of this. If you had enough time, you could test, identify, and train them, but if Earth already under attack, the stress in the general population is probably too high for you to obtain accurate test results."

Killian looked from Emma to her companion. "So that's it then? There's no hope?"

"No," she said firmly. "There's always hope. And you're here, which means there's definitely a chance that we can help you."

Her gaze shot to the tall, dark-haired man, one eyebrow quirked as if she were asking a question. "Devan?"

"Only if there's no other way," he said.

Emma nodded and turned to Killian.

"How much room do you have on your ship?"

TWENTY-ONE

OVER THE NEXT EIGHT HOURS, Callista decided there was such a thing as too much adrenaline.

By the time her plan was finally put into action, she was exhausted and flying on fumes, but there was so much left to do. So much only she could be responsible for.

Her first stop had been the Canyon.

To deploy Killian's engineered aerial microbes, they would need pilots—and lots of them—with no political agendas. Phillip had managed to convene a meeting with the other Conclave members, but talking them out of ships when they were facing the immediate threat of the Bhandecki had proven a losing battle. None of them wanted to risk leaving their own territory unprotected.

Fortunately, there were other resources, and when Diamondback sent out the call, every underground racer in Haven Two showed up to answer it. Only a few had access to their own ships, but Callista still had the keys to her grandfather's secret war fleet —over a hundred space-capable small craft and the fuel required to fly them.

It still took too long—everything took time they didn't have—but by the time the Bhandecki fleet was within two hours of Earth, Callista and her motley group of pilots were in the air.

It was the most stressful race of her career, even though there were no obstacles, no course limits, and no spectators. No time to beat, no prize to win—no prize except survival.

They flew as fast as they could without spreading their payload too thin, and still, the time was too short. The Bhandecki horde came nearer and nearer, and as the glowing red mass of their numbers grew ever brighter, Callista began to doubt everything.

What if this didn't work? What if the engineered microbes did nothing to stop the fireworms? Would she have to watch as Earth's cities fell, melted to slag by the fireworms' potent chemical weapons?

They had no choice now but to trust Killian's word. No choice but to keep moving forward and hope that each piece of their desperate plan would play out as intended.

As she deployed the last of the bioengineered microbes in her ship's canisters, Callista also found herself worrying and wondering about more than just Earth. Had Killian and Seph made it to Daragh? Had they found a way to eventually defeat the Bhandecki? Or did all of them—on every human planet—face a slow death as the invaders simply waited them out?

She felt like crying from sheer exhaustion, but at last, the task was complete. Callista landed her ship, bumped shoulders with the other pilots, and then joined the rest of Earth as they held their breath and waited.

Waited for the enemy to appear.

Waited to find out if what they'd accomplished would be enough.

SHE PROBABLY SHOULD HAVE TRIED to sleep, but sleep refused to come. Her tiny fleet had parked themselves outside Haven Two to refuel, check their systems, and wonder when they might be called on again. Callista had returned to the cockpit of her ship to wait and watch reports on the viewscreen when the first of the fireworms reached the outer limits of the atmosphere.

Vids from around the world began streaming in, reporting panicked crowds, riots, and even a few celebrations, from those who believed the alien fleet had come to liberate Earth from its oppressors.

For the first few hours, she was able to view the global satellite feeds, watching in horrified awe as the worms spread out, encircling the planet in a deadly net. But one by one, the satellites began to go dark—the Bhandecki were already destroying whatever technology they encountered. How would Earth even know if the shield was working once those were gone?

Tapping her wrist comm, she called her brother and transferred the connection to her ship's console. "What does Lindmark have in the way of eyes out there?"

Phillip looked exhausted, and from the bustle in the background, his work was nowhere near done. "The worms are taking potshots at satellites as soon as they find them, but we still have a few left. And we have a handful of drones from Rill. She sent them into the upper atmosphere and claims the Bhandecki won't be able to see them. Why?"

"Do we have a count yet? Any idea how many fireworms there are and of what type?"

He paused. "I don't know. Why?"

"Because from what I've seen so far, there aren't a lot of alphas with the fleet…"

A voice from the background intruded on the call. "Sir, one of the drones picked up a fireworm that's already entered the middle atmosphere!"

Phillip's face went granite-hard. "Does it appear to be changing course or slowing down?"

The woman moved to stand beside him, eyes glued to the screen in front of her. "It's… sir, it's… I don't have a word. It's deflating?"

Phillip's lips thinned, and his eyes narrowed as he watched. "I'm patching this through to your screen," he told Callista. "Tell me if this is what I think it is."

The footage appeared a few seconds later, and Callista watched in awe as the tubular shape of the fireworm seemed to collapse in front of her eyes. From a graceful, sinuous form sailing smoothly through the atmosphere, it seemed to melt and grow limp until it was little more than a lumpy, barely contained sack.

"Yes!" She punched the air in victory and relief. "Killian said the microbes disrupt their physical stability! The shield must be working!"

No longer proceeding under its own power, the worm suddenly began to drop and passed out of range of whatever drone had been tracking it.

"We need eyes back on it!" Callista demanded urgently. "Where is it going to fall? We need to know if it's going to hit in a populated area!"

"I'm on it," Phillip said tersely.

For a tense few minutes, Callista waited.

"It's breaking up," he said finally. "If anything is left, it should fall into the ocean."

She breathed a sigh of relief.

"I'm receiving reports of this happening in six... no, eight... eleven other places," he told her. "And I've asked the other Conclave heads to keep radar active to watch for falling debris."

If only this was the worst they had to watch out for. If only the threat could end here. But did she even dare hope for that?

Did she dare believe that by the time Killian and Seph returned, there would be no more need for the information they sought? No need to take the battle out beyond the microbe-seeded atmosphere?

Callista settled back in her seat and listened to the background chatter in Phillip's command center—mostly more reports of fireworms braving the atmosphere and ending up as clusters of burning debris chunks, leaving blazing trails across the sky.

"We have another one coming through the shield!"

This time the voice sounded different. Panicked.

"It came in too fast. It's not changing. It's holding together!"

Callista sat bolt upright and stared at her screen.

"Phillip?"

"I'm on it," he said grimly. Then, "She's right, dammit. I think the difference is in how fast it hit the middle layers of the atmosphere. Instead of approaching obliquely, it punched straight through. It's headed into Hastings territory!"

"Alert Hastings!" Phillip barked towards someone off-screen. "Give them coordinates and trajectory in case they don't have eyes on it yet."

"Should we scramble the ships in case they request aid?" Callista's hand was already poised to activate her ship's thrusters.

"So far, every one of them has declined to cooperate," Phillip said bitterly. "If I send ships, they'll probably claim I'm trying to take their territory by force and attack us instead of the Bhandecki. We're going to have to wait."

And so they waited.

Finally, unable to stand not knowing, Callista commed Jocasta. "What's happening?" she asked urgently. "Do you have any intel? Did it break through?"

The older woman's face was drawn and pale. "It did," she said. "I haven't seen any of the damage yet, but it ended up targeting a manufacturing district."

Oh gods, no. "Was it deliberate? And was it able to maneuver in the lower atmosphere?"

"We don't know yet."

Callista had to deliberately and forcefully uncurl her fingers from the edge of the console. Unclench her teeth. Take deep, steady breaths. She needed to be out there, doing something.

Without warning, new vid footage flashed onto her screen.

Footage from Hastings.

As the massive bulk of the fireworm emerged from the clouds, people on the ground began to scream and run. But it was too late. The frills hung limp, and the worm appeared unable to change its trajectory. As it approached the ground, its leading end began to glow red. A circular opening appeared, and the fireworm spewed its caustic mist ahead of it just before crashing into the stacks of a polycrete manufacturing facility.

From the way the vid was shaking, the effect must have been similar to an earthquake. Flames and debris shot skyward, and the stacks collapsed as if in slow motion. Smoke began to billow, alarms began to wail, and then the footage suddenly cut off.

"Jocasta?"

"That's all I've been able to get," she said, her voice hollow and haunted. "If it had hit a more populated area…"

Callista swallowed the bitter taste of failure. The shield had worked, but only in part. And there were still thousands of fire-worms waiting just beyond the atmosphere. What if the Bhan-decki decided to use them as living bombs? They wouldn't be able to wipe out humanity completely, but the loss of life would be unimaginable.

And yet, what were their options?

She could take her pilots up, and they could attempt to take a few fireworms out with missiles before they had a chance to ram the atmosphere. But realistically, how many could they take down?

Not enough.

She thought she knew what helplessness felt like, but she'd been so wrong. No matter how bad things got, she'd always been able to find a way around the problem. Even when dealing with her mother and her grandfather, she'd always had resources, abil-ities, and new paths she could take. So many options had been open to her because of who she was and where she'd been born.

Now, for perhaps the first time in her life, she was utterly powerless. She faced an enemy beyond her abilities or her control and knew that even her utmost effort would not be enough. No amount of money, power, or privilege could change what was happening.

In hindsight, she probably owed Killian an apology. She'd been too hard on him, back when she'd confronted him about his unwillingness to help where he saw no chance of success. She might not have been wrong, but she also had not fully understood.

Now, there was only one thing she could still do, and it didn't feel like action. But in a moment of darkness, it was a tiny point of light, so she seized it and hung on.

All she had left was trust. Hope. A firm belief that Killian and Seph were still out there, still looking for answers.

She couldn't win this on her own, but she could prepare the way, hold off the destruction as long as possible, and believe that they would come through in time.

"Phillip?"

His worried face appeared on her screen. "I can sense you planning something," he said.

"I saw the footage from Hastings."

His face seemed to sag and age by ten years right in front of her. "I don't know how we can stop them. If all they have to do is hit the shield head-on, and they decide to crash half their fleet into Earth…"

"I'm going up there," she said.

"No." He bent over the screen and stared straight into her eyes. "That's a death wish, and you know it."

"Phillip, I've thought this through. If they keep sending worms through the shield, we're going to lose millions of lives. I know we can't fully stop them, but we may be able to distract them."

"Until when?" he demanded. "Until we lose every pilot and every ship we have?"

"What good are we if we just sit here?" she cried. "I know we can't win this, Phillip. Believe me, I know. All I can do now is try not to lose. And I can hope that…"

She couldn't say it.

"Hope that they come back." Phillip was fighting for that hope just as surely as she was.

The woman he loved was out there somewhere on the other side of that fleet, and he could do nothing to help her.

"Killian and Seph are the best chance we have now, so anything we can do to prepare for them to come back is a risk I'm willing to take."

Phillip's blue eyes bored into hers. "Before you do this, I need you to understand: you are not expendable."

"I'm not planning on any dramatic sacrifices," she said, smiling a little at his fierce expression. "But I am planning to get our people home safely."

His chin dropped, his eyes closed, and she watched as he fought with some deeply ingrained impulse. To protect her? Surely not. Lindens didn't care about one another that way.

At least, the Lindens of the past had never seen it as a virtue.

But these Lindens?

"I love you, too," she said softly.

His eyes flew open. "You…"

She shrugged. "It's okay if you need a little time to get used to it. I just decided I wasn't going to fly out of here without saying it."

"Then prove it by coming home in one piece," he responded gruffly.

"Will do, brother dear." She threw him a mock salute. "Now, I need you to do your thing and get on a call with the rest of the Conclave. Tell them what's happening. Let them know I'm taking up a force in an attempt to confuse and distract the enemy. If they want to help, it would be better to coordinate an attack in all sectors at once, but if not, at least convince them not to shoot at me or my pilots. Offer them any spare missiles we have if it will tempt them to mount a defense. And give them a heads up that Killian and Seph may be returning. If we give them some hope, maybe they'll decide it's worth working together to end this thing."

"Done," he said, locking eyes with her once more. "Be safe. I don't want to be the one to tell Killian you didn't make it home."

It was her turn to look startled.

"And don't pretend you don't know what I mean. I've seen that confused look you get whenever he's in the same room."

For probably the first time since she was ten years old, Callista Linden felt the heat of a blush spread across her cheeks.

"Aren't you going to tell me I could do better?" she demanded, hoping to disguise her embarrassment. "Threaten to beat him up if he looks at me the wrong way?"

A tiny smile pulled at her brother's lips. "The two of you are the only people I know who can keep up with each other. Besides, I have full confidence in your ability to beat him up for yourself."

"Seph has trained you well," she teased.

"You have no idea. But if you ever see her with a tray full of beer mugs? Duck."

Callista's lips quirked, even as tears threatened. She wished they'd had more time. This version of her brother was one she would have liked to call a friend. "I'm headed out," she said, blinking fiercely and refusing to let him see her cry. "Hold things together for me, will you?"

He nodded. "I'll see what I can do to find you a few more pilots."

She hit the button to end the transmission and immediately sent out a brief message to the waiting pilots.

"This is Diamondback, calling everyone with a ship that can still fly. We're waiting on news from Daragh, but in the meantime, the Bhandecki have found a way to break through the shield. They may begin using individual fireworms to dive-bomb the planet, and as far as I'm concerned, that's unacceptable. We have one task—target any worms that penetrate the shield and use missiles to break them up before they can activate their weaponry or hit the ground.

"We'll need to coordinate attacks, so I'm designating a handful of you as flight leaders. Ten ships per flight. We'll be heading to base for our payloads, but we'll only have two missiles per ship, per sortie, so use your resources wisely."

"How much ground are we covering?" one of the pilots asked.

"For now, we can only cover Lindmark's territory. The other Corporations haven't given us permission to enter their airspace. I'm hoping they'll join our efforts, but for now, it's just us. Flight leaders, you'll be put in touch with one of my people who will assign you a sector and coordinate our efforts from the ground. Once you've fired both missiles, return to base and reload. At least until we run out of ammo. Any questions?"

"Just one," a particularly cheeky-sounding pilot broke in. "Can I buzz the tower?"

Callista chuckled. "After we win, we'll all buzz Lindmark Tower together. Now, if you don't have anything better to ask, let's get up there. No heroics. Just try to hold things together until the cavalry gets here."

————

MINUTES BECAME HOURS. Hours felt like years. The shield took out hundreds of fireworms, but there were still hundreds more, and the Bhandecki seemed determined to achieve their goals by any means necessary.

The alpha worms hung well back from the outer edges of the

atmosphere, like command ships directing their fleet into battle. And more often than Earth's defenders could counter, one of their fleet would break through.

Despite the other corporations' deployment of surface-to-air missiles, three worms had already crashed in Hastings after doing tremendous damage. Two had done the same in Olaje. Sarat had borne the brunt of the attack, with five direct hits, two of them in the middle of their capital city.

Callista heard the reports dimly through her aural implant, but she couldn't spare enough focus to mourn the losses. The only reason no fireworms had reached the ground in Lindmark territory was her team's remarkable skill and resilience. They'd destroyed eight worms before they could enter the troposphere, reducing them to formless chunks that burned as they fell.

But she'd lost twelve ships, and they were almost out of missiles. And beyond the shield, the bulk of the Bhandecki fleet still waited.

The only bright spot was that Phillip had finally convinced the rest of the Conclave to join forces. All around the globe, teams of pilots had taken to the air, following the example of Callista's crew. Because Rill's drones were now the sole remaining source of intelligence on the invaders, Lindmark was able to run point, and Priya had stepped up to coordinate their efforts. She now directed all of Earth's defenses, finally meeting a challenge worthy of her formidable talents.

Callista hadn't slept in who knew how long. Her eyes burned, and every muscle in her body ached from the tension of being locked in her cockpit for so many hours.

But she couldn't stop. Couldn't quit. She knew they couldn't win, but if they could just hold out one more minute. One more hour. They could buy one more moment of hope that Killian might still pull off the impossible.

"Shield break in Sector Twelve! Three coming through together!" The message blared through her aural implant, and she reacted automatically, changing course and accelerating towards the breach.

Sector Twelve. Half of their flight was on the ground, refueling and reloading. But Markheim was in Sector Twelve. Phillip was in Sector Twelve. Phillip, Jocasta, Priya, Alli, Xavier, and millions of others.

She had to stop them. There was no other option.

How many missiles did they have? She had one. Two of her flight had two each. Four others had one. Would it be enough?

Only if none of them missed.

Only if they could get there fast enough.

Her comm suddenly blared with static.

"Calling anyone at all! This is Persephone Katsaros. We are approaching Earth, so whatever you do, don't shoot us by accident! If anyone can hear us, we made it back, but it looks like we're going to need an escort if we can get one."

Callista's breath left her.

For one eternal moment of agonizing hope, she froze at her ship's controls.

"*Seph?*" Had she imagined it, or had they really made it through?

"Callista!" This time it was Killian. He sounded almost frantic. Desperate. Worried. And she'd never been so relieved to hear his voice.

"You really made it. Did you find a way? Can we beat these things?" She almost couldn't get the words out between gasping, sobbing breaths of pure relief.

"We brought Emma back with us. She's going to try to free the alphas, but we're going to have to get close enough."

"How close?" Dread shot through Callista's limbs at the memory of their last fight. She wasn't sure she was ready to get that close to an alpha fireworm again. Last time she'd been fresh. Full of energy and determination. How could she fly on that razor edge when exhaustion was threatening to overwhelm her?

"We don't know." Killian's voice was still tight with worry. "She says last time she was just an observer, and Daragh did most of the work. We're just going to have to try it."

"Understood. How much time do we have?"

"I don't think it'll be long before they spot us."

She was going to have to split her forces. And she had seconds in which to make the right decision.

How many to protect Markheim, where millions of lives were at stake?

How many to escort Killian, Seph, and Emma, who might hold the key to the survival of everyone else on Earth?

She opened a channel—ready to make the gut-wrenching call—when a new voice came crackling over her comm.

"Callista, call off your pilots and get out there to protect the captain. I've got Markheim." The woman sounded determined and so very familiar...

"*Dinah?*"

"Rill is with me, and we've got the *Fancy* in the air," she said, sounding almost bored. "We'll take care of the three worms in Sector Twelve."

The *Fancy* was in the air? But *how*? And how could it possibly be capable of maneuvering?

"Don't you dare ram them!" Callista snapped.

"We weren't planning on it," Dinah replied, sounding almost

sarcastic. "But we're closer than you, and I've made the necessary repairs. Besides, I think the *Fancy* deserves another shot at these bastards."

Mind racing, Callista tagged two of her pilots. "I'm sending you backup," she said flatly. "Just in case. Fly safe and try not to crash again, or Killian won't ever forgive either of us."

"I've been flying longer than you've been alive, kiddo, so just trust me when I say we've got this," Dinah said dryly. "Now go."

Heart in her throat, praying she'd made the right call, Callista turned her ship skyward and opened a channel to the remainder of her tiny fleet.

They'd already done the impossible, and now it was time for one last request.

"I know we're almost out of ammo," she said. "I know we're all at the end of our rope. But we have one last chance to win this thing for good. I don't have time to explain, but a ship has just entered the system, out past the Bhandecki fleet. They need to get in close to an alpha worm without taking damage. That means they're going to need a distraction. Anyone feeling crazy enough to join me, tag my signal and follow my drive trail—I'm about to head out there and see if I can make the Bhandecki regret their little side trip to Earth."

One at a time, the tiny lights on her sensors flashed gold as each pilot tagged in. So many... When the lights finally stopped flashing, aside from the two still racing towards Markheim, every single one had volunteered to follow her into hell.

A fresh surge of adrenaline raced down Callista's limbs and curled the corners of her lips into a fierce smile.

"Let's do this."

TWENTY-TWO

ONE WORD HAD ALMOST UNDONE him.

It didn't even matter what she'd said—the sound of Callista's voice had cracked through the shell around Killian's heart and let him breathe again.

She was alive, and Earth's defenses were holding.

But as they came nearer and nearer to the Bhandecki blockade of Earth, every fresh report that reached them brought new horrors.

The shield had only been partially effective, and in the wake of this discovery, only a few brave pilots now stood between Earth's billions and utter destruction.

He could hear exhaustion when Callista asked how much time was left. Earth's defenders were near the breaking point, and now it was up to this one, last-ditch effort to turn the tide.

Killian turned to Emma, who sat behind him—quiet and almost unnaturally serene as she gazed out the forward viewscreen at the Bhandecki fleet.

"Anything yet?" he asked.

She shook her head. "But I think we'll be close enough soon. I'll go back and talk to Daragh to see if she'll be able to help."

The blonde woman shrugged off her flight harness and made her way out of the cockpit towards the cargo bay. She was followed by the protective bulk of Devan, who shot Killian a warning look as if to say he'd better get them all out of this alive.

It wasn't as if he had any plans to die today. He was going to live. Callista, too, was going to survive. And when it was all over, he was going to find her, kiss her again, and then fly away with her until he could figure out why and how she'd become so damned important.

Devan popped his head back in. "Emma says she's located the fleet leader. It's hanging back, almost by itself, but it's the largest one. If you can get in closer, she'll try to make contact."

He disappeared again, back to the cargo hold, where, in an unassuming tub of dirt, a slender sapling spread its branches across the width of the bay. An offshoot of Daragh herself, the planet had offered it before they departed, and Emma hoped it would enable her to reach farther with her psionic abilities.

From the copilot's chair, Seph offered him a tight smile and buckled her flight harness. "Guess we won't know until we dive in," she said.

Killian gritted his teeth, increased power to the drives, and headed for the biggest fireworm he could find.

It went against every instinct he had to approach the imposing bulk of the alpha worm with no weapons—no plan of attack or defense. And the closer he came, the harder it grew to hold course.

The thing was possibly twice the size of the one he'd fought with Callista. It dwarfed his tiny ship, and Killian knew he would probably have nightmares of the moment he realized he could have flown right into one of the structures that crowned its gargantuan bulk. He doubted his ship would have even scraped a fin.

Closer. He had to get closer, but not too close…

Beneath a gently rippling frill, a familiar green glow appeared, growing gradually brighter as they approached. Killian swore under his breath and changed course, darting up and away from the danger.

"I can't get much closer," he called back towards the cargo bay. "Not without risking a hit, and we don't have enough shielding to survive that."

No answer.

He glanced at Seph. "Take the helm for a minute," he said, before stepping through the door and into the cargo bay.

Devan knelt on the floor near the tree, Emma in his arms. Her eyes were closed, her face was pinched, and one slender hand rested lightly on the sapling's trunk.

"Is she…"

Devan shot him a hard look. "I don't know," he ground out. "But if she doesn't come back soon, I'm pulling her out."

Emma's eyes suddenly flashed open, focused on something far beyond the ship's bay.

"Old…" she gasped out. "So old. Tired. Hurts."

Devan held her closer. "Don't go too far!"

Killian could see his fear for her in the way his jaw clenched and his eyes went a little too wide.

Her body suddenly stiffened. "It wants… No. Can't. Closer!"

Killian dashed back to the cockpit.

He was going to have to risk the fireworm's defenses, or this might all be for nothing.

With a softly muttered curse, he reversed course and increased speed, wondering whether they could survive long enough for Callista and her pilots to back them up.

This time, when the portals beneath the fireworm's frill began to glow, he angled the ship to fly lengthwise along its body, keeping just far enough away…

The portals opened and belched a familiar glowing mist, but instead of widening the distance, he flew faster. Faster than the cloud could expand, closer and closer to the worm's scarred grey body…

Suddenly he heard a cry from behind him.

"Emma!"

His heart stopped. Seph bolted from her chair towards the cargo bay, only to stop in the doorway.

He didn't dare look. He was too close to colliding with their target. A half-second later, they flashed past the fireworm's tapered end, expecting to see it glow red as it prepared to fire on its assailant.

But instead…

"It's done."

His head whipped around. Emma was in the doorway, leaning heavily against Devan. A trickle of blood ran from her nose, but she nodded in response to his incredulous stare.

"It's free," she said simply, an exhausted smile curving her lips. "I was able to break through the conditioning and show it a different future. It's been held captive for so many centuries, I don't know what it will do, but it's free to choose for itself."

It was a relief, but only a partial one. How could any of them guess what a creature that old—enslaved for who knew how many years—might choose given the chance?

His comm buzzed.

"We're on our way," Callista reported, "but something isn't right here." A burst of static disrupted her transmission. "Half the fleet is turning away from Earth. A few of the worms are"—her words sounded incredulous—"Killian, they're *firing on each other*!"

Emma had done it. She'd actually done it.

"That was Emma," he told Callista, blinking back tears as his hands began to shake in the aftermath of too much adrenaline. The relief was almost too strong to contain, and he struggled not to simply collapse on the spot. "She set one of the alphas free. All of the fireworms it's been controlling must be free now as well."

"It worked." She was clearly stunned. "I can't believe it actually worked. That means…"

The transmission suddenly cut off.

"Callista?" He tried the ship's comm, and then his personal comm. Nothing.

"Seph, can you locate her ship?" He knew he sounded frantic, and he didn't care.

"She's still out there," Seph reported, "but the Bhandecki fleet…"

She looked up at him, eyes wide. "They aren't just turning away from Earth," she said. "They're headed straight for us."

"Well, that's just ducky," he muttered, scanning the sensors and telling himself he couldn't afford to go running off to make sure Callista was okay. He had to stick to the plan. Finish the course.

So he turned to Emma and Devan. "In your experience, what happens next? Do we run for it and hope they chase us? Or will they just return to bombarding Earth?"

The two shared a glance that seemed to say far more than any words could. Devan looked grim but resolute, and Emma… She appeared almost apologetic.

"They may continue to fight amongst themselves," Emma said, "but I believe they will also try to either recapture or destroy their flagship. If they can do so, there may be a risk that they will once again gain control over the smaller worms and resume the attack. We need to continue on."

"I was afraid you'd say that," he muttered, turning back to his console. "Do you have a priority target, or are we just aiming for any alpha we can find?"

Emma's eyes widened as sensors indicated the fleet beginning to converge on their position.

"Maybe we should run first."

His comm produced a sudden burst of static.

"Sorry we're late!" It was Callista! She sounded shaken, her voice wavering with some strong emotion. "We just lost... Gods, Killian, we lost half a dozen pilots. One of the worms just exploded, and there was no time to get out of the way. It burned everything."

He wanted to say something to comfort her, but there was no time.

"Are you all right? Is your ship intact?"

"I'm good," she said. "And we're almost to your coordinates. Tell us where you want to go, and we'll do what we can to give you an escort."

There! Near the glowing red dots of the fireworms, his sensors now showed smaller golden sparks, darting alongside their enemies, making their way swiftly towards Killian's position.

"Emma?" He motioned her forward and pointed to the screen. "Tell me which one you want."

Her head turned slightly to the side as she watched the

sensors. "I think if I'm seeing the patterns correctly…" She pointed to a single red dot, and Killing tagged it.

"Sending you our destination," he reported to Callista. "We need to get close and not be interrupted, so the clearest path we can get would be helpful. Just as long as you can do it safely! Don't risk anyone if you don't have to. We can always come back for another run."

"Understood."

He hoped she really did understand. He hoped she knew what it would do to him if she died. But he'd never told her, and just as Phillip had warned, that failure would haunt him if he never got another chance.

Did he dare say it now, in the heat of a life or death battle, when she might believe it was only spoken in the stress of the moment?

"Callista?"

"Still here."

"I need you to know—there's no one I'd rather have at my back." He willed her to hear what he was really saying. What those words actually meant to him. "And even if I never get to return home… you *will*, do you hear me?"

He heard a tiny gasp from Seph but ignored it.

"We're all going home today," Callista replied fiercely. "All of us, Killian. So don't even think about giving up."

"I'm not," he said, allowing himself a momentary smirk. "I'm just here to remind you that Callista Linden doesn't believe in the impossible."

"Damn right," she responded. "Ready when you are, pirate."

He turned to his passengers. "Strap in, boys and girls. This is probably going to get a little bumpy."

———

THEY WERE GOING to have to fly faster this time. Watch out for particulate clouds, and dodge the worms already headed straight for them. Hope their escort could distract some of their new admirers long enough to locate Emma's next target.

Locking on to the alpha worm she'd indicated, Killian revved the drive and shot forward, not away from the fleet, but straight for the heart of it.

It should have been Dinah, or even Rill at the helm, but he was all they had, and so he employed every trick he'd ever learned, every skill at his disposal. Twice, they narrowly avoided a collision with fireworms attempting to turn to intercept them. Once, he nearly flew through the path of a worm's caustic breath.

But only a handful of seconds later, the sleek shapes of the Lindmark fighter craft fell into position all around them, above and below—a deadly escort to their destination.

And somehow, Callista was everywhere at once. She seemed to predict the enemy fleet's movements while simultaneously avoiding catastrophe—seeing traps before they could form and directing her pilots to fire their last remaining missiles to clear the road.

Killian knew she died a little each time she lost a pilot. Three of the golden sparks were gone by the time they approached Emma's target, and he hurt for the scars Callista would carry away from this.

But he held steady, because that was his task.

After all those years of lurking, watching, and learning how to be human... All that time, waiting for his chance to do what he'd been sent to do...

All of it had come down to this—this moment, where a single

twitch in the wrong direction could spell disaster, not just for his ship but for every human on Earth.

He'd always thought he would one day bear responsibility for the lives and deaths of his people. He'd just never dreamed that his people would be human.

Because somehow, between his first bitter insistence that he didn't care about the fate of humanity and this moment of fire and fury, he'd taken a handful of irreplaceable humans for his own.

"She's got it," Seph called from her station in the doorway at the rear of the cockpit. "She's connected, so try to hold your distance."

The alpha loomed before him—smaller, younger, and more maneuverable than the last. Killian dodged as it turned and tried to maintain position near the front, but not close enough to be in range of its primary weapon.

"Getting a report from Phillip," Seph murmured, glancing at her wrist comm, her eyes wide with awe. "He says three other alphas have engaged the freed one. They're fighting each other! And no worms are currently even testing the shield!"

It was working.

For the first time in recorded history, the Bhandecki were losing a fight.

Exultation knifed through him, lending him a fresh surge of focus.

"Done!" Emma didn't sound nearly as tired after this one. "I'd like to try for one more."

Killian didn't need to see to know that Devan was probably scowling. But like Phillip, the former soldier respected the strength of the woman he loved. He would stand beside her no matter what she decided.

If they survived the day, would Callista allow him to do the same for her?

Searching his sensors, he tagged an alpha in an area that appeared to be less crowded.

"One more," he told Callista, and sent her the tag. "Then I think Emma's going to need a rest."

"It may be enough," Callista assured him, "and even if it's not, she's done miracles already. We'll clear the road and then escort you all home."

The jump-ship arrowed towards its target, once more taking up position near the head, matching the worm's trajectory as Emma reached out to make contact.

"Hold on!" Callista's voice blared from the comm, sounding a little tense. "We've got a tight formation coming in behind you. Going to try to head them off."

The bright golden sparks of the fighters split apart and aimed for the tight knot of red approaching swiftly from aft. The alpha suddenly changed direction, and Killian had to fight to maintain a steady distance.

"She's in," Seph reported. "Just a bit longer."

Killian never knew how the smaller worm escaped his notice. But when he looked up briefly from the controls, it was there in the viewscreen, on a collision course and not slowing down.

The Bhandecki had recognized the threat and were planning to ram them head-on.

"I can't hold," he barked.

"You can!" Callista responded. "I see it. We'll head it off. I've got one missile left."

The bright golden spark of her fighter veered around and accelerated towards the oncoming worm.

"Don't…"

309

He saw it with razor-edged clarity—each moment an eternity in which he couldn't move quickly enough, couldn't force the words of warning past his lips.

Callista fired her missile at the last second, pulled away, and shot past the front of the oncoming worm just as it spat a burning chemical cloud.

The leading edge of the burning cloud caught the trailing edge of her ship's fins.

Killian didn't remember screaming.

Didn't remember Seph grabbing his shoulders and begging him to hold on as the missile impacted and the fireworm twisted away from their path in its death throes.

He only remembered clinging to the controls of his ship. Trembling in agony as he held to his course, capable of only a single thought.

He couldn't let her die for nothing.

Every muscle in his body howled for him to go after her, to save the woman who'd made him want to truly live again, but if he went after her at the expense of losing this battle…

Whether she lived or died, she would never forgive him.

Earth's future meant far more to her than her own life, and if he wanted to be worthy of her, he could believe no less.

Even if he didn't know how to face any future that didn't have her in it.

The small, bright speck that was her ship plummeted towards the middle atmosphere and vanished as he sat, grim and frozen. The seconds passed. The battle raged on, but he could see and hear nothing but the task in front of him.

"Done!" Devan's voice was tense and almost angry. "Get us out of here. Emma needs a doctor."

Seph raced for the cargo hold, and Killian raced towards Earth.

He knew it was too late. He knew there was nothing they could do. He could only return Emma to Earth and hope.

Hope that Callista would once again accomplish the impossible. Hope for a miracle.

TWENTY-THREE

IT HAD BEEN A ROOKIE MISTAKE, and Callista acknowledged it with a morbid sort of humor as she fought her ship's systems to gain control.

She'd gone too many hours without sleep. The stress and exhaustion had finally caught up with her—that and her reluctance to delegate what she could do for herself.

Perhaps she should have sent another pilot, but she'd seen the threat, and she was the closest, so she reacted.

There were so many things she wished she could say to the people she loved before the end. So many things she should have said sooner. But it was too late for conversations. The receiver for her comm array had been located near the rear of the ship, so she suspected it was fried.

But she would transmit a few final messages anyway, hoping that someone, somewhere, might hear them. Or maybe just so she could feel more at peace.

"If anyone can hear me," she started, "this is Callista Linden. I'm transmitting my location and trajectory, but I won't have power much longer. Fireworm caught me, and I don't know if I'll survive re-entry. So, before my comm dies, Phillip, if you're listening, and this is goodbye, I forbid you to blame yourself. You're going to have a lot to do, and Seph is coming home, so you're not allowed to waste time moping.

"To everyone who has been a part of my team these past few years, I wish I could name you all, but I want you to know I'm so proud to have worked with you. Proud to have known you. Earth could ask for no greater warriors as it rebuilds after this victory."

She paused, wondering how to say this next part. For some reason, she'd started crying, and she didn't want him to hear her tears. Didn't want him to know how her hands trembled and her throat ached when she thought of everything they would never have a chance to say to one another.

"Killian, if you're out there, don't you dare give up, do you hear me? And don't you dare make this about you. I chose this. So let yourself remember today as a victory, not a loss. Take your people home. Take back the life you always wanted. I wish we'd had more time, but... you were always going to go home in the end. I don't think more time was ever going to be enough for me."

The controls were fighting her now, and the drive began to falter.

"I can't hold on course much longer. Catch you all on the other side."

She ended her transmission, took a deep breath, and let the tears fall as her ship entered a steep glide through the middle atmosphere.

There was a chance. There was always a chance. But in this case...

She knew it wasn't much of one. It seemed the impossible had finally caught up with her.

As her glide steepened, she tried using her thrusters to compensate, but there wasn't much left of them. The fireworm's caustic emissions would have eaten through much of the outer structure by now, and it was a miracle the hull had not yet been breached.

A sudden whine from her aural implant made her wince and clap a hand to the side of her head.

"Callista! You'd better be listening because I won't say this twice!"

It was Phillip. Phillip was fine. Markheim had survived. Even in the midst of her own fears, Callista sagged in grateful relief.

"You're not going to die today, do you hear me?" Phillip snapped. "So stop your whiny little pity party, get out of your seat, and open the compartment just inside the cockpit, near the floor. It's not easy to see, but it has a green handle, and there's a flight suit inside. Apparently, Grandpa wasn't a complete screw-up after all—he included at least one safety measure in these birds' design."

Heart pounding, Callista jumped up, just as the ship lurched beneath her. She stumbled, but grabbed at the back of her seat and pulled herself to the rear of the cockpit.

Sure enough, inside the tiny compartment was a flight suit with an emergency oxygen pack, a basic helmet and seal, and flight boots. Not as good as an escape pod, but enough, maybe, that she could survive a hull breach.

"I know you can't talk to me, so I'm going to walk you through this," Phillip continued. He now sounded calm. Steady as a rock. As if he did this sort of thing every day. "You're not going to jump if we can help it. You're going to stay with the ship. I want your wrist comm activated. It has a chip in it, and we'll be able to track you from here."

Callista began to laugh helplessly as she activated the comm.

"Xavier says you're welcome, by the way."

She couldn't exactly complain when she'd done the same to Killian.

Her ship was groaning now, between the forces exerted by the descent, the heat building against the hull, and the ongoing destruction caused by the fireworm's attack. She couldn't pull on the suit fast enough, and made quick work of sealing it to the helmet.

How high was she?

Still high, but falling fast. How long would her ship hold together?

A sharp cracking sound shot through the ship, and without warning, the bay depressurized. The cockpit automatically sealed itself, but it was only a matter of moments before the damage broke the seal.

"Now, you need to do anything you can to flatten out your trajectory. You're still about twenty miles up, which doesn't give us much time, so fall as slowly as you can, and hopefully, it'll give us enough time for a miracle. Dinah and Rill are on their way."

Dinah and Rill? In the *Fancy*? How was the *Fancy* even still flying? And even if they could catch up with her, what could they possibly do?

But this wasn't the time to lose hope. Callista dropped into the pilot's seat and hit every button she could find.

Landing thrusters, landing struts, deployed. Flashing red letters warned her that only two were functional and that she shouldn't attempt a landing. She almost laughed.

But nothing she tried seemed to do much. She was still falling. Still…

What in the name of all hells was that?

A ship appeared off her right fin, or what was left of her right fin.

At least, she thought it was a ship, but it was like nothing she'd ever seen. Where most ships were angular, this one had curves. Where fusion drives were bulky, obvious things, this one ran on a power source she couldn't see.

The ship had scars, but it flew with a grace Callista didn't believe she could have managed on her best day.

And as she gaped at it, almost forgetting her own predicament, her aural implant nudged her to switch channels.

"Callista." It was Dinah. Flying that impossible, alien ship. A ship that had to be the *Fancy*, but not a *Fancy* Callista had ever seen. "Don't ask questions, just trust me. Hold as steady as you can. We're going to clamp on to the top of your ship, and then we're going to pull you out. Got it?"

They were going to do *what*? How was that even possible?

No questions. Callista smothered her doubts and did as Dinah asked. Tried to hold steady as the strange ship moved to fly directly over her. Felt a jolt and then a distinct slowing.

"We don't have long," Dinah said. "Get your butt back to the cargo hold."

Callista scrambled out of her chair, took a precious few seconds to break the seal on the cockpit door, and pulled it open. Then her mouth dropped open as she saw what had become of her ship.

The rear half was in shreds and tatters, gaping open to the atmosphere. But above and to the sides, it had been seized in strange, metallic arms that gripped it almost as if they'd grown there.

And just in front of where Callista stood was a… a basket? A pod? She didn't even know how to describe it, but it was clearly meant to carry her.

"Just hang on," Dinah said in her ear. "And try not to fall off in shock, would you? I don't want to have to do this again."

Callista closed her mouth, climbed into the pod, and hung on... And then had to make a serious effort not to collapse in shock as the material of the pod curved around her, encasing her tightly at the same time that it moved upwards, carrying her with it. Once she rose above the wreckage of her ship, the arms that clamped the two vessels together released and flowed back towards the *Fancy's* hull, melting back into it as though they'd never been apart.

The pod continued to move until it carried her inside the *Fancy*, where it dropped her unceremoniously on the floor, reformed itself, and sealed the hole in the hull.

What. The. Heck. What had just happened?

She was inside. Safe.

It was more than her brain could take.

Clearly, she'd fallen into an alternate universe. Or perhaps she'd suffered a loss of oxygen, resulting in these hallucinations of being rescued by a magical, shapeshifting spaceship.

That must be it. She was still plummeting towards the Earth, dying from a lack of oxygen.

At least she'd hallucinated a comfortable floor to lie on while she died. Callista unsealed her helmet, pulled it off, laid it to the side, set her head back on the floor, and blacked out.

———

"ARE you waiting for someone to carry you?"

Callista's eyes opened to see Dinah looming over her, hands

on her hips, a disgusted look twisting her lips and putting a crease between her brows.

Callista considered the apparition and wondered about her own sanity.

"Am I dead?"

"Only if you want to be."

"What just happened?"

Dinah made a grumbling sound and folded her arms, looking resigned to an explanation. "You humans have such inflexible minds. What you're seeing now is the *Fancy* as she was meant to be. What she looked like when we first came through the Rift into human space. We had to disguise her over the years until she looked enough like a human ship not to cause comment. But under all the horrible, clunky hull plates and other nonsense, she was always still here. After the crash, there wasn't enough left of her disguise to matter, so I dug her out. Decided there was no point in hiding anymore."

"How did you…" Callista didn't even know how to say what she wanted to say. Maybe it was her inflexible human brain, or maybe it was her complete and utter exhaustion, or maybe she was just in shock. Likely, it was all of the above.

But Dinah seemed to hear her question anyway. "The *Fancy* uses nanotech, same as we do."

So it really *was* a shapeshifting spaceship. But was that really any weirder than anything else Callista had encountered up to this point?

Wait. "I thought you were almost out of nanotech," Callista recalled, though her memory was more than a little fuzzy. "I'm sure Killian said…"

"He did." Dinah's eyes met Callista's, and there was a world of meaning in their somber depths. "Don't make me regret my choice."

She'd used it.

She'd used it all.

To fix the ship so she could save Earth. Save Callista.

"Why?" Callista could not even begin to calculate the magnitude of such a sacrifice.

"Our captain gave up on himself a long time ago," Dinah said gruffly. "But he never gave up on getting the rest of us home. Even when we would have chosen to forget and stay human rather than continue to hope. So we owe him. And this is how we've chosen to repay that debt."

Her gaze was steely, and Callista gave a slight nod to acknowledge the weight of that confession.

"We're not saying *you* owe us anything, because you don't," Dinah went on. "All we're asking is that you don't let him quit on himself."

Callista sat up. "Where are we?"

"We just landed outside Haven Two. Which means we're about to be overrun by the anxious, the curious, and everyone in between."

"And the battle?"

"Half the Bhandecki fleet is still fighting each other, but the other half is on the run. At least one alpha has already rifted out, along with its crew."

The Bhandecki were leaving. Defeated.

They'd actually done it.

"Did... did the others make it back down?"

Dinah raised one eyebrow. "Why don't you get your ass off my floor and go find out?"

Callista wasn't sure she could move. As it turned out, miracles were exhausting. Almost as exhausting as facing the end of the world on no sleep, fighting a space battle with an alien fleet, and nearly dying as her spaceship tore itself apart.

But she got up anyway. Tucked her helmet under her arm and looked quizzically at Dinah. "How do we get out?"

Dinah laid her hand on the wall of the compartment. An opening appeared, and the hull material simply formed itself into a ramp leading to the ground.

A shapeshifting spaceship.

A world that would never be the same.

Once Callista set foot outside the *Fancy*, her life would never be the same either.

She had no idea what her immediate future was going to look like or where she might be needed. But she knew exactly where she wanted to be right then.

"Thanks for the save," she said, holding out a hand to Dinah. "I won't pretend I don't know what it cost, and I'm grateful."

The Wyrdane engineer accepted her hand and shook it once. "Then go out there and live. And try to fly smarter next time."

Callista grinned and took off running—down the ramp and into a bright new day.

———

IT TOOK time to fight through the crowd. To give and accept hugs, slap hands with her fellow pilots, and allow herself to feel the joy of being alive after all. But behind Callista's joy was urgency. She needed to see that Phillip was all right. That he and Seph had been reunited. That Emma Forester had survived her dedication to saving the planet that had nearly killed her once before.

But the streets of Haven Two were crowded, and eventually, Callista gave up on pushing her way through or finding a taxi. Instead, she found her way to the center of a green space, sat on the edge of the fountain, and watched the celebratory crowds with a tiny smile on her lips.

Her people would find her eventually, but in the meantime, she could just sit and appreciate that all of this was still here. That with all of its flaws, Earth would continue to turn. Humanity would continue to laugh and cry and fight and celebrate with one another and—hopefully—remember that it had taken all of them together to ensure their survival.

Setting her helmet aside, she looked up into the cloudless sky, closed her eyes, and took a few deep, cleansing breaths.

When she opened her eyes again, he was there—standing at the edge of the swirling crowd, only four paces away.

Killian looked as if he were seeing a ghost. His witty, sharp-edged veneer was stripped away, and all that was left was a man who'd walked through hell and wasn't sure whether his heart was still beating.

She wished she had some clever words to clear the look of anguish on his face.

"You told me not to give up," he said finally, each word formed so carefully, she knew he was fighting not to break. "You told me to get my people home and take back the life I always wanted. But the moment you said that, I knew that the life I wanted was falling away from me in an out-of-control spaceship, about to be lost forever."

He stepped forward, holding her gaze like the world would stop turning if he looked away. "You thought I was going home, but I've been looking for home since the moment I first crossed the Rift. It's not where I thought it was."

When he was inches away, he stopped, as if he were waiting for something.

"Where is it?" Callista finally asked, her voice hoarse with emotion.

"Where do you think?" Killian lifted one trembling hand and rested it, featherlight, against the curve of her cheek.

He loved her.

Maybe he hadn't said it with words, but she knew, and no matter what happened after this, no matter where they went or what life threw at them, she would always have this one moment of pure, uncomplicated joy.

Her daring, ridiculous, unpredictable, impossible pirate actually loved her.

He would always be closer to a villain than a saint, and that was just fine with her.

A smile dawned on her lips, and she couldn't have stopped it if she tried. "Oh, I don't know," she mused innocently. "Concord? Mars? Oh no, wait… is it Lindmark Tower?"

"Shut up," he said, laughing, and pulled her up to wrap his free arm around her waist. "I would tell you how I feel, but as I recall, you believe sometimes it's easier to just show."

He bent his head with a wicked smirk, and kissed her.

It was the kiss she'd been waiting for her entire life. More than just the meeting of lips, it was pure acceptance. They'd seen one another's darkness and relied on one another's strength. So it was without hesitation that she reached up, grasped his shirt, and pulled him closer, wanting nothing more than to remind herself that she was alive and he was hers.

"Callista," he murmured against her lips, once the kiss finally ended, "you said that more time was never going to be enough for you. But I'm hoping you'll be willing to reconsider."

"Hmmm." She pulled back and ran her fingers through the rumpled spikes of his hair. "I *am* a Linden," she said. "So I'm always up for a negotiation."

"What would you say to the offer of forever?"

"You have a lot to learn about bargaining," she told him with a grin. "What are you asking in return?"

"Only everything," he said seriously. "Every bit of you. No hiding, no pretending, no holding back. I want it all."

She thought she couldn't love him more, but she was wrong.

"It's a deal," she said, and pulled him down to kiss him again.

EPILOGUE

CALLISTA STOOD in the tall brown grass at the edge of the landing pad and attempted to conceal her anticipation.

Along with no small amount of worry.

Emma had assured her that everything would be fine. But even Emma had sounded a little skeptical when she first learned of Phillip Linden's intent to travel to Daragh.

Despite all her warnings, he'd remained adamant, and Callista couldn't help but feel proud of him. After the past year of righting Lindmark's wrongs and beginning a new chapter in the corporation's history, there was still one apology left for him to make, and he intended to make it in person.

The *Fancy* finally slipped from between the clouds, the Wyrdane jump-ship close behind, their sleek, graceful shapes dark against the violet Daraghn sky. Callista smiled as she watched the ships descend, more than ready to see a certain captain again. More than ready to begin this next chapter in their plans.

It had been a full year since the Bhandecki siege of Earth. A full year of rebuilding, forming alliances, and preparing for whatever the future might bring.

Callista had spent that year on Daragh. As it turned out, the intuition she'd relied on since childhood was more than just a series of hunches—she had a real psionic talent. After meeting Emma and understanding how the battle for Earth had been won, it hadn't taken long for her to decide the best way to make use of that talent. And while she didn't care for the delay, a year of training on Daragh was a small price to pay for what she hoped to someday accomplish.

Killian had spent his year ferrying passengers and cargo through the rift between Daragh and Earth. The Wyrdane ships were still the only ones capable of rift travel, so now that the two worlds were so closely connected, there was an enormous demand for his services.

But that—and so many other things—were about to change.

When the two ships finally came to rest on the landing pad, a small crowd awaited their arrival. Not all of them looked happy, and Callista could hardly blame them—the citizens of Daragh had no reason to welcome anyone with the Linden name. While most of them had grudgingly accepted Callista, she knew her brother would face a much more hostile reception.

The *Fancy's* boarding ramp extended, and three people made their way down it to the landing pad. First was Seph—smiling and waving at Emma and Devan, whose smiles slipped a little when they saw the man following behind her.

Phillip Linden.

As the four of them made their way towards one another, Callista's gaze strayed to the third person to emerge from the *Fancy*. It had only been three days, but she'd missed him anyway, so when he strolled up to her, slid an arm around her waist, and kissed her temple, she elbowed him quite firmly in the ribs.

"I missed you too," Killian said with a grin. "However have you managed during my eternal absence?"

"By recalling that I'm about to be stuck with you for a very, *very* long time," she rejoined sweetly. Then a little more seriously, "Are you ready for this? Or do you want to give it more time?"

He shook his head, brown eyes clear and unshadowed. "No. It's been long enough. I'm more than ready to deal with the past so we can move on, and Rill and Patrick are going to start chewing the bulkheads if I make them wait any longer. We've trained enough of Lindmark's people on the jump-ship, so I feel reasonably comfortable leaving them to make the run from Daragh to Earth."

Of the five Wyrdane who had participated in the battle for Earth, all of them had decided to return home. But that was where their paths diverged.

Rill and Patrick were unlikely to leave their homeworld again. They'd had more than enough of both humanity *and* adventure to last them even a Wyrdane lifetime.

Harvey and Dinah, on the other hand, had made the shocking announcement that they intended to go wherever the *Fancy* went, which meant Callista would be seeing a lot more of them in the future.

And Killian? He had some unfinished business with his brother. But after that…

Across the landing pad, Phillip and Seph came to within a few feet of Emma and Devan before they stopped, and it wouldn't have taken an empath to feel the tension radiating from the four of them.

"You can state your business now," Devan said brusquely,

moving ever so slightly to place himself between Emma and Phillip. "Before Daragh changes her mind about letting another Linden set foot on her surface."

"Two more Lindens," Seph murmured with a tiny smile, and both Emma and Devan turned to regard her with shock.

Callista was one of only a handful of people who'd been present at Phillip and Seph's private wedding ceremony on Earth. Their exchange of vows had been kept secret from nearly everyone, in part because they'd chosen to celebrate that profoundly personal moment out of the public eye. But Callista guessed there was another, possibly more important reason—they'd wanted to announce it on Daragh first.

"Yes," Seph said gently, "we're married. Sorry we didn't tell you, but we haven't actually told *anyone* yet. And I wasn't sure you would understand until we had a chance to see you in person. Phillip has changed," she went on, "and I love him, but I knew you would need to see evidence of that if you were going to believe me."

Devan's face proclaimed rather loudly that he would believe it when garms learned to fly, but Phillip didn't waver.

"I believe my first business is with Daragh herself," he said calmly. He held himself without fear or pretense, but after her year on Daragh, Callista could feel the lie.

He was nervous.

Because he wanted so badly to be forgiven. Wanted permission to care about these people he'd once hurt so deeply.

Callista could see Emma's surprise written on her mobile features.

"I will be happy to relay your message," the blonde woman said. "What is it you wish to say?"

"That she is owed an unimaginable debt by all of humanity

and by me in particular. That I regret the pain and suffering she has experienced due to our hubris and have no right to hope for her forgiveness. But while I do not ask for absolution, I do dare to ask for patience—while I work to undo what was done by the corporation and the family that bears my name."

Devan's forbidding expression did not change. "Don't you want to explain how you were lied to and misled and how none of it was your fault?"

Phillip's smile was wry. "Of course I do. But how would that help? The rot at the heart of Lindmark began because no one was willing to accept responsibility. Because all of us were a part of its corrupt system and chose to be blind to the pain it created. That corruption can only stop when someone says, 'Enough. I choose to be responsible. I choose to take a different path.'"

Devan's stare never wavered, but Emma cocked her head to the side and smiled.

"Come with me," she said, and took Phillip's hand. She led him to the edge of the landing pad, where a young badhinjan tree spread its branches under the orange Daraghn sun. Placing both their hands on the trunk, she nodded once at his questioning gaze.

"Just wait," she said.

Callista could feel his fear, but he never wavered. This was the path he had chosen for himself, and he would follow it to the end.

They all stood in silence, waiting, until the ground suddenly rumbled underfoot, and a newcomer materialized as if out of nowhere, landing a mere three feet from Phillip with a thud that shook the ground anew.

The chimaera was enormous.

Like the mythological griffin, it possessed a powerful, leonine body and four muscular legs, but its birdlike wings were covered in shimmering scales rather than feathers. A draconian tail whipped back and forth while its beaked avian head bent forward, scintillating silver eyes fixed on Phillip with predatory focus.

Phillip turned to face it, and Callista's breath caught in her throat as he confronted the magnificent creature.

It could end his life in an instant, and he knew it, but he stood his ground, bearing the weight of its scrutiny.

No one moved as they stared at one another—chimaera and man—until it bent its head, made one swift motion with its razor-edged beak, and then flew away.

"Was that Josephine?" Phillip asked hoarsely, and Emma nodded.

"Daragh cannot forget," she said. "It is not in her nature. But she is also practical, and accepts that humans are more changeable than she. I don't recommend testing her by staying for long, but know that she has chosen to give you the chance to prove your sincerity. As," she added gently, "have I."

Phillip's eyes closed briefly as if in relief. "That is more than I had any right to hope for," he acknowledged, and held out a hand towards Emma.

She accepted it without even a moment of hesitation. "I believe you are different," she said. "Love changes us beyond anything we expect or understand when we first let it in. I can't tell you how happy I am that you and Seph have found each other."

Phillip turned back towards the landing pad, and Callista's eyes widened as she saw the bright stain of blood that marked his shirt-front—a gash that crossed the very center of his chest.

A judgment, and a reminder, that it was only his change of heart that had saved his life.

"So, what now?" Killian eyed the two parties curiously. "I'm not sure all persons present are satisfied."

"Now," Callista guessed, "they'll go off and try to figure out where we all go from here. Devan will glare some more, Emma and Seph will reminisce, and by the time it's over, they'll agree that a truce is in everyone's best interests. They'll probably never be best friends, but they'll respect one another, and both Earth and Daragh will be better for it."

"Oh, and did you develop prescience too, while I was away?" Killian cocked an eyebrow in her direction.

Callista shuddered. "That sounds like too heavy of a burden, even for me. And I already know everything I need to know about the future."

"Such as?"

She turned to face him and smiled up into his beautiful brown eyes. "I know that you love me," she said simply.

"That's all you know?" His exaggerated look of surprise nearly made her elbow him in the ribs again. "Have you forgotten we had plans, love? We were going to sail off into the Rift, confront my brother, restock our supplies of nanotech, and then follow the Bhandecki into the unknown."

"But those are just the beginning," Callista said. "And plans... Well, they're always changing. After all, who knows what new challenges we'll find along the way?"

Killian's eyes softened suddenly, letting her see all the way into his heart. "I hope we do," he said quietly. "But I hope you know that the only challenge I need is being worthy of facing the future alongside you."

"Even if I decide to drag you along on my ridiculous quest to use my newfound powers for good? To free the fireworms from Bhandecki control and end their trail of conquest forever?"

He shrugged nonchalantly, as if he hadn't known all along what she was planning. "Sounds like it could be interesting. Will there be a reward at the end of this quest? I am a pirate, after all."

Callista tapped her lips with one finger as if in thought. "I can offer you one small heart. It doesn't have a lot of practice, but it loves you."

"You can't offer me something I already have. That's not how rewards work."

She stretched up to plant a gentle kiss on his frowning lips. "You have it today. But hearts are tricky things. We have to keep giving them every day. So I'll be giving you mine again tomorrow, and the next day, and the next. Until we find out when the end of forever is."

"It won't always be fun, you know." He slid his arms around her waist and looked down at her intently. "I don't know what to expect when we go through the Rift. And I can't promise we won't eventually find ourselves lost in an uncharted portion of the galaxy, unable to find our way back."

"We might," she acknowledged, running her fingers through the spikes of his hair and wondering how she'd managed to find this man, exactly when she needed him the most. "But that seems like a lot to hope for, don't you think?"

His crooked smirk made her fall in love with him again, for at least the thousandth time.

"After all," he murmured in her ear, "what fun would life be if we already knew how it ends?"

And then she really had no choice but to kiss him again.

———

THANK YOU

Thanks for reading! I hope you enjoyed this conclusion to the Conclave Worlds Trilogy. To learn more about my books and receive updates on new releases, be sure to visit my website and sign up for my newsletter.

http://kenleydavidson.com

If you loved The Linden Legacy and want to share it with other readers, please consider leaving an honest review on Amazon or Goodreads. Not only do I love getting to hear how my stories are impacting readers, but reviews are one of the best ways for you to help other book lovers discover the stories you enjoy. Taking even a moment to share a few words about your favorite books makes a huge difference to indie authors like me!

ALSO BY KENLEY DAVIDSON

http://kenleydavidson.com/books

ABOUT THE AUTHOR

Kenley Davidson is a fantasy and science fiction author who loves to write clean romance, complex characters, and surprising plot twists. Her worlds (both real and imagined) are largely fueled by coffee, more coffee, and books (plus the occasional cup of tea). She currently resides in Oklahoma with her husband, two kids and two dogs, and believes everything is better with dragons.

Kenley is the author of The Legends of Abreia (a fantasy romance series), The Andari Chronicles (an interconnected series of fairy tale retellings), and Conclave Worlds (a clean sci-fi romance series).

She also writes sweet contemporary romance under the pseudonym Kacey Linden.

kenleydavidson.com
kenley@kenleydavidson.com

ACKNOWLEDGMENTS

I started this series over four years ago. Like many other writers, I was often encouraged to write the book I wanted to read, and I'd been in love with romantic science fiction for years. I patiently hunted down even the tiniest *hint* of romance from popular sci-fi authors, but there didn't seem to be much out there for those who didn't necessarily enjoy the technical side, or for those who prefer cleaner books.

So I decided to dive in and give it a try, only finding out *after* I'd written *The Daragh Deception* that clean science fiction romance didn't really have a home, even in its own genre. So this became the series that didn't sell—the series I never thought I would finish.

But you—my readers—wouldn't let me give up on it. Every few months I would get an email from someone who loved the series and was dying to know how it ended, and I would squirm with the uncomfortable realization that I didn't quite know. I would have to start writing in order to find out, and I wasn't sure I could write this book. Wasn't sure I could wrap up such an epic story in a satisfying way.

But after yet another email, and after several author friends asked again when I planned to finish the series, I made the impulsive decision to set up a preorder, so that I would be forced to confront the story and bring it to a conclusion.

And I'm so, so glad I did. This was an incredibly difficult book to write, but it was a huge growing experience for me, and I'm so pleased with how all of these characters came together in the end.

So to all of you who wouldn't let me quit and who believed in this series enough to badger me to finish it...

To everyone who emailed to say that they loved these books and these characters, and everyone who encouraged me when I was halfway in and wanted to give up...

Thank you.

This book wouldn't exist without you.

Made in the USA
Las Vegas, NV
28 November 2022

60575989R00204